A GROOM'S KISS

Edward whirled around, only to find himself nose to nose with Calamatta.

"You're not being helpful, Edward. Why can't you show me?"

A man could only take so much. Show her? Yes, he'd show this beautiful minx why she tread on dangerous ground. Edward gripped Calamatta's shoulders and drew her toward him. With a half-cocked grin, he leaned down and kissed her.

Slowly, seductively, his left hand rose to cradle the back of her head. But Edward felt no resistance from her. Damn! The chit was supposed to resist—be shocked. He eased Calamatta's head back until he looked into her eyes. She was lovely. His voice lowered. "That's why, Callie! That's why!"

"Let me see if I have the right of it," she whispered.

As her hands slipped down his chest and around to his back, he kissed her again and again. How had this hoyden in an angel's disguise stolen his heart so completely?

Books by Paula Tanner Girard

LORD WAKEFORD'S GOLD WATCH

CHARADE OF HEARTS

A FATHER FOR CHRISTMAS

A HUSBAND FOR CHRISTMAS

THE SISTER SEASON

THE RELUCTANT GROOM

Published by Zebra Books

THE
RELUCTANT
GROOM

Paula Tanner Girard

Zebra Books
Kensington Publishing Corp.
http://www.zebrabooks.com

ZEBRA BOOKS are published by

Kensington Publishing Corp.
850 Third Avenue
New York, NY 10022

Zebra and the Z logo Reg. U.S. Pat. & TM Off.

First Printing: August, 1999
10 9 8 7 6 5 4 3 2 1

Printed in the United States of America

Prologue

London, England
July, 1815

"He did what?" Edward and William Hatcher shouted in unison. The two dark-haired young men, tall, slender, and pleasing to the eye, stood shoulder to shoulder in the solicitor's paper-strewn office.

The odor of musty books and beeswax permeated the walnut-paneled room. From behind his plain but serviceable desk, Obediah Dickering, an honest and most diligent attorney, squinted up at them, cleared his throat, and repeated, "Your grandfather, the late Sir Henry Hatcher, left your entire family estate in Careby, Lincolnshire, to a Miss Calamatta McGannon."

When his older brother, William, showed no signs of challenging the solicitor's statement, Edward stepped forward.

"Who the devil is she?"

Mr. Dickering adjusted his small reading spectacles and stared at the document in front of him.

An uncomfortable foreboding stirred in Edward. If their grandfather was trying to give them a stand-down from the other side of the grave, the old curmudgeon was doing a bang-up job of it. Edward squared his shoulders and awaited the lawyer's answer.

"She is a great-great-great granddaughter of the American William Hatcher. A common ancestor of yours, too, I believe?"

A searing pain burned a path down Edward's left hip. *Cursed wound!* He scowled and imperceptibly shifted his weight.

Mr. Dickering's grin disappeared. "Let me see—this William removed to the Crown Colony of Virginia before 1636. He felt that the part of the inheritance which should have gone to him was passed over to your side of the family."

The lawyer lowered his voice. "Your grandfather, Sir Henry, hinted there was always a bit of guilt connected with those shenanigans, for he knew the American Hatchers had been cheated out of their inheritance."

While William pondered, Edward splayed his hands upon the desk, stared intensely into the eyes of the agent, and demanded, "So our great-great-grandfather played the fox. What has that to do with this ridiculous will?"

Dickering stammered, "Sir Henry led me to believe that the three of you had come to some sort of an agreement."

Edward straightened up. Their grandfather had warned them he'd do something from beyond the pale if they didn't make a smart turnabout. But who would have thought he'd slip his anchor so soon?

"Sir Henry hoped when he married again and removed to the Highlands," Dickering continued, "you would in some way bestir yourselves to restore the family holdings at Careby to some semblance of their former grandeur and productivity."

William finally broke his silence. "Always before, the estate has gone to the oldest male in a direct line."

"Several years ago, before you went to Cambridge," began the lawyer, "Sir Henry began searching for relatives descended from the American William Hatcher." As if in prayer, Dickering pressed the tips of his fingers together. "A penance, so to speak, for your ancestor's buffoonery. He hired a well-known firm of investigators in London—Parnell, Parnell and Davidson—to send an operative to our former colonies. Your grandfather settled upon this young woman in Virginia. Calamatta McGannon."

William laughed. "Why worry, brother? The estate is entailed."

Dickering shook his head. "Sir Henry petitioned His Majesty, King George the Third, when he was still of sound mind, to void the entail so he could disinherit you if certain promises were not kept. The King, having had many a disappointment with his own sons, was sympathetic to your grandfather's request. In these latest papers, Sir Henry informed me that when he went to his Maker, I was to give a copy of the will and his further instructions, which he has sealed in this envelope—" Dickering began rummaging among the papers in a scarred leather valise on his desk.

"Why her?" barked William.

Without looking up, Dickering quipped. "Miss McGannon is an only daughter. Parents dead, brothers heavy in the purse, and no sibling or parental opposition or jealousy to stand in her way. Her father's will gave her no land, only money. Nothing to keep her from moving to England."

"The old reprobate probably figured she'd be thrilled to become the mistress of an English estate," said Edward, aside to his brother.

"Aha," the lawyer cried, pulling out a large packet and triumphantly waving it in the startled men's faces. "I was told to deliver this to Mr. Parnell Senior himself, to be held until they find Miss McGannon."

William jumped forward. "You mean she still hasn't been located?"

"All I know is that in fourteen months, on her nineteenth birthday, she will receive an annuity of"—he paused, a gleeful grin splitting his craggy face—"the equivalent in American dollars of ten thousand pounds sterling."

Edward heard William's heavy intake of breath.

"The last epistle to arrive in England from Parnell's contact informed them that she was no longer to be found in Virginia," the solicitor said.

"Where is she?" asked William.

Mr. Dickering shrugged. "It has been bandied about that she ran away. Her eldest brother, Ward McGannon, is her legal guardian. He runs a large plantation on the James River, also has a law office and another residence in Richmond. Ward is trustee until she comes of age or until she marries. If Miss McGannon marries before she is one and twenty, she receives a dowry worth"—his fingers began fiddling again—"fifty thousand pounds, but upon reaching her majority, married or not, she will have complete control of the monies left to her under a special trust by her father, John McGannon. However, your grandfather did stipulate she must reside in England to inherit Careby Manor."

William raised his eyebrows. "Perhaps she won't want to leave America to assume ownership."

"What woman would not want to come to England to claim her inheritance?" The lawyer smirked. "She may be as plain as a pea hen, but I assure you, her brains and looks will be of little consequence. With all the titled dandies falling into dun territory, she would be quite a catch on the marriage mart."

Edward interrupted. "Hasn't her family searched for her?"

"She has two unmarried brothers living in a wilderness land called Kentucky. It was believed she was headed there, but never arrived. Parnell's agent wrote that he had a clue as to her whereabouts, but misfortune overtook the man on his way to check it out. Thrown from his horse. Broke his neck. With the escalating conflagration with our former colonies, it was difficult to smuggle in another operative."

Why doesn't he just say the bloody war? thought Edward. Aloud he asked, "Where is this Kentucky?"

"Over the mountains west of Virginia. A place, I hear, full of uncivilized savages and ferocious beasts." The lawyer stared into space, seemingly contemplating those horrors.

"Then she definitely has disappeared?" quizzed William.

Dickering snapped to attention. "I can say no more, gentlemen." Removing his spectacles, the lawyer pinched the bridge of his nose. "Until the aforementioned lady is located or until such time as you can prove the will is invalid, all possessions and holdings of the estate now belong to Miss Calamatta McGannon, residing somewhere in the continental United States of America. Good day to you, sirs."

An hour later, William and Edward sat in oversized wing chairs in their bachelors' chambers at the east end of Piccadilly. They frowned at each other, then at the empty glasses in their hands.

William grumbled, "I didn't think the old fussbox would do it."

Already Edward was running several schemes through his head. "We were forewarned."

During the ensuing silence, his servant, Fitzgerald, who had served him in the Navy, stepped into the room to replenish their drinks. Though his bushy brows and unkempt beard hid his demeanor, Edward knew the wily old salt had heard every tiddle of their discourse. Fitz had expressed his surprise the first time he saw the two brothers together. "Lawd, Cap'n. Ye're so much alike, I'd've taken ye for hatchlings from the same egg."

Their lean bodies were honed by five hard years at war. Though they looked much alike, Edward knew his lined, slightly darker complexion, etched by months at sea, made him appear older. But his brother, at twenty-seven, was the elder by eleven months, a matter of fate which sometimes proved hard for Edward to swallow. However, as firstborn and the one to receive the entail, William was most affected by this sudden change in their fortunes.

William took another sip of his drink. "To have dug up so much muck about our affairs, he must have had spies everywhere."

Edward snorted and plunked down his glass, splashing his wine. *Grandfather should have gone to work for the War Department instead of me,* he reflected.

William dabbed at the ring of liquid left by Edward's glass. "It was his own personal acquaintance with Prinny's father that got us into that circle in the first place. You know I preferred quieter friends and activities. My curse is, looking so much like you, I'm thought to be in places I'm not, when all the time I'm reading in some secluded corner at Hatchard's."

The corners of Edward's mouth began to twitch. The likeness was exactly what he'd counted on in his undercover work for the government. "You miss most of the fun by half, brother. You're becoming one of the dullest of pattern-saints."

"And you are a rascal, Eddie," accused William.

A devilish smile spread across Edward's face, but quickly disappeared. "We have been wronged, brother."

"Aye. There is the rub."

Edward took a long draught of his wine and contemplated their various alternatives. They could leave the country to escape their creditors. No, that wasn't an honorable option. Gain employment. As landed gentry, it wasn't out of the question, but not likely to bring in the needed money quickly enough to satisfy their debts. Go to a pauper's prison—a likely possibility if they didn't act quickly. Or marry a girl with a fortune. There was an idea worth pursuing. Why hadn't he thought of it before?

Edward's humor returned. He looked at his brother and winked. "Grandfather wanted the search for Miss McGannon to continue. If she's kicking up her heels somewhere, our only hope is to get to her first."

"What for?"

"Why, to marry her before she turns nineteen, of course. What better way to guarantee that the family seat in Careby remains in the Hatcher name?"

Springing from his chair like a jack-in-the-box, William hovered over his brother. "Marry her? Why would you want to do that?"

"Not I, brother. You." Teasing Will always gave Edward great satisfaction, but the twist he'd proposed began to take on a more practical shape.

William gave his brother a dark look. "Me?"

Edward shook his head. "I harbor no desire to be riveted to

anyone, even a woman with fifty thousand pounds coming to me on her wedding day."

"Why me? It's your brainstorm."

"You're the one who is supposed to carry on the family name."

"To wed her, I'd have to go to America to find her."

Edward always enjoyed needling Will. "That seems feasible."

"It would mean a turn at sea for me, would it not? You know how violently ill I get even when I no more than step foot in a rowboat." William swallowed and ran his finger around the inside of his neckcloth.

Edward studied his brother. He knew that on horseback Major William Hatcher cut a formidable figure, but at sea . . . well, that was another story.

"The sail to Portugal nearly did me in before I could join Wellington in the Peninsula," William blustered, regaining his seat. "Besides, I need to remain here to see what can be done to contest this preposterous will. You're the seaman. You go. I know you'd fair jump at a chance for a voyage."

"True," admitted Edward. "But it's not I who will be marrying her. A delay in putting on the collar would give Parnell's agent time to find her."

William frowned. "If we waited until she came here, knowing all our acquaintances who are short in the pocket, I would have to stand in line to court her."

"What a down-in-the-mouth you are, Will. You know you must eventually choose a wife, but once she saw your grim face, she'd cry off altogether."

William's scowl deepened and he disappeared into his cups. That meant he was thinking the trick through in his usual drag-it-over-the-coals manner. Having no better inspiration, Edward held his tongue. Why did he feel that whatever wrinkle William dredged up, it boded trouble for him?

"I'll get a proxy," declared William. "Used to be done quite often, you know. When the settlers in the colonies were seeking brides, young women married them by proxy here in England."

Again that irritating sensation assaulted Edward's stomach like a weasel digging into a rabbit hole.

His brother continued. "You plead my case. You're much better at that sort of skulduggery than I. I'd only bungle the whole game and appear a muttonhead. I'll give you full powers in my name to marry her to me and bring her back to England."

"And what do I get for setting this snare?"

William drummed his fingers on his glass. "As soon as I control her monies, I'll pay your debts, give you five thousand pounds, and when Careby is running well in the races again, I'll assign you an annuity."

Edward spoke in a slow drawl. "Five thousand."

"That's what I said," nodded William.

"I mean, until I turn up my toes, I want five thousand pounds a year."

Edward thought Will had sprouted wings, he rose so quickly. "Dash it, Eddie! That's half her annual income! It'll take most of that to get Careby producing a fair living."

William balled up his fist, held it in front of his face, and studied his thumbnail for so long a time Edward was about to burst with exasperation. "Tell you what," he continued, whirling around. "I'll deed you the hunting box and forty acres outside the deer park. You'll have a residence in the country. That includes the woods to the stream. You always liked to fish."

"I say, Will, you're a regular good fellow. Shall we say my debts, five thousand a year, the hunting lodge, the four hundred acres that include much of our section of the deer park, and the willowed glen?"

"Dash it all, Eddie. Be sensible."

"Or," Edward threatened, "you go to America to woo the heiress McGannon yourself. Of course, if you die of the bilious heaves aboard ship, I'll be next in line to go courting the young lady myself."

William exploded. "Fifty percent? You're a highway robber, brother. A scoundrel of the first degree. Twenty-five percent."

Edward swore he saw smoke rising from his brother's ears. "Fifty."

"All right," yelled William. "I will do all that is possible within the law to regain what is rightfully mine. However, only under these stipulations: You seal the proxy marriage, you acquire the fifty-thousand-pound dowry before you sail back to England, and my bride is delivered to me unsullied. If any one of these conditions is broken, you lose the whole."

Edward grinned. He hadn't expected William to take the bait so readily.

Reluctantly, William continued, "I'll pay your debts and give you five thousand, then assign the remainder of your portion over to you after we've restored Careby Manor and have the crops and livestock increasing. Agreed?"

Edward rose from his chair and held out his hand. "Agreed." A yawn escaped him. There was no time for sleep. Already the sun was beginning to rise, and they had a busy schedule ahead of them.

As soon as they had changed into fresh day clothes, the two weary-eyed brothers met for breakfast.

"We'll need a lawyer," remarked Edward. "How about Preston North? You remember him at university? Came to London to study law at Gray's Inn, then joined a firm here in London. I ran into him at Jackson's and we went a few rounds in the ring."

William groaned, "A few rounds at Jackson's, Eddie?"

"I know. I know. The doctors told me to take it easy on my hip, but I'll never get back into shape if I mollycoddle it. Well, how about North?"

"Not Dickering?" questioned William.

"Anyone but Dickering. I'd not want him to get word of our plans. He'd try to knock the wind out of our sails for sure."

"All right," William acquiesced. "I'll look up North and see what has to be done to get a proxy."

"I'll inquire into the earliest passage I can get to America."

"We're dear in the pockets, remember."

Edward grinned. "Never fear, brother. A certain amiable countess might be persuaded to back our venture."

William raised his eyebrows. "How so?"

"Appreciation, my dear boy. For rescuing the fair damsel from what could have been an embarrassing situation with her finicky husband."

The elder Hatcher threw up his hands. "Where this time, Eddie?"

"Vauxhall Gardens—a week ago."

William shook his head. "You live on the edge, brother."

Edward knew that Will frequented the house of a certain widow on the north side of London, but Edward's tastes ran to more forbidden fruit. He threw back his head and laughed. He could always count on a few scolds from his dour brother to lighten his mood.

Within three days, special marriage papers were drawn up, and Edward purchased passage for Fitz and himself on a cargo ship sailing directly to Virginia. At the dock, William once more brought up the subject which seemed to plague him. "What do you think she'll look like, Eddie?"

Occupied with appraising the lines of the vessel in front of him, Edward shrugged his shoulders. His concern wasn't with appearances, but with the strategy he would follow. He'd find Calamatta McGannon, charm her with tales of his handsome brother, heir to an ancient family estate, lord of the manor. This paragon of virtue, this knight of the realm, burdened with the heavy responsibilities his status required, had sent Edward out into the world as his emissary to find a wife worthy of his name.

Edward grinned. He had great faith in his own ways of persuasion. After he'd described his brother's many attributes, what woman could resist the promise of marriage? Aye, he'd have the chit upon her knees in no time, begging him to take her to England. If she were less than a fetcher, wouldn't she jump at the chance to have the marriage performed by proxy, so as to eliminate any chance of William's crying off?

"Eddie!" William persisted. "If she's homely, I anticipate no trouble from you, but if she's halfway as comely as ladies with whom you consort, I shan't be surprised if I receive a wife who might not be exactly pure, but will make me twice as rich when you fail that part of our agreement." He grabbed Edward's arm. "I want you to know that for as little time as I plan to spend with her, it doesn't matter to me a whit one way or the other."

Thinking of all the spoiled young ladies throwing out lures for husbands in England, Edward shuddered. There was no need to step over the bounds of propriety with virgins when loose women of astounding capabilities were so easy to come by. He'd spent last night in the warm arms of his paramour, all sails hoisted. Now, thoroughly satiated, he was ready for the voyage ahead.

With long, determined strides, Edward started up the gang-plank. He had the proxy and his identification papers secured in a leather pouch strapped to his chest and a small but adequate amount of money, which should see him through this adventure if he watched his expenditures.

He heard his brother's voice calling after him. "If you make a cuckold of me, I shall find out, you know—and I'll hold you to my terms."

With a gleam of amusement, Edward shot back, "No cause for alarm, Will. Little provincial chits hold no attraction for me."

The next day, Edward stood at the rail when they hit the open waters. A wave crashed against the side of the ship and soaked him to the skin. Loosening his neckcloth, he threw back his head and laughed. "Finally, brother Will, your time has come to get the short end of the stick. A lifetime shackled to a wet goose of a girl. I vow no woman is going to lure me to such a fate."

One

Appalachian Mountains, Kentucky
October, 1815

The windy mountain pass challenged the two men. Edward sat hunched over his horse and steeled himself for the blast of cold air he knew would come. In England, they had called it the year without a summer. And now, here in America, the weather continued to be as fickle as their mission.

Behind him, Fitzgerald shouted, "Crackajack gag you thought up, sir, that we drop Parnell's detective a false trail. If we hadna, he could've caught up to us by now, the snail's pace we been traveling."

Edward knew Fitz wasn't blaming him for their disastrous journey, but he still felt guilty. It had taken their ship nearly two months to cross the Atlantic. On their arrival, they'd heard that Parnell's agent had already arrived. The good news was that Miss McGannon's brothers had found her living with a roving band of Indians in a territory called Tennessee. The bad news was that no one knew for certain where they had taken her.

Edward reckoned that if he was to lure the heiress back to England and into the arms of his waiting brother, they had to make haste. By the middle of September, he and Fitzgerald had headed west.

A gnawing hunger clawed his stomach. "I swear, Fitz, we haven't had two decent meals since we left Richmond."

"Aye, Cap'n. And we set sail on these nags over four weeks ago."

Unseasonable rainstorms had descended upon them. Edward's fine wardrobe had been reduced to a few items, which he traded for sturdier trousers and a stinking coat, oiled with some god-awful stuff to make it water-resistant. They'd found the McGannon name well-known along the Ohio River, but the brothers, Creed and Benjamin, had gone to New Orleans.

Here it was one week later and they'd still found no sign of any Calamatta McGannon. At a hamlet called Dunfree's Corners, they were informed that the brothers had settled their sister inland with a good Christian family, the Colemans. Their homestead lay thirteen miles west in the next valley toward Lexington.

Edward reined up atop a rise. "Hell! The McGannons have to be gypsies," he muttered. "Wealthy gypsies. No one named McGannon has a right to Careby Manor." Hiding his vexation from his servant, Edward pulled out his gold watch and called back, "Six bells." Seven o'clock and already darkness obscured much of the valley. He made out the roof of a large barn. Nearby, a bonfire shot flames upward. Like firecrackers, spurts of laughter popped into the air. "It must be a celebration, Fitz."

He headed his horse down the rocky path toward the sound of the festivities. His wretched hip pained him. He'd seek food and lodging.

It took an hour to travel down the winding trail. By the time they rode into the barnyard, supper was over. Two older farm women remained outside clearing the tables. The taller one introduced herself as Miz Hetta and her sister, Miz Abigail. "Widows," she emphasized, looking toward Fitz speculatively.

Abigail set out two plates. "You're jest welcome to he'p yourselves to what's left. They's plenty. Ain't they, Hetta?"

"Hungry men is hungry men," agreed Hetta. "And," she

added, "maybe you'd like to stay for the dancin' and singin'. You're more than welcome."

Edward was about to turn down their invitation when the plumper one, Miz Abigail, said, "The dancin' commences right after the girls' auction."

He puzzled over that promising possibility. "Auction of . . . what?"

"Abigail forgot you're a stranger. We unattached ladies," Hetta giggled, patting her hair, "bake a pastry and bring it in a box."

Smiling at Edward's look of confusion, Abigail explained. "The goodies are put up for bids." She winked at Fitz.

"Now, Abbie," fussed her sister, "don't you go giving these gentlemen the wrong idea." She turned to Edward. "We had a barn raising for the Tracy family. They was burned out."

"The single men must bid and whoever made the sweet in the box is their partner for the first dance," Abbie said.

Edward almost declined, but three mugs of Miz Abigail's potent, fruity cider changed his mind. His entrance into the barn didn't go unnoticed. The admiring glances from the women reminded him of his salad days at Cambridge, and if any of these fair lasses were as pleasant as an English country maiden, he mused, perhaps he could look forward to a few hours of agreeable diversion. He shrugged out of his coat and hung it on a peg.

Lanterns hung from iron hooks along the walls of the large room. The pungent odor of kerosene mingled with that of recently sawed wood, fresh straw, tobacco, hot cider, and, if he wasn't mistaken, rum.

Edward, alerted by the rib-punching antics of three young fustians standing nearby, let his gaze follow theirs. A magnificent young woman stood in front of a long, white-clothed table covered with gaily decorated boxes. She placed a strangely shaped package with the others.

Her hair, flying free of the ribbon meant to tame it, shone like burnished copper in the golden reflection of the flickering lantern lights. Her body was—Edward searched for the right word— statuesque? Yes, that was it, a classical beauty like the sensuous carving of a goddess he'd seen unearthed near an ancient Roman villa near Bath. Her face . . . innocent? No, not with a body like that. The vixen twirled round in a most unconventional manner, her skirts flying up to show an enticing view of long, well-turned limbs. He wanted her. Edward opened and closed his fists until sounds of quarreling broke his concentration.

"She kissed me longer than you."

His body now battle alert, Edward decided a child-woman like that was gunpowder ready to explode. With a mask of indifference, he leaned nonchalantly against a post to hear the rest of the young sprout's gossip.

"Heck, Sauly. All of us knows which box is hers. She left it outside on a log and I nearly squashed it."

Sauly, a good-looking, sandy-haired youth, pulled several coins from his pocket. "I get her tonight."

The other two glared. "Demme. Where'd you come by all that money?"

"I been saving since the last dance."

The second boy squinted in the direction of the fiddler's stand. "Don't know what you want that for anyway when Pattijean Tendal gives you the whole bit with no struggle."

Edward boldly glanced back toward the table. The girl turned and looked at him. No skinny, swooning creature that one. A regular Boudicca. The hoyden was exactly what he was looking for—exactly what he needed. There would always be tomorrow to find the Coleman farm. Edward turned and stalked out of the barn. He could feel her soft flesh beneath him already. There was little coin left in his saddlebags, but he knew she would be worth every bit of what he had. Edward's eyes narrowed. Her gaze hadn't wavered. He'd read it as a dare. That luscious woman was made for a man like him, and tonight she would be his.

* * *

When the sadly crushed box came up for bids, Edward found the three young farmers were not the only ones eager to purchase it. But when he held up his one remaining gold guinea, all other bids ceased.

Fitz's angry mutterings fell upon deaf ears.

The wench's look of astonishment amused Edward. He crooked his finger for her to come to him. She raised an eyebrow. Edward grinned and with a roar of triumph he leaped upon the platform, ignoring the wrenching strain on his hip. He swept both hoyden and cake into his arms and carried them from the barn.

Edward set her down. Her rich, lusty laugh set his blood afire; to his amusement, he found himself not leading, but being led. The vixen seemed to know where she was going. Who was he to question? She hurried to a spot not far from the bonfire, hidden by a stand of bushes. The moon skidded in and out of the clouds, making an unreal fantasy of the landscape.

Carelessly, he let the package drop to the ground. Her face turned up to his. She was the pawkiest wench he'd seen in a long time, there for the taking. Just as her mouth pressed against his, her eyes closed. His didn't.

The kiss took no longer than a butterfly's tongue takes to suck nectar from a flower. Her body wasn't even touching his, but his toes attempted to dig their way out of his boots. He knew it was a stupid question before he asked, but he had to say something. "What was that supposed to be?"

Her eyes flew open. "Why, a kiss."

Beads of sweat broke out on Edward's forehead. "A cat's whiskers have tickled me more," he lied. Once again the moon peeked out from behind the clouds and bathed her face with silvery light. He wasn't prepared for the look of failure in her eyes.

"Oh, dear. I only had the books to go by, you see."

The moon chose that moment to hide, and just when he decided she was perhaps more inexperienced than he first thought, he found his head pulled down and his lips soundly kissed.

What else could a man do in such circumstances? Assist her, of course. As his arms encompassed the most delectable body he'd ever hugged, any guilt he previously entertained flew away. The whisper of her breath in his ear started his heart pounding, and the scent of her hair did more to unbalance him than any of the exotic French perfumes worn by the *demimondaines*.

Raising his head, his hand brushed away the lock of hair which had fallen over her forehead. "By the way," he whispered, his voice rough with a new emotion he couldn't identify, "I forgot to ask your name."

"Calamatta," she said with a hearty earthiness. "Calamatta McGannon."

Edward stared at the inviting lips a few inches from his. God preserve him! He held his brother's future bride.

"Hatcher's the name," Edward choked out. "Your servant, ma'am." What taradiddle could he possibly dredge up to get himself out of this muddle? As he stepped away, his boot struck something. He patted the ground until he found the box. Oh, good lord! He'd stepped on her cake! Hurriedly, he scooped what he could of its contents back into the container. Trying for a bit of levity, he laughed. "I say! Hope I haven't ruined it."

She made no response.

Confusion in a crisis was a new sensation for Edward, one he didn't like. His hip pained him and he needed to sit down. Then the moon showed its face, enabling him to see well enough to pull a large log from a wood pile. He settled Calamatta upon the makeshift bench then eased down beside her.

As crumbs fell from the crushed box, Edward tried to hide the shambles. He was certain it had taken a great deal of effort to bake so large a pastry. "Hmm. Looks quite the thing," he prevaricated. "Tip-top."

Two shiny chestnut-sized eyes looked at him expectantly. If Edward was to make any headway with his brother's intended, nothing would do but for him to plunge in. Have a go at it. Right the wrong. Eat every morsel.

The first mouthful told him the contents had mixed with half the soil on the ground. An anxious smile spread across her lovely face, throwing him off balance. Brother or not, Edward knew he had to hold this enchanting girl once more, even if it were only to dance. He had to finish the cake. Bravely, Edward stuffed another handful of crumbs into his mouth and swallowed.

A half hour later, Calamatta stood at the barn entrance. She couldn't keep the grin off her face. "I did it! I really kissed a man!" Not an overgrown boy like Sauly. He had hugged her, too, and she hugged him back. Nothing terrible happened like Lucy had predicted. In fact, it was quite pleasant.

Her baking must be improving, she thought happily, for Hatcher had eaten his box dessert with an unexpected thoroughness. After escorting her to the door, he'd excused himself in that deep baritone voice of his, saying he'd only be a minute. She hadn't thought to ask Hatcher what his last name was, but she'd rectify that omission when he returned. Calamatta peered into the darkness, hoping to catch a glimpse of him coming toward her. His kiss hadn't been like any of the others. When his dark eyes looked into hers, she'd had a terrible urge to do it again. Whatever possessed her?

The fiddlers began plucking their instruments. The first dance was about to begin. She glanced up at the sky and started to hum. It was hard to believe that it had been only yesterday that she'd been standing upon the low wooden stool in the Coleman farmhouse.

Lucy had knelt on the floor to pin up the hem of Calamatta's skirt while giving her a scold at the same time. "Lordy, Callie, you must stop letting so many boys kiss you."

"They don't kiss me. I kiss them, but I don't find much to recommend it," Calamatta said defensively.

"You're going to get into a peck of trouble, Calamatta McGannon."

"Well, *Miss Lucy,* tell me. How can I learn if I don't practice?"

"Mama says . . ." Lucy blushed. "Well, she says men do other things if you let them touch you."

Calamatta had to give that some thought. "They don't put a finger on me when I kiss them. Just get wide-eyed. I must be doing it wrong."

"They know they dasn't touch you, because your wild redheaded brother Creed will skin them alive if they do."

"Humph," Calamatta snorted in a very unladylike way. "Those rascally brothers of mine are probably raising Cain in Natchez or New Orleans right now. It'd serve them right if I took a notion to let one of those boys do more than kiss me. In fact, I have a mind to let Sauly Hughes hug me."

"Calamatta! Don't you dare! Mama says never let a boy go farther than holding his hand at your side when you dance." Lucy turned a becoming shade of pink. "She says if a girl isn't careful, other things happen."

Calamatta looked askance at her friend. Of course, Lucy had no older brothers to spy on. "Pooh! Creed doesn't care about me." Creed had been her favorite. Then he had a fight with their oldest brother Ward and fled Virginia for Kentucky. Calamatta never did know why, but it still hurt that Creed had left without so much as a good-bye. "I was here only a few weeks and off they went down the river again. He said it was no place for a girl. I got myself all the way to Kentucky from Virginia, didn't I?"

"Callie, your brothers went crazy looking for you. They gathered all your McGannon kin in Kentucky to help search. Even Papa joined them."

"After I got lost, I followed the river, just like Creed taught me."

"You're lucky you were found by friendly Indians," Lucy scolded.

"Applesauce!" Calamatta laughed so heartily that she popped out two pins and nearly upset the stool.

"Landsakes, Callie, stop wiggling!" Lucy said, unable to keep a serious face. "The barn dance is tomorrow night and I'll never get your skirt hemmed if you don't stand still."

Calamatta guffawed and stepped out of her skirt.

Lucy sighed wistfully. "How could any girl in her right mind want to give up such a splendid life as you've told me you had in Virginia, Callie? Please tell me again about your plantation home, Mockwood. I truly believe Mr. Darcy's Pemberley Manor couldn't have been any finer."

"How many times have you read *Pride and Prejudice*, Lucy?"

"Six."

"You must have it memorized by now."

"Beside the Bible, it's the only book I have. Mama lost most of hers in the Ohio River when we came to Kentucky."

"I know what it's like not having anything to read," Calamatta said, looking over at the well-worn volume on the bedside table. "That and another book were the only things I had to read all last winter while I was with the Indians. Someday I'll get you more. Oh, I'll be glad when I have my own money. Ward wrote that after what I did—running away and scaring them like that— he isn't going to give me my inheritance until I'm twenty-one."

"You said you can have it in less than a year if you marry."

Before Calamatta could state her opinion on her chances of matrimony, smoke billowed through the doorway. "Glory be! My cake!" Calamatta cried, making a dash for the kitchen.

Lucy dropped her needle and thread and ran after her.

After Calamatta dumped the blackened lump onto the cutting board, she studied the odd-shaped mound from all sides. "I have to admit it isn't the best cake I ever baked."

"Perhaps when you have a home of your own you'll have servants so you can live like a grand lady and not have to cook."

Calamatta wrinkled her nose. "That sounds like my sister-in-law Susanna. I was ten years old when Ward married her. She was so dainty that next to her I felt like an overstuffed chair. All she cared about was what I wore and what I said and how

I acted. Nothing I did pleased her, and she sent me away to a finishing school. She said that the only way to make a lady out of me was to get me away from my brothers."

"I think Susanna was just trying to be nice, Callie. You're grown up now. Wouldn't you like to have a husband and a home of your own?"

Calamatta thought about that. "Well, yes, I suppose—if I found someone like Mr. Darcy in *Pride and Prejudice*. Someone who'd never leave me."

"Isn't there anyone you left behind in Virginia?"

Calamatta stared at the singed lump of dough on the table as if it had come alive. "Oh, lord! Jeremiah!"

"Who?"

"Jeremiah Dinwiddie, the preacher's son. Ward said he thought he'd be a settling influence on me."

"What's wrong with that?"

"He's round as a ball, has burnt straw for hair, sloping shoulders, and his eyes bug out like a trout. No, I want someone who is reasonable to look upon and so rich he wouldn't give a sneeze for my fortune. Then I may like to marry. That's why I must learn how to kiss, don't you see?"

Lucy shook her head, so Calamatta explained. "I have older brothers and you don't. That's all they talked about." Calamatta blinked her eyes. "And other things I couldn't make heads or tails of, but . . ."

"But what, Callie? You are most vexing."

Calamatta nodded knowingly. "But kissing was right up there at the top of their list."

Lucy looked puzzled. "I don't remember Mr. Darcy kissing Elizabeth in *Pride and Prejudice.*"

Calamatta remembered catching Ward and Susanna kissing. "Well, I am positive it is very important to learn to do it just right."

"If you don't find a Mr. Darcy, what will you do?"

"I'll open up a leather shop," Calamatta said, nodding confidently.

"Oh, Callie, you're so clever," Lucy said with sincerity. "To think you learned all that from the Indians. The gloves you made me from deerskin feel like silk. I do believe they are the loveliest gift I've ever received."

"Well, now," Calamatta said gruffly, trying to find an excuse to hide her embarrassment. She was not used to receiving compliments. "I must make my frosting." She took down a bowl from high on the shelf.

"I can see why the Indians call you Tall-as-the-Trees," Lucy said in awe.

Calamatta shrugged. "Strong Arm said *Stand tall as a tree and walk softly as a deer.* He's the African slave who I told you lived with Indians."

"Yes, I remember," Lucy said, gasping as Calamatta took two eggs and dropped them shells and all into the bowl, followed by several scoops of sugar and a pinch each of salt and pepper. "However did you persuade Creed to let you stay in Kentucky?"

Taking a moment to consider her answer, Calamatta added a tablespoon of paprika for color and began to beat the mixture with a wooden spoon with such enthusiasm that much of it splattered onto the table. "I promised to cook and clean house for him and Benjamin."

Lucy nearly choked. "You? Cook?"

Calamatta found a spatula and began to lather the rust-colored frosting onto her cake. "I told Creed that Susanna had been instructing me for two years on how to run a household, and Ward's Negro, Abednego—the one he sent to a chef's school in Paris—was teaching me how to cook." She squinted at the sad-looking lump in front of her and shivered. "Oh, Lucy! I must catch a husband soon. When Creed finds out I can't cook, he'll send me back to Virginia and I'll have to marry that horrible Mr. Dinwiddie."

Lucy put her arms around Calamatta's shoulders. "Never! I won't let him send you back. I shall ask Mama if you can come to live with us."

With a whoop, Calamatta hugged her friend. "Oh, Lucy, would you?"

"Now enough of that," Lucy said, trying to look stern. "We had best be thinking about boxing our cakes for the social. But, I'm warning you, Callie. You behave yourself tomorrow. If you get into any more trouble, your brothers won't take kindly to it."

By the time they arrived at the Tracy farm the next day for the barn dance, Calamatta had made her decision. She was going to let Sauly hug her.

After the evening meal, when Lucy had placed her basket on the long table with the other desserts, she scolded, "Quit fidgeting, Callie. They're about to start the auction and you haven't brought in your cake."

Calamatta stopped smoothing her dress and looked blankly at her friend.

"Where is your cake, Callie?"

"Oh, lordy! I left it on the log outside." Calamatta ran out and soon returned, dangling the lumpy box by its rumpled ribbon.

Lucy caught her breath. "It looks like someone sat on it."

Calamatta laughed, trying unsuccessfully to straighten the bow. "Maybe that improved it. Do you think Sauly will know which one is mine?"

Lucy pushed her own prettily decorated box further back. "I'm sure everyone knows your . . . your unique packaging."

Calamatta was enjoying herself too much to take offense at her friend's awkward statement and asked, "Who do you want to buy your cake?"

"It doesn't matter," Lucy said softly. "He isn't here, anyway."

Calamatta swung around. "Lucy!" She was so filled with her own plans for Sauly that she'd never given a thought that her shy friend might be entertaining a fancy for someone. "One of my brothers?"

Lucy blushed and turned away.

"It is!" Calamatta didn't give her friend a chance to verify her conclusion. "Benjamin! It has to be Ben. He's such a romantical poet." Delighted with the idea of Lucy someday being her kin, Calamatta had whirled about, sending her skirt flying out to a most immodest height.

It was then that Lucy had grabbed her. "Callie! Don't look, but there's a tall man I never saw before standing near Sauly. He's staring at you."

Calamatta had instantly done what she'd been warned not to do. She turned and found her gaze locked with that of a dark-haired stranger leaning with savage grace against one of the wide supporting posts.

Lucy gasped. "The man looks like a wild beast."

Calamatta had never seen anyone so—she searched for a word. Handsome? No, the man appeared a little worse for wear. Noble? Patrician? No—more rugged than that. A scarf was knotted carelessly around his neck. His white shirt had definitely seen better days, and his breeches clung to long muscular legs. Her eyes scanned him from head to dusty boots and back up again. He towered over Sauly and perhaps was a little taller than Creed, but not as wide. His whiskers, not yet a full beard, were as dark as his unruly hair, but it was his piercing eyes which held her.

His mocking gaze had not wavered. She'd played the game of Old Hawk Eyes with Ben too many times to back off. She decided that if the bounder wanted to try to stare her down, she'd oblige him. Calamatta ignored the chirpings of Lucy, until her friend tugged so desperately on her skirt that she feared the cloth would rip. "For heaven's sake, Lucy. Do you want to see me standing here in my shift in front of everybody?"

Calamatta had ignored Lucy's apologies. She'd taken her gaze away from the stranger for only a second, but when she swung back around he was gone. But not for long. Oh, it had been fun seeing Sauly's eyes bug out when the auction began and Hatcher returned, waving that gold coin for all to see.

Now the fiddlers began to play and the men led their partners out onto the floor, but Hatcher still had not returned. Calamatta peered uneasily into the darkness. Where had he gone? He said he'd only be a minute.

The dance began. Sauly stomped by with Pattijean, who squealed like a cat with its tail caught in a door. "Oh, Cal-a-matta, where is that mysterious man of yours?"

Calamatta licked her dry lips. She was sure every head in the room turned her way. As the minutes ticked by, Calamatta came to the conclusion that Hatcher wasn't coming back. He probably was out there enjoying his little joke, guffawing at how she'd kissed him. Evidently she'd done it wrong again—and she really did try to do it right this time. Then he had filled his belly with her cake and left. He'd made a fool of her. Calamatta knew she had to get out of the barn. Rushing out into the night, she balled up her fists and swore, "By gory! If Hatcher ever dares show his rascally face around this territory again, he'll rue the day."

Creed always told her, "No one makes a fool out of a McGannon."

TWO

In the days which followed, Calamatta tried to put on a brave face. Thank goodness, not once had Lucy said, "I told you so."

From what Calamatta had seen of the surrounding farms, the Coleman's two-story house was more ample than most of the dwellings in Kentucky, and therefore large enough to have a weaving room off the kitchen.

"I'll help with the spinning," Calamatta said. She liked the low-pitched hum of the great walking wheel which spun the wool yarn. She would have preferred scraping skins under the great trees of the forest to being cooped up in the house, but any activity that would keep her thoughts from returning to that dark-eyed rascal Hatcher was better than none. But, try as she might, she couldn't keep the blackguard's image from her thoughts.

"Hatcher's the name. Your servant, ma'am," Calamatta mimicked. "Hah!" The humiliation set her Gaelic blood to boiling and she imagined the rogue's head spiked atop the spindle whirling in her hand. With wicked delight, Calamatta's feet began to walk faster and faster, until, after several disastrous attempts to keep the wheel steady, she had yarn all over the floor.

Lucy shook her head in dismay. "You card the wool, Callie. I'll spin."

Calamatta watched in admiration as the smaller girl stood at the walking wheel, stepping back quickly, one, two, three steps, holding high the long yarn, twisting it. As it quivered, Lucy gracefully glided forward and let the yarn wind onto the spindle, all the while keeping up a chatter to distract her friend. "Callie, I don't know why you can't sew a stitch of clothing out of woven cloth, but you make the finest leather gloves I've ever seen."

"Maybe it's liking what I do. I bribed her, you know."

"You what? Bribed whom?"

Calamatta told her about Sunflower, who lived in the Indian village. A real Indian princess descended from a Natchez Indian chief, Great Sun. Her great-grandmother, Sun Woman, had shown Calamatta a special way to soften skins, and in return Calamatta read her books to them.

"But how could an Indian understand English?"

"Sun Woman had been an Indian guide and spoke French and English. Later, when most of her tribe was killed in an uprising, Sun Woman escaped with Sunflower and moved north to the Tennessee Valley. She asked me to help Sunflower read. With the Muskegeon Indian dialect I learned and pictures I drew in the dirt, we got along fine. I left the tragic gothic romance about the dark, handsome Lord Haverwulf with Sunflower, because Creed made me leave before I finished reading it to her."

Thinking about the Indians made Calamatta yearn for the deep forest, and by the time the sun rose the next morning she had decided to go hunting. She could shoot no better than she cooked, but that did not deter her.

A chill was in the air much earlier than last year, teasing the trees to shed their colorful wardrobes. She knew the Colemans would disapprove of her going off alone, so she waited until the younger children were in school and Papa Coleman was in the fields and Mama Coleman was tending the herb garden. When Lucy went to the henhouse, Calamatta wrote a note.

> *Dear Lucy,*
>   *I will be all right. Do not worry if I am gone overnight. I know of a cabin my brothers use when they are hunting.*
>   *Your friend.*
>   *Callie*

"That should keep them from being overly concerned," she said. And picking up *Pride and Prejudice,* she placed the message between two pages where she was sure Lucy would find it.

A few minutes later, Calamatta entered the barn and saddled Cherry, the mare Creed had given her. As soon as she had food in her saddlebags, a bedroll secured to the back of the saddle, and plenty of ammunition for her rifle, she led the horse out by way of the back pasture.

Riding toward the hills, Calamatta tried to think of a happy tune to sing, but no matter how much she tried to erase his image from her mind, a certain broad-shouldered, impulsive stranger kept intruding into her thoughts. Why had she kissed him? True, he had definitely been an improvement over Sauly. On the other hand, Hatcher was nothing like the reserved, immaculately attired Mr. Darcy of her dreams.

For two days, Edward swore he was dying of the plague.

Fitzgerald was more blunt. "Looks like a case of diving too deep into yer cups. Too much of Miz Abigail's cider."

Edward vaguely recalled leaving the delectable Miss McGannon at the entrance to the barn. He struggled to remember what had happened before he'd scooped up the confection. "Good God, Fitz! The cake! I ate it. Every crumb." What a numskull he'd been. Besotted by those beseeching eyes—and all the other delectable parts of her. "The witch deliberately poisoned me!"

When Fitz looked at him as if his head were turned around backwards, Edward pulled himself together and halted his mumbling. *The dance! Oh, lord!* He hadn't even made the first reel. Was she angry with him? Of course she was. No, she wasn't, even though it pricked his vanity to think it. Surely a beauty like that had dismissed him from her mind and spent the remainder of the evening kissing someone else. Why was he angry? The chit was going to marry his brother, not him.

Later, Fitz told him he'd found him behind some bushes, looking three sheets to the wind, and managed to get him onto his horse and into the woods. "Gawd, Cap'n! Ye looked sicker than a parrot full of bilge water." Then the old sailor had made a lean-to of boughs, found a stream, and poured enough water down Edward's throat to float them back to England.

Edward put his head in his hands. Witch or not, he still had to make his apologies to Miss McGannon. Start all over to gain her confidence. If he was unsuccessful in his mission, he'd have failed his brother and could say good-bye to five thousand pounds a year and his chunk of the Careby estate.

By the third day, Edward felt more hobnail than cavalier. He insisted they ride back to Dunfree's Corners, where they found lodgings in a rooming house run by a widow named Maude Adams. After a warm bath, some decent food, and a good night's sleep, Edward was in much better humor. Early in the morning, they once more headed for the Coleman farm.

On a rise overlooking the valley, though they were still several miles away, Edward saw a mounted rider galloping in the opposite direction. Something about his odd ballooning trousers caught his attention. Not trousers—a skirt.

"That's not a man!" he exclaimed. "It's a woman riding astride." Her hat fell back from her head. A long braid bounced out, and he imagined the rest of her bouncing just as enticingly. "Damn! It's Calamatta." The sight of her, for some reason, both accelerated his heartbeat and threw him into the doldrums at the same time.

Fitzgerald grinned. "Aye, Cap'n, ye still got good eyes in yer head."

Edward ignored the jibe. "If I circle the outer fields and hold to the edge of the wooded area, I should catch up to her in an hour or two." His gaze took in the surrounding territory. Mountains lay east of these dense foothills.

"Surely she isn't going into that wild terrain alone. In England, no green girl would go out without an escort. Doesn't she know it's dangerous?" Edward mumbled. "Of course not. She lived with the Indians for nearly a year. I've already been a victim of her ruthlessness. Too bad the British Intelligence couldn't have smuggled her into France to cook for Boney's army. The war would have ended sooner."

Perhaps the chit's independent spirit would serve her into his hands. A bit of a fright. A gallant rescue. Now he was feeling more the thing.

Edward turned toward Fitz and barked an order, "Back to Dunfree's Corners with you. Wait for me at Mrs. Adams's." He pulled out his gold watch and handed it to the older man. "I doubt it will take me long to persuade the young lady to accept William's suit, but if you should fall short of funds, see what you can get for this."

Grumbling his disapproval, the old sailor took the timepiece and turned his mount back toward town.

With confidence once again his companion, Edward set his horse into a gallop. He was so intent on the pursuit of his game that he took little note of the fringe of clouds beginning to frost the tops of the mountains like gray hairs on an old man's pate.

As Calamatta rode deeper into the forest, she headed Cherry in the direction she thought she remembered the cabin to be. The Lord willing, she'd find it by eventide, build herself a comfortable fire, and eat some of the food she'd brought. But a strange uneasiness engulfed her, for it seemed the deeper she traveled into the forest, the more she saw the same places twice.

Darkness fell and still no cabin came into sight, but she discovered the welcoming mouth of a cave on a rocky hillside. She tethered Cherry inside the cave, built a fire, then ate a small portion of bread and cheese.

Here she was, running away again. Even now, panic assailed her when she recalled the moment Susanna informed her of her plans for another cotillion for her seventeenth birthday. A wildcat would have posed less of a threat. She was glad she'd left. Being robbed, abandoned, and left alone in the Cumberland Mountains wasn't as frightening as facing all those people.

No sooner had she gone into the mountains than she'd found

herself alone, much lighter in purse, and heavier in spirit. Her patience had been too stretched to its limits with the unfairness of it all for her to be the least bit thankful that she hadn't lost her virtue. She still couldn't figure out exactly what that was, so it was just as well she hadn't taken it with her. Miss Needle at the academy said young ladies did not discuss such things. But it had to be something very important, because she'd overheard her brothers say they'd kill any man who took hers. She supposed Ward kept it locked up in the bank with her inheritance and wasn't going to give it to her until she came of age.

Nevertheless, both her horse and mule were tricked from her when she went to the river to bathe. The only belongings left were the clothes she'd worn and the things in her possibles sack, the drawstring bag which was large enough to hold soap and towel, her comb, and the two books from Susanna's library. She'd finished the romance by P.A. Eder, *The Silent Lord Haverwulf,* and had just begun *Pride and Prejudice,* which so absorbed her thoughts she'd lost all track of time, allowing the thieves to carry out their dastardly act of devilry.

Well, no sense crying over spilt milk. Calamatta finished her meal with an apple. Then, leaving bread crumbs in a corner of the cave for the small night creatures, she curled up in her blanket and slept soundly until morning.

The next afternoon, she found a sad-looking log cabin. The furnishings consisted of a chair with one leg missing and a cot made with the hide of a large deer, stretched and secured over a wooden frame. The primitive log and clay chimney looked usable, and she saw a smattering of firewood scattered about the room.

Thinking a plump rabbit or a squirrel would do well for the evening meal, she checked to see that her rifle was loaded and cocked before she set off on her mare. With a smidgeon of guilt, she looked back at the squirrels and birds flitting in and out of the one small window of the cabin and decided she'd have to go some distance away before she'd have the heart to shoot her supper. A sudden rumble from the sky made her realize she'd better hurry if she was to beat the rain.

Following Calamatta wasn't as easy as Edward had anticipated. He'd kept sight of the place where the girl had entered the forest, but was having difficulty following her trail.

Heavy layers of leaves swirled in the wind, concealing any tracks made by her horse. Edward would have sworn he'd rounded the same large chestnut tree three times. Was the wily wench using an old Indian trick of going around in circles to throw off any pursuer?

The melancholy winds moaning through the trees sounded like the lowing of bagpipes, and Edward's thoughts wandered back to England, back to the first time his grandfather had fallen ill, the winter of 1814. Worst and heaviest snows he'd remembered. The Thames had frozen over. Edward was convalescing in a military hospital and William was in France. When word finally reached them of their grandfather's collapse, they both returned home to Careby, arriving within two days of each other.

Boskins, the family's elderly retainer, told them, "Sir Henry's in Scotland. He left me and the Missus to keep the house open for you if you returned. I know he'll be glad to see you before he passes on."

Anxiety had pushed the two brothers to hire a post-chaise and four in Stamford. From there, they hastened north, only to find their grandfather had rallied quite miraculously under the sweet ministrations of his closest neighbor, the wealthy widow Lady Dundreggan, Dowager Baroness of Hawthorne, who to their surprise had become his wife.

Relieved to find the old fussbox in fine fettle, they good-naturedly accepted their new title. "You dunderheads!" he'd scolded. "You gave up your careers in His Majesty's service?" Aye, he was definitely getting well, and on their way home, they'd regaled each other with childhood memories of being raised by their grandfather.

The next time they heard from the Dowager Baroness, she informed them their grandfather was dead, and because of that sudden occurrence Edward was on this hillside chasing a booly named Calamatta McGannon who was now mistress of his ancestral home—and the chit wasn't even aware of it.

Edward didn't see Calamatta again that day. Tracking a quarry in the up and down, rocky hillsides of the Kentucky forests was far different from hunting in the deer park which marched along the boundary of the Hatcher estate in Lincolnshire. His plans for a quick surprise, gallant rescue, and the eternal gratitude of a damsel in distress soon disappeared, as did all the biscuits he'd brought from Mrs. Adams's. And he didn't dare fire his gun for fear it would alert the girl of his presence.

At dusk he made camp by a stream, built a small fire, rolled up in his malodorous saddle blanket, and tried unsuccessfully to sleep. How had he come to agree to being the gull-flusher? Why was he here on the hard, cold, stony ground, and brother Will in a comfortable bed in England?

"You're more forthright, Eddie," William had said. "You know it takes me twice as long as you to dredge up the right words."

"Because you chew on arguments like a dog worrying a bone." Although Edward enjoyed taking advantage of William's think-it-through nature, he knew that, cautious as he was, the heir apparent more often than not got what he wanted.

It was toward the end of the second day when Edward saw Calamatta but before he could execute his surprise plan of attack-and-rescue, the storm caught up to them. Dark clouds skidded across the skies and the rumblings of thunder were heard in the distance. Edward sighted her riding along a precarious ledge across the dingle from him. When lightning severed a tree only a few feet in front of Calamatta, her horse reared. Edward dug his heels into his own horse's ribs. His only thought was to get to the lightwit before she was killed. Then a gunshot blasted away the silence and a bullet whizzed past his ear. His horse screamed and fell, rolling them over the side of the rocky precipice. Edward's right leg twisted under him, his head cracked against something hard, and the last thing he remembered was blinding pain.

When Edward regained consciousness, he was first aware of the crackling of fire, then the odor of roasting meat. For an instant, he thought he was at Careby Manor. He saw a figure on the hearth poking a stick into the flames. A serving girl? He called to her. "What am I doing here?"

Calamatta ran to the cot. "I rescued you," came the husky voice.

The McGannon witch! Now he knew exactly where he was: her clan's coven. "You're mistaken. I was supposed to rescue you."

"For heaven's sake!" She laughed, waving her knife around in the air.

Instinctively he tried to raise his hand to grasp her wrist. Hadn't she lived among savages? But he found his arms bound by a blanket.

She lowered the knife. "What made you think I needed rescuing?"

When he realized she wasn't going to cut his throat, he scoffed, "Ladies don't rescue gentlemen." Edward's hand felt for his pouch. It was still strapped to his chest. At least she hadn't robbed him. He'd half flung the blanket off when the cold air hit his bare skin. "What the deuce!"

With concern in her voice, Calamatta lifted the cover from his foot. "Are you in pain?"

"No," he fibbed. He quickly pulled the blanket to his chin, uncovering his bandaged foot. "Miss McGannon, where are my clothes?"

"Drying," she said, indicating the direction of the fireplace.

She didn't seem the least perturbed by having stripped him. "How did you get that long scar right here?" she asked, as she ran the tip of the knife the length of her hip. "Did you fall on something?"

"You might say that," he said, picturing the sword which nearly severed his leg. Well, so much for a dignified approach to William's suit. "What happened to me?"

"My rifle went off accidentally."

A very doubtful possibility. Edward thought as he fell back on the cot, whacking his head on the edge of the short frame. He let out a yelp.

She leaned over him. "Oh, dear, you hurt yourself again."

"No," he growled through clenched teeth. "Aside from my foot looking like a cannonball, I'm feeling top-of-the-trees." He changed the subject. "Where did you find bandages for my foot?"

"I tore up my petticoat."

"I'm sorry you had to do that," he said sharply.

"Give it no nevermind. But how did you know my Indian name?"

Edward gave her a blank look. The chit talked in riddles.

"You called me 'Tall-as-the-Trees.' That's my Indian name."

"I said *top-of-the-trees.* That means I feel quite up to the mark."

Giving him a questioning look, she reached out to feel his forehead.

Edward began to have hope that Miss Calamatta McGannon had a kind heart after all, until he glanced past her to the hearth. There, over the smoky fire, he saw a creature dangling at the end of a rope, its lower extremities turning black. He shuddered. Some sort of heathen ritual she had learned from the Indians? He'd probably be next. She obviously hadn't forgiven him for his boorish behavior at the barn dance. He could only pray that he could appeal to her sympathy.

"By the by, my Christian name is Edward. Edward Hatcher," he said weakly, then smiled to himself when he felt her hand again on his brow. "Why did they call you Tall-as-the-Trees?" He watched her straighten up. *Numskull,* he cursed to himself, *why did I ask that?* He closed his eyes again and told her in whispered tones, "After I left you, the night of the dance, I was attacked." That wasn't altogether a Banbury Tale. Calamatta's soft cooing told him he was on the right track. But the mood broke abruptly when the sharp smell of burned hemp and flesh permeated the air of the cabin.

That evening Calamatta served Edward a supper of charred rabbit smeared with melted cheese on a hunk of bread. "Your horse fell on it when you tumbled into the ravine," she said by explanation.

What could he say to that? Edward ate every bite handed him. Perhaps in time he'd become immune to her cooking. Since she didn't bring up the subject of the barn dance, he felt she'd forgiven him. That would mean that he'd overcome the first hurdle to winning her for William.

The rain didn't sound as if it had any plans of letting up. While Calamatta preoccupied herself with rekindling the fire, Edward struggled into his dry clothes, then sank back onto the cot and pulled the heavy blanket over his shivering body. His head throbbed, the fire burned low, and his side of the cabin began to feel like northern Scotland in the winter.

A drop of water fell onto the hot hearth and hissed near Calamatta's feet. He looked up to search for the leak, but it was so dark in the room that it was all he could do to make out her silhouetted figure dragging her saddle nearer the dying embers. The crackling of the leather sheet reverberated like thunder throughout the small room.

"Blast, it woman! What are you doing?"

"Making my bed."

"Jamaica will freeze over before I let a female sleep on a hard floor while I sleep in a bed." Edward flung off the blanket and started to struggle from the cot, only to have her body fall upon him and pin him down.

"You'll only make your ankle worse. I-I've slept on harder

ground," she chattered pointing to the wooden planks. "I'll be p-perfectly all right."

"You're freezing," said Edward, wrapping the blanket around her.

"But, Mr. Hatcher, now you don't have a cover." Her nose was nearly touching his. "The only fair thing to do is to share."

Edward agreed it was the only sensible thing to do, but deep down he knew the sensible thing wasn't sensible at all. He turned his back to her.

Calamatta crawled in. The only way she could fit was to put her arm over his body. After a bit of wriggling on her part to get settled, Edward felt her hand begin to make circles on his chest.

"What do you think you are doing?" he bellowed, grabbing her hand.

"Rubbing your chest to get you warm."

"I'm very warm, thank you."

"No, you're not, Mr. Hatcher," she said. "You're cold."

Edward grimaced. "I'm warm, Callie. Believe me, I'm warm."

She snuggled up to him and, as she pressed her nose into his back, she smiled. It was the first time he'd called her Callie. "Good night, Edward."

When he heard her faint even breathing, he placed his hand over hers. Soft and feminine, it fit perfectly in his. Edward swallowed a sailor's oath before it could escape his lips. This was the woman he'd promised to win for his brother. He didn't know whether to pity Will or envy him.

As the weather grew colder, the driving rain turned to sleet. By the second day, when both their fuel and food ran out, Edward's survival instincts told him their only solution to keep from freezing was to stay in bed.

That night, a screaming panther frightened Cherry. Much to Edward's consternation, Calamatta decided to bring the horse inside the cabin. By the time she got the mare through the low, narrow doorway, both were drenched. "Why are you bringing that horse in here?" he growled.

Calamatta saw that Mr. Hatcher's disposition hadn't improved. "Wild animals are out there. Branches are shooting through the air like arrows." Calamatta stroked the mare's nose. "Poor thing's frightened. If she runs off, we'll have to walk out of here when the storm is over."

Edward wrinkled his nose and sneezed. "Take her out. She stinks."

Calamatta gave Cherry a reassuring pat on the neck and, in doing so, splattered water all over Edward. "Well, you don't smell like a rose yourself," she snapped.

Edward bolted upright. Blast it, the woman was stubborn! He turned back the moldy blanket. "Get out of those wet clothes and into this bed." He saw the word no start to form on her lips. "Now!" he ordered.

Three

Calamatta was shivering so hard she could not speak. She pulled off her boots and let her coat, skirt, and blouse fall into a sodden heap on the floor. Before she hopped under the blanket, Edward made her put on his smelly oiled jacket over her underclothes.

Except for the necessary reasons to get up, they clung to each other for the next day and a half, talking and sleeping—talking to fill the time and sleeping to forget their hunger. But, stiff jacket not withstanding, Edward was uncomfortably aware that the kissable body inside was that of the woman intended for his brother.

At first, Cherry was inclined to wander about, snuffling in the corners of the cabin for something to eat. By the third day hunger made them all listless. While the storm continued, Edward decided to take a starboard tack to get in Calamatta's good graces. He told her amusing tales about their boyhood. She laughed heartily. No shy, missish giggles. Edward liked that. He thought he was building William up to sound not only like quite a noble fellow but a prime wit, as well. Old sobersides Will a wit? What a clanker.

Now Edward felt it was the time to hint at his real purpose. "My brother greatly admires American women," he said. "He told me to find him a diamond of the first water—someone who would wish to become the mistress of his distinguished old manor in a beautiful rural area of England."

Edward waited for some reaction, but when he got none, he reached for her hand where it rested upon his hip and gave it a pat. He had found that Calamatta was interested in birds and animals, and she liked to fish. Not many women did. He began to revise his opinion of Miss Calamatta McGannon. An impulsive lass, aye. Mean, nay. There was not a disobliging bone in her body. Upon entertaining that thought, he couldn't refrain from giving her hand another squeeze. Perhaps she wouldn't be such a bad wife for William after all—loosen up that stiff-rumped, pattern-saint brother of his. Edward chuckled to himself. William hated fishing. "I was to look for someone comely," he said, thinking a little flummery would not hurt.

Calamatta curled her fingers around his. "Is he romantic?"

Now Edward knew he was making some headway. "A regular up-to-the-mark Romeo. Do you know of anyone who may be interested?"

"I was thinking of Lucy," Calamatta said. "She's always dreamed of living in a grand house and being a fine lady. If she hadn't already given her heart to another, she may have been interested in meeting William."

Their conversation wasn't taking the direction he'd planned.

While Edward talked, Calamatta was thinking that although the words he whispered against the nape of her neck were of William, they revealed more to her about Edward than he realized. She was beginning to like Mr. Edward Hatcher. His deep concern for his brother's happiness made her decide to accept Edward's apology for leaving her at the dance and double her efforts to find a bride for William.

The darkness which descended upon the cabin played tricks on Calamatta and Edward. The passage of time was lost, so it was not surprising that they had slept all afternoon and into the early evening of the fourth day. They didn't even notice when the rain stopped and snow began to fall.

The first indication that all was not well was when Cherry's whinny awakened Edward. The door of the cabin crashed open.

Cold, fresh air shot across the room. Quickly, he rolled on top of Calamatta to protect her.

The face of the wild-looking man filling the entrance was lost in shadow, but the muzzle of his rifle was pointed at them, and Edward realized too late that Calamatta's gun was beyond reach. When the entire band of mountain men crowded into the room, he knew his life was over.

Calamatta awakened and struggled to free herself from being crushed beneath Edward. Had the man gone mad? The bump on his head must have been worse than she thought. She peeked out from under Edward's chest.

"Creed! You're back."

Edward looked down at her smiling face. Enlightenment slowly penetrated his brain. Her brother. "Creed?"

As Calamatta wriggled free, Edward rolled off onto the floor and ended in an awkward crouching position. Attempting to rise, he extended his hand to the scowling monster. A challenging roar rent the air and, nearly too late, Edward saw the fist coming.

Animal instincts surfaced. He blocked the punch and landed one of his own in the giant's gut. The blow only angered the man more, and Edward knew he would have been killed if his leg hadn't given out on him. As Edward sank to one knee, Creed's first attempt to smash his face missed, but the next caught his left eye.

Male pride in his pugilistic skills goaded Edward to ignore the pain in his leg. He forced himself to get up again and strike the pompous fellow with such momentum that they both toppled over backwards.

"Stop it!" yelled Calamatta, throwing her arms around the downed Edward. "Can't you see he hurt his ankle?"

"Ain't his ankle I'm aiming to put out of commission," shouted Creed.

The two men sat on the floor glaring at each other. Edward expressed smug satisfaction, but Creed, from the look in his eyes, harbored far darker thoughts than his opponent.

Calamatta's arms were still around Edward's neck, nearly strangling him. The more Creed yelled, the harder she squeezed. Edward thought he might prefer being killed by the ruffian to being choked to death by the man's sister. But at that point Edward, as dizzy as he was, didn't care. In fact, if the truth be known, he was feeling quite proud of himself.

"Calamatta Mary McGannon!" Creed bellowed, hauling himself up.

When her brother used her full name, Calamatta knew he really was angry with her, but she didn't loosen her hold on Edward.

"Remove your hands from that heathen Tory," Creed said, towering over the both of them. "I'm going to grind him into the dirt."

Oh, my. Creed really was fit to chew a wildcat, and she could tell Edward's mind was wandering. His eyes weren't in focus.

"Cain't leave you two days afore you're in trouble."

Eyes ablaze, Calamatta released her hold on Edward and confronted her brother. "It's been over three months, Creed."

"Don't make no difference. Cain't trust you off a leash."

Edward held his head to steady it. A queasy feeling of apprehension, which had nothing to do with his reeling brain and throbbing ankle, roiled around in his stomach. He tried to rise.

Creed's eyes narrowed.

Calamatta threw him a suspicious look. "What're you thinking?"

"Good Gawd!" roared Creed. "It doesn't take a simpleton to figure out what you two have been up to."

Edward could see the moment it registered in her brother's mind that Calamatta was standing there before eight men in nothing but a dirty jacket over her torn shift. The giant's face turned purple. As he swung back to Edward, he exploded, "Your name Hatcher?"

Dumbstruck, Edward nodded.

"Well, you're going to marry my sister. Four days you've had her."

With the ringing in his ears, Edward wasn't sure he'd heard correctly.

Calamatta straightened up and placed her hands on her hips while Edward tried to steady himself. Her eyes blazed and her face turned red with anger. "Lord-a-mighty, Creed, I never heard the like. You take back what you said."

Edward took a quick look at the surrounding army of gladiators. Grins spread across all six faces.

A tornado roared from the big man's lungs. "Callie . . . someday . . . someday!" Creed shook his gigantic fist in her face, then barked an order to the men in the doorway, "Get those horses ready. We got to find a preacher." He turned to the man nearest him. "You know of one, Zach?"

"There's a circuit rider lives up near Dunfree's Corners," volunteered Zachariah. "Ain't that right, Coleman?"

The older man nodded. "He should have made his rounds 'bout now."

Edward started to protest.

The bear whirled on him. "You English think you can have your way with a McGannon woman and get away with it?"

"It wasn't like that, Creed!" shouted Calamatta.

"You mean you agreed, willing?"

"No, you old cattymount."

"Then he forced you." Creed swung. Edward wasn't ready for the fist that slammed into his face. Blood spurted from his nose.

Calamatta didn't know whether to bellow at her brother or try to defend Edward. Then the room began to spin around in the strangest way, her hunger having caught up with her. Too late, she realized her indecision was taken by Creed to be guilt.

"That does it, Cal. You made your choice." Creed looked over at the young man standing with his arm around the mare's neck. "Ben, saddle up that horse. We're going to find a preacher."

For the first time, Benjamin spoke up. "Creed, don't you think you're being a trifle hasty?"

There came a resounding, "Nay!" Then, the large man rounded on his companions. "What you all gawking at? Git yourselves out o' here." With the toe of his boot he pushed the pile of discarded garments toward Calamatta. "And you, girl, put on your clothes and make yourself decent for your wedding."

Edward remembered little beyond that point. The congestion in his chest made him fight for every breath. It was dusk when they left the cabin and pitch dark by the time they reached the settlement. His rough jacket proved a poor weapon against the chill, and because his ankle was still swollen, he was forced to carry one of his boots. He rode Cherry. Calamatta, mounted in front of Creed, fell into an exhausted sleep in her brother's arms.

As they approached Dunfree's Corners, the only sounds were coming from a tavern. He wondered if Fitzgerald was inside enjoying himself or asleep at Maude Adams's boardinghouse. Either way, surrounded by seven determined men on horseback and a rifle aimed at his back, there seemed little chance he could get word to his servant of his predicament in time to prevent the inevitable. At the end of the street, they found a church with a house attached to the rear. With his sleepwalking sister sternly in tow, Creed mounted the three steps to the porch and banged his fist on the door. "We need a preacher," he bellowed. The pounding brought no response.

"I don't think anyone's home," Edward rasped.

But a second assault on the door produced a light within and a weak voice from the other side called, "Coming. Coming." The door opened a crack and a thin face appeared. The man, a nightcap covering his head, squinted at them over a candle. "What can I do for ye?"

"We need a preacher," repeated Creed, pushing open the door. "There's a pair of lovers here who can't wait to get married."

The man in his nightshirt barely had time to jump back. Then, with no more than a by-your-leave, Edward and Calamatta were pushed into the small entryway, which opened to rooms on either side. Creed herded them all into the parlor.

Their host came running after them. "It's late."

"You're damn right, but not too late," shouted Creed, waving his rifle.

"You don't understand. There has to be identification and witnesses, and the marriage certificate has to be signed." The perplexed man began to pat the front of his nightshirt. "Oh, dear, where are my spectacles? Cain't see a thing without them."

Creed glared at him. "What's your name?"

"Isaiah Butters, sir."

"All right, Butters, don't you know the wedding words by heart?"

"Y-yes, sir."

"Then say 'em." Creed still had one hand firmly clasped around Calamatta's body to keep her from falling. He pulled her forward, then pointed his rifle at Benjamin. "That's my brother, Ben. And this is our sister, Calamatta Mary McGannon. She is who we say she is, and a McGannon's word should be good enough for anyone. This here's Mr. Hatcher, who wishes to marry our sister. Now, where are those papers you say have to be signed?"

The man hurried to a big open desk against the wall, and with shaking hands, picked up a sheet of paper and held it a couple inches from his eyes. Sighing, he took the quill pen from the inkstand and handed it to Calamatta to fill out her name. He then addressed Edward.

"I believe some sort of identification is needed for the groom, also."

Identification, thought Edward. The proxy in his pouch!

"What're you doing?" grunted Creed, prodding Edward in the back with the barrel of his rifle.

"Getting my papers," coughed Edward, his voice nearly gone.

"Then get 'em."

Edward sneezed. His cold fingers fumbled in the packet until he found what he wanted. To make his plan work, he would have to insert the proxy in with the marriage certificate and get that signed as well. If the cleric was as poor-sighted as he suspected, no one would be the wiser.

Standing on either side, Benjamin and Zachariah supported Edward. The ceremony was short. The frightened little man in his nightshirt first called him Mr. Latcher, then Hatcher. Held tightly against her brother's side, Calamatta heard everything as if in a dream. He shook her. When told to say yes, she did.

"I now pronounce you man and wife." Isaiah Butters began to rustle through the sheets of papers.

"Permit me," Edward said helpfully shuffling the documents like he played cards—with expert precision—and scribbled Will's name. No one noticed. Edward pocketed the documents. Quite inspirational, he thought. Brother William, you now have a wife.

Minutes later, the party was outside and mounted.

"Which way to Mrs. Adams's?" Ben asked.

Thank God the McGannons had taken Edward's suggestion that instead of continuing on to the Coleman farm, they seek lodgings nearby. Edward pointed Cherry toward the north end of the street. The others followed. Creed sat in his saddle with his sister in front of him, enfolded in his enormous coat. As soon as Ben had handed her up to him, Calamatta had fallen asleep again. Even though Creed announced he'd accomplished his purpose to see them buckled, Edward noted that the big man seemed reluctant to let her go.

Aroused from her sleep, Mrs. Adams, a plump, motherly woman, acted as though she was quite accustomed to receiving boarders in the middle of the night, and, with her candlestick held high, good-naturedly led them to the second floor. She opened the door to a room at the head of the stairs.

After being given a taradiddle of an excuse for their late arrival, the disheveled appearance of the newlyweds, and lack of baggage, Mrs. Adams looked at the sleeping girl and cooed, "Poor little lamb. She's plumb tuckered out from all the celebrating."

Thank God, Edward thought, his swollen, bearded face so altered his appearance that she didn't recognize him from his previous visit.

While she explained that the other gentlemen would find beds in a large attic space on the third floor, Creed carried his sister into the bedroom.

Dragging one boot, Edward limped up the stairs. He didn't know what was expected of him. As Creed laid Calamatta gently atop the comforter, Edward overheard the big bear whisper, "Sorry we didn't get to give you no shivaree, little sister." And Edward detected another chink in the bullheaded warrior's armor.

Mrs. Adams shooed the men out of the doorway. "You men skeedaddle to your room now and let me find the purty thing something decent for a bride to wear. I'm sure some of my gowns will fit her fine." She soon came back with some garments thrown over her arm.

With embarrassed coughs, the men sought out their room, all except Creed. He grabbed Edward by the collar and pushed his bearded face up against Edward's hairy one.

"You already had your wedding night, Tory. You took her innocence, damn you. Now you take care of our little sister or—" Not finishing his sentence, Creed opened the bedroom door and shoved Edward inside.

Mrs. Adams was pulling the sheet up under Calamatta's chin. The lace of her night rail encompassed her face like the petals of a flower. "Didn't wake up the whole time I was putting on her gown. Sakes alive, you young people are a frolicsome lot," she chuckled. She gave Calamatta's cheek a motherly pat, then tiptoed out.

Edward dropped the boot he still grasped and managed to slip out of his stiff jacket. He didn't wash, nor did he snuff out the candle. "You're all that you should be, aren't you, you little devil? If you weren't, Creed would have wiped out that whole band of Indians." He limped over to the bed and stood looking down at Calamatta. "How did you survive all those months in the wilds?" he asked, in a raspy voice. "Did you threaten to cook for them?"

He reached out his hand to touch the long brown hair cascading over her pillow. The one question which posed an obstacle to his bargain with his brother had been answered. She was still a virgin, but Edward was afraid this created another problem. How was he going to keep his hands off her?

As his fingers came within inches of her face, Edward lost his balance, fell upon the bed next to his brother's bride and was unconscious in seconds.

Calamatta awakened and stretched. The first dim rays of morning light bathed the room in a soft orange glow. She felt there was something she should remember. She started to roll over, but a solid form wedged against her prevented her from doing so. She lowered the comforter to look. A man lay upon his stomach beside her. She reached over and gingerly lifted the strand of hair that nearly covered his swollen nose.

"Edward!" A racking cough was the only answer she got. His face revealed a most distressful-looking black eye, and one touch of his forehead told her he was burning up with fever. She looked about the strange room, then down at herself. She was wearing a voluminous, but pretty, white gown, and he lay like a dirty rag dumped upon her bed. For a moment longer she stared at him; then the past evening's events flooded in on her. *To have and to hold. In sickness and in health.* Her eyes widened and she gazed in wonder at the man beside her. Edward was her husband.

But where were Creed and Ben? Her heart began to beat wildly. Surely they wouldn't leave without telling her. Or was Creed mad at her still? The sounds of clattering pots and pans came from below. She slipped from the bed and ran barefooted across the wood-planked floor to the window and looked out over the dusty street.

Calamatta tiptoed back to the bed and stood looking down

at Edward. My, did all men have to be taken care of as much as this one? One boot lay on the floor. Didn't he know enough to take off his clothes, or to get under the covers? No wonder he was so poorly. No more sense than a bullbat.

With no small effort, Calamatta managed to roll him over and pull the coverlet up around his face. Her own clothes were nowhere to be seen, but a brown woolen frock, pantaloons, stockings, and a pair of slippers lay upon the cane chair. The morning air was brisk, but delicious odors of frying bacon and coffee were beginning to seep up between the cracks in the floorboards. Shivering, she pulled on the stockings and dress.

Although her stomach churned with hunger, Calamatta didn't want to leave Edward. She pulled the chair up to the bed, sat down, and tried to decide what to do. Should she see to cooking a poultice for his chest to help him breathe easier? She tried to hark up some of the recipes Mandy-lu, her old Negro nurse, used to make. Garlic and oatmeal? That was it.

But if she dared to leave the room, would she have to face the wrath of her brother? While she was debating this serious problem, she felt under the sheet for Edward's hand and held it tenderly in both of hers.

Four

That same morning, Mrs. Adams pointed Fitz to a seat at the dining-room table with her other boarders, including six McGannon men and Mr. Coleman. The group, deep in their conversation, only nodded as the good woman made brief introductions before scurrying back to the kitchen. Fitz recognized Mr. Coleman from the barn dance and ducked his head before that gentleman could get a good look at him. Six of the other men had the same name as the pretty lass the Cap'n had chased after. Their discussion pertained to a rafting trip they'd made recently transporting produce to New Orleans.

Fitz's ears perked up when the stout-hearted redhead started boasting of the day when steamboats would not only carry Kentucky farmers' products south, but would then bring much needed merchandise, as well as passengers, back north again. Then the men's discourse switched to a recent wedding they'd attended and the old sailor lost interest. His attention turned back to filling his mouth with juicy pork sausages and steaming hotcakes. Suddenly someone mentioned Mr. Hatcher was upstairs with his new bride. Fitz nearly spit out his coffee. "What mess has the Cap'n got hisself into now?" he spouted under his breath.

As inconspicuously as possible, Fitz hied himself up the stairs where he waited around the corner in the hallway until he saw the girl his master had made a fool of himself over slip quietly from a room and down the hall.

Silently, Fitz made his way in through the same doorway.

Edward lay in the bed like a dead man. His face sported several days' growth of beard, a swollen lip, scarlet nose, and a purple eye.

The old seadog had seen many a battle casualty in his day, but at the sight, he gasped. "Gawd, Cap'n, ye look like ye been burnt to a socket."

At the sound of Fitz's voice, Edward, with extraordinary effort, opened his one good eye and gave him a lopsided grin. Sounding like a choking frog, Edward whispered, "I did it, Fitz. I married the chit to William, only she doesn't know it yet."

Fitz raised an eyebrow.

Edward quickly filled him in on his misadventures of the last few days. "Fetch me some paper and pen. I have an urgent message which I must get to my brother in England."

The efficient servant was soon back in full sail with the required essentials. Edward laboriously scribbled off a letter to William. "I've written him that as far as I know there has been no word of Grandfather's will reaching the United States. So we've beat the bugler, and after a few minor details are worked out, I'll deliver his bride and her dowry to him."

Fitz tucked the letter inside his jacket. "Aye, if ye say so, Cap'n, but I sure as hell don't like leaving ye here to fend for yerself." With no more ado, the seaman left the room, promising to start for Virginia that very morning. As soon as the door closed behind Fitz, Edward fell back upon the pillow and closed his eyes. The hacking cough which he'd suppressed while his servant was in the room racked his body. When the spasm was over, he tried to focus his mind on organizing his plans. What a coil he was in. According to their agreement, he had to obtain the dowry and get William's bride back to England, or they would end up with their pockets to let. Unfortunately, the two tasks went together. The acceptance of her brothers was paramount, but with Creed's bombastic attitude, the achievement of his goal appeared nigh to impossible.

Just before he fell into an uneasy sleep, he remembered Calamatta's hand seeking and tightly, yet gently, holding his under the blanket. Who was this perplexing vixen he'd snared for his brother?

The following day, Edward felt worse. Earlier that morning, Mr. Coleman had left the boardinghouse for his farm, but not before saying he'd have a wagon sent back for Calamatta and Edward. Zachariah, Rueben, and the other two McGannon cousins left with him, planning to stay a few days with the Colemans before continuing on to their home further north.

While Creed went to settle their account with Mrs. Adams, Ben pulled Calamatta into the front parlor. "You shouldn't let Creed rattle you so, Cal. You know he's all wind-'n'-holler."

Calamatta stuck out her lower lip. "I know, but he pricks me worse than a skeeter."

"That isn't what I wanted to talk to you about. With all that's been happening, I didn't have time to tell you that I sold all your gloves."

The expression on Calamatta's face turned a full circle. "You didn't!"

He grinned and pulled a pouch and thin package from his pocket. "I found a ladies' dress shop in New Orleans. The modiste was quite a pretty little thing." Ben turned red. "She sold me these scissors. Well, anyway, she was quite impressed with your workmanship and the quality of the leather and knows she can sell them. Fancy European goods are still slow in arriving."

Ben took her hand and poured several coins into it. "A store which deals in hunting clothes and riding equipment took the men's gloves."

Calamatta looked wide-eyed at the money. "Oh, Ben. I promised I'd buy Lucy some books if I sold any of my gloves, but there isn't any place around here I can do that."

"Zounds! I nearly forgot." Her brother bounded toward the door. "Wait right there."

He returned with a package wrapped in plain brown paper. He started to thrust it into her hands, but, too impatient to wait while she pocketed her coins, he pulled off the string and let the wrappings fall to the floor. "Almost left them in my saddlebags." He held up five books. "The bookseller assured me I'd made a good selection."

Ben handed her the first volume. "Of course, I'm partial to poetry, so I picked up this book that has selections by Wordsworth and Coleridge. What I wouldn't give to be able to talk to men like them."

Calamatta took the second little book. "Hannah More," she said looking at the author's name. "Susanna has some of her stories."

"Rather like Sunday sermons, I thought," said Benjamin. "But these," he handed her two more books, "are just what the store owner said the ladies really like. Both are romances by a P. A. Eder. Fairy tales, I'd call them."

"Oh, Ben! He wrote *Lord Haverwulf.*"

Ben held the last book behind his back.

She tried to reach around him. "Don't be a tease. Let me see."

"Well, knowing how much you and Lucy liked *Pride and Prejudice,* I just happened to run across another book by the same anonymous author."

"Ben!"

He brought the book around and handed it to Calamatta. *"Sense and Sensibility!"* she whooped. "That's really top-of-the-trees."

"What?"

"Really, Ben, don't you know anything? That means tip-top. The greatest!"

"Well, why didn't you say so? Really, Cal. Sometimes I wonder where you pick up some of the odd things you say."

She gave him a knowing look. "Why don't you give the books to Lucy yourself?"

"What for?" he expostulated. "I'll be with Creed. We aren't going back to the Colemans. Besides, it was your money."

"Never mind," she said with a shake of her head. Men! Why did they always have to be so secretive about their feelings?

Ben gave her a hug. "Take care, Cal," he said, and kissed her on the cheek. She clung to him for a minute, then followed him out of the house. She stayed on the porch while he mounted his horse, which Creed was holding impatiently. Calamatta waved until they were out of sight.

When she could no longer hear them, Creed barked at Ben, "Quit frowning at me. We've been delayed long enough. I need to get back to Louisville to conclude that business on the river-front property." He ordered his horse into a gallop, bellowing to the sky, "Females always sprout trouble."

True to his word, Mr. Coleman sent the wagon to fetch Cal-amatta and Edward at Mrs. Adams's. Mrs. Coleman sent a new sheepskin coat she had been making for her husband, but said that from what she'd heard about the state of his clothes from the other men, Mr. Hatcher needed it more.

For several weeks, Calamatta hovered over Edward. At night, she slept in the trundle, which she pulled out from under his high bed.

One late evening, he saw Calamatta eyeing his empty food tray when she carried it from the room. He was feeling stronger every day. How much longer could he pretend to be sicker than he truly was? She would be back soon, and he was betwixt and between how many more excuses he could dredge up to keep her from crawling into bed with him.

Edward lay back on his pillow and mulled over the prepos-terous events of the last few months. His undercover activities had come to an end shortly before Sir Henry's final illness. Government officials were certain that during the war with Bonaparte, turncoats high in their own offices were leaking in-formation to French spies. "It will be easy for you, a former

Navy man, to frequent unsavory hideaways along the waterfront to uncover enough evidence to convict the renegades," Sir Richard had said. It would have been only a matter of days before the whole of it was concluded, and Edward could have given his undivided attention to the Careby estate. Then Sir Henry died.

After the funeral, he'd asked Will, "Why didn't you tell Grandfather of your outstanding war record? When I was in hospital, I heard rumors that Major William Hatcher would surely be cited for his actions at the siege of Paris. Grandfather thought we were just playing the fool."

William had shaken his head and likewise chastised Edward, "And so, Captain Eddie, why didn't you tell him that you were wounded in battle?"

Edward was sure that if Grandfather had known of their true activities, he'd have destroyed that poppycockish will. Pride was an expensive armor, he decided, for it had cost them their ancestral home.

Sir Henry would never know how much he had admired him, because Edward had never worked up the courage to tell him. How does a rebellious child tell an irascible old man that he holds him in great affection? How could he say that he wanted a hug or a shoulder to cry on when the school's headmaster, Mr. Pickle—Sour Pickle, they called him—delighted in nettling small boys? "Acting missish again, Master Edward? That will never do."

He'd laughed in the headmaster's face, but when night came, Edward cried alone into his pillow because he missed his home—missed his parents, who'd been taken so suddenly from his life.

Joviality, Edward had found, was a clever mask for tears. He had taken out his hurt on his brother, teasing him, trying to crack that stern exterior. But Will was not easily rattled, and no matter how much Edward tried to get his brother to join in his pranks, in the end, Will got his way. He had always made adjustments look so easy that it had never occurred to Edward before that perhaps Will was suffering in his own way, trying hard to be the kind of man their grandfather had wanted them to be. Now Edward could make it up to both of them. He'd bring home his brother's bride and restore the ownership of Careby to its rightful heir.

Suddenly, Edward's thoughts were interrupted when he heard the door of their bedroom opening. He hunkered down under the covers.

"The stars will be bright with the clear sky tonight," Calamatta called out gaily, as she crossed to the window to pull the curtains back. His silence made her pause for a moment, but she decided to give it no nevermind and scurried about performing her wifely duties.

Edward enjoyed watching her from under his half-closed lids. She dug into the trunk and withdrew her pink flannel nightdress, and, after smoothing out the wrinkles, laid it across the bed. But when she saw him watching her, she blushed.

He'd never seen her blush. Turn red with anger, yes, but surely his Callie was not shy.

She picked up her nightgown and disappeared behind the screen in the corner of the room.

He heard the splash of water and smelled the aroma of scented soap.

"Do you ever think of that night at the barn dance?" she called out.

Edward had been doing his best to forget it. He cleared his throat.

"The kiss. Did I get it right?"

A sudden sense of guilt assailed him when he recalled how near he'd come to losing his agreement with William.

"It wasn't, was it?" She sounded unsure.

"No," he lied. "No . . . it was not the thing."

She came out from behind the screen, looking like a pink angel.

Edward turned his gaze toward the ceiling.

"But now that we're married, maybe we should start practicing."

"There are other things that follow, Callie."

"Oh, I know that. I'm not dumb." She cocked her head to one side like a thrush eyeing a succulent grub. "But I'm not quite sure how that works."

Edward closed his eyes. "You'll learn."

"How?"

"Your husband will teach you." Too late he realized what he'd said.

Calamatta smiled. "You're my husband."

Edward faked a groan. "First, I must build up my strength," he explained. "That part of the marriage responsibility takes a great deal of energy on the part of a man."

"Yes," Calamatta said, nodding thoughtfully. "I can imagine it must." She plumped up the pillow beneath his head and brushed his hair back from his forehead. "But, Edward——" Heavy breathing greeted her. With a sigh, she blew out the candle and settled onto the trundle. Men just didn't have the stamina women did. Why hadn't her brothers explained these things to her? They likely didn't want to admit their own weaknesses. Men were like that.

That made her think of her sister-in-law. Now she wished she'd asked Susanna more questions about how to be a good wife. Perhaps if she gave Edward a present, he'd feel more inclined to kiss her. He'd been happy with Mama Coleman's gift of a warm jacket to replace his old smelly one.

Gloves! She'd noticed his were worn and cracked. Gloves would make a splendid gift—something that she could make herself. She still had some pieces of soft deerskin which she'd brought with her from the Indian village. Yes, that would make him feel loved and cared for. Calamatta curled up to her pillow. Marriage wasn't turning out to be what she'd expected. Glory be! Men were confusing.

Edward couldn't sleep. He wiped his sweaty palms on the sheets and tried to turn over as quietly as he could, but, damn, she had ears like a fox. She was standing over him before he knew it. The moon and starlight silhouetted her figure.

"Edward," she whispered, "are you awake?"

Perhaps if he faked sleep, she'd go away.

When she got no response, Calamatta tapped Edward, none too gently, on his shoulder.

He could see his luck was running out. Until inspiration struck, he'd have to use flummery to keep the tempting wench away. He took her hand in his. "We both have a lot to learn," he said. "Do you remember what you said about kissing, Mrs. Hatcher?"

She nodded. "I told Lucy that you have to get it just right before the other things happen." She wanted him to know his wife was no babe in the woods.

For a moment that statement threw Edward a bit off track, but he tried not to show it. "Right! Right! The kiss has to be learned first." He drew in a deep breath. "Then the other things will follow." Agreeing with her should give him a grace period, he reasoned.

Calamatta sat down on the mattress next to him. "Ward and Susanna kissed a lot." However, to her disappointment, they had always closed their bedroom door, preventing her from seeing what came next.

Edward scrambled to think of something that would send her away. "Ah, there you are then. I gather it takes a bit of practice."

"Then perhaps we should start," she said, lowering her face to his.

Torture. She was torture personified. With the comforter between them, what harm could it do if it was the only way to stall her? *So be it,* he reasoned, enfolding her in his arms.

On their first attempt, Calamatta closed her eyes and kissed his nose. She was embarrassed at missing her target, so on the second try she kept her eyes open. She was glad Edward was being so helpful by cupping her face in his hands to help guide her. His beard tickled, little sparkles in his eyes danced in the moonlight, and one side of his mouth curled up before the other.

The second time, she tried to kiss him correctly, but the instant her lips touched his, he pushed her so abruptly she fell backwards onto the trundle.

With a groan, Edward rolled toward the wall, pulling the blanket over his head.

"What are you doing?" she demanded.

"Going to sleep!" came his muffled voice.

Well, if that didn't beat all! Maybe she had done it badly, but he was supposed to be trying, too. *What odd creatures men are,* she thought. *If they don't get something right the first time, they give up.* Tomorrow, she'd get him to try harder.

Calamatta crawled into her bed and burrowed her face into her soft pillow. There was that strange little rippling feeling running through her again. It happened when she leaned over Edward. In fact, it was occurring a lot lately, at strange times and for no apparent reason, but always when she was near him. She hoped she wasn't catching whatever he had.

When he heard the trundle creak, Edward rolled over and stared out the window. Starlight flooded the room. The constellations were all in the wrong places here in Kentucky. He wished he were sailing a ship in the middle of the ocean where there were no women and no problems. For a long time, he lay looking out into the night, then, taking a deep breath, expelled it with great force. He needed delaying tactics. Plotting a course at sea was far simpler than this one his brother expected him to finish.

Edward never considered himself a religious man, but that night he found himself praying for deliverance harder than he ever had in his life.

Deliverance of sorts did come the next day. Indian summer was upon them and, with its warm days, Creed and Ben returned to the Coleman farm.

Creed was wearing body-fitting fringed white buckskins, which set off his broad shoulders and made him appear more an indomitable warrior than any suit of armor could have ever done. He handed his sister a letter.

Calamatta read it and gasped, "Ward knows?"

"Ben wrote him. Told him you were married to an Englishman. Now we'll see what he's going to do about it," the redhead said curtly.

"Glory be!" She'd forgotten all about Ward. Calamatta looked at Edward. His face was like a blank page in a book—unreadable.

Creed followed her direction with furrowed brows. "Ward says you and that husband of yours are to return home post-haste."

Edward gave them a pleasant smile. Who'd have thought that one of Calamatta's own brothers would provide the means to get her back East?

Two days later, Edward, Calamatta, and Ben caught the Lexington mail coach going south on the Kentucky-to-Virginia route. Creed stayed behind.

Their coachman said, "Our stage line prides itself on swift, competitive service. If you take an overnight, women and children get the beds. Men sleep wherever they can. But if you go straight through, we stop only long enough to change horses. Relays is ten miles apart. The Pioneer line brags they change horses in five minutes. Well, my men do it in four."

Edward did not dispute the coachman's claim and chose the fastest timetable possible. Now his only concern was, if they survived the wild ride to Virginia, that he would be up to the challenge of pirating Calamatta away from her brother Ward.

Five

London, England
December, 1815

As soon as they docked in London, Edward sent a message ahead to inform William that he and Calamatta had arrived in England. He prayed that the elation which surged through his veins would not cause him to act recklessly. To his own amazement, he'd not only survived his confrontation in Richmond with the shrewd Ward McGannon, but even managed to get his brother's bride back across the ocean without having to commit murder—or, worse, be strung up himself on the gibbet for kidnapping and embezzlement.

The riskiest part of the caper had been when he had to gamble on revealing to her that she was really married to William and not to him. When he had finally persuaded her to accept the idea of a substitute husband, he should have been pleased. After all, wasn't that what he'd hoped for? Yet he'd felt irritated.

But now Edward had her in England, out of reach of her brothers, and as soon as he delivered Calamatta to his brother's doorstep, he would have completed his part of their bargain and could wipe his hands of the whole affair. "I've obtained a suite for us here at Grillon's Hotel," he told Calamatta. He'd signed them in as Mr. and Mrs. William Hatcher, thankful once again for his close resemblance to his brother in case the register should for any reason be scrutinized by someone who knew them. "My room is across the sitting room from yours. That way I won't disturb you if I should come in late this evening."

"Are you sure you will be all right, Edward?" Calamatta said, concern showing in her voice. "You were sick all of the way across the ocean, you know."

Edward suddenly found it imperative that he check the latch on the heavy satchel which he'd carried since leaving the ship. He was afraid that if he looked at Calamatta directly she would see the guilt reflected in his eyes. "I am fine now that I am on solid ground," he assured her.

Thankfully, Calamatta had accepted the taradiddle he'd fed her about his having a landlubber's stomach. Fitz would have a good laugh over that. "You should be quite comfortable here while I take care of a few business matters and see to hiring a traveling coach for tomorrow. Careby is seventy-five miles to the north. If we don't stop except to refresh ourselves and change horses we should be home by the end of the day." *Home.* he thought. *William's and her home—not mine.* "I am afraid I must leave you here by yourself now, but I shall try to finish everything I have to do by this evening so that we can be off early in the morning."

"Oh, you need not worry about me," Calamatta said, with too much enthusiasm to suit Edward. "I am certain I can find any number of things to do in London."

He eyed her warily. "I prefer that you stay in the hotel," he said. "I have arranged for a maid to be assigned to you to attend your personal needs. You can ask her to find you something to read or you can continue the stitchery you brought with you."

"I lost my best scissors on board ship," Calamatta said.

"I am certain the maid can find you another pair," he said.

"But these were a special kind," she said. "Ben gave them to me. They are so sharp they can cut leather. But that is all right. I have some letters I wish to write, and I should like a nice warm bath."

"Very good," he said. "I shall leave you then." *Is she home-sick? Has she really accepted the consequences of being mar-*

ried to William and not to me? Calamatta was always so damned cheerful that it was hard for him to tell.

As Edward entered the corridor, a young girl in a black uniform with a stiffly starched white apron and mobcap was just approaching the apartment. He held the door for her to enter. "As soon as I can conclude my affairs, we shall be off to Careby," he called back over his shoulder. "Just obey me and stay in the hotel."

Her voice carried after him. "Oh, I shall, Edward. Don't you pay me no nevermind."

But of course he did. He didn't trust the minx out of his sight. On his way out of the hotel, he told the doorman that if Mrs. Hatcher should be seen leaving Grillon's, he wanted a male servant assigned to accompany her.

After hailing a hack, Edward made his way to the Bank of London with his satchel. It held monies worth nearly fifty thousand pounds British. His plan was to open an account in London with a portion of the blunt, pay off some of his and William's creditors, and place the rest in smaller banks more accessible to Careby.

Settling back on the leather squabs, Edward chuckled to think what bedlam must have occurred in the McGannon household when it was discovered that he had not only escaped from America with Calamatta but had absconded with nearly all of her dowry, as well.

He thought back to their harrowing coach ride from Kentucky and his first encounter with Calamatta's oldest brother. It had taken them little more than a week before he was being shown into Ward McGannon's study in Richmond—an imposing room with an imposing desk for an imposing man. The pleasant family reception and elegant dinner which followed had not lulled Edward into letting down his guard. Ward was not as muscular nor as wild-looking as his redheaded brother Creed. In contrast to the latter, he had been impeccably dressed, and, from his former inquiries, Edward knew this McGannon was not a man easily flummoxed.

"Sit down, Mr. Hatcher. Now that the social formalities are out of the way and my wife is assured of Calamatta's well-being, we can get down to the business at hand."

Edward moved a chair closer to the desk and seated himself. The scowl on Ward's face had charged the whole room with suspicion while his fingers tapped a monotonous tattoo on the top of his desk. "Ben wrote that they found you in very compromising circumstances with our sister." The fingers kept tapping.

Edward was well aware that the steady rhythm was meant to mesmerize him. He crossed his legs and sat back. "I assure you, I was in no state of mind nor body to be coherent—or dangerous. I had been injured. Your sister took care of me."

"So she told me. Why didn't you explain that to Creed?"

"Your brother doesn't listen very well. I tend to believe that your wife was right when she described him at dinner as a misplaced cocklebur on a pussy-willow bush.

Ward gave a bark of laughter and the tapping ceased. Tension eased. "I know what you mean. Ben said you professed to be in this country to pursue an advantageous business venture when you inadvertently came upon the barn dance, all of which started this bizarre chain of events."

Nodding, Edward uncrossed his legs, leaned a bit more toward Ward, but remained silent.

Ward raised his eyebrows. "You don't seem to be dissatisfied with the outcome.

"No," Edward said truthfully.

"Well and good. Susanna says Calamatta seems happy, and I have checked out the early William Hatcher family here in Virginia. He was elected to the House of Burgesses four times from Henrico County. They came from a well-to-do family in Careby. If a younger son was able to live so well, I can imagine the generous wealth of your family in England. I understand that is the same area from which you profess to come. Strange as it may seem, we had a great-great grandmother, Sarah

Hatcher, who was a granddaughter of that William. We may be distant cousins."

Edward managed to look surprised.

"Nonetheless, Calamatta is your wife now."

Edward willed himself to remain calm. "Aye. Thanks to your brother Creed, she is legally Mrs. Hatcher."

"After Benjamin wrote the details, I sent immediately for more information from England, but that will, of course, take time."

Edward's mind began to calculate. If Ward McGannon hadn't received any correspondence from England yet, that meant he didn't know of the will. Parnell's agent had still not returned to Richmond. Fitz, the old geezer, had done a bang-up job, but it also meant that Parnell's investigator could turn up any day.

"You see, when Creed wrote that Calamatta was married to a foreigner, my wife, who I'm sure you realize is in confinement, was upset." A shadow came over his face. "She is of a delicate nature. At the time Calamatta was found living with the Indians, Susanna insisted that she should go to Kentucky, but I was afraid she would lose our baby. We have lost several. Now, with this latest news, I feared if she didn't see for herself that Calamatta was content, her health would be endangered. That's why I sent for you to come to Richmond—aside from the fact I wanted to meet you myself."

Ward sat back and placed the tips of his fingers together. "There is another matter I wished to discuss with you. In less than a year's time, Calamatta will begin to receive an annuity of thirty-five thousand dollars, the equivalent today of about ten thousand pounds."

Edward kept his expression placid.

The big man paused to offer him a cigar. Edward knew Ward's keen eyes observed every move he made. "The tobacco is from our own fields," he said, pointing to an open tin on his desk. "Help yourself."

Edward took a handful of cigars and placed them in his coat pocket.

"Now to another matter," Ward said. "What you don't know—for Calamatta isn't aware of this herself—is that our father, John McGannon, set aside a dowry for her of one hundred seventy-five thousand dollars. Since she is not yet of age, that money will be under your administration until she is twenty-one. At that time, she will regain control of her estate."

Ward had lit his own cigar, then handed it over the desk for Edward to light his. "I'm certain that someone such as yourself may not think it much, but nevertheless, I shall have the account registered under both your names at the First National Bank of Richmond. I know from experience that sometimes it is difficult to get the transfer of funds from another country. Since you are legally in charge of your wife's monies, I will instruct my banker that you may draw on it any time you wish."

Ward sat back and blew a cloud. "You indicated an interest in shipping. Perhaps you would want to stay in Kentucky and invest in some of the family businesses—and"—he grinned—"perhaps hire a cook?"

The man was not without a sense of humor, Edward decided.

"When Calamatta's affairs are concluded, I'll understand if you want to return to England for a time to finish some business there."

Edward nodded soberly.

Ward rose from behind his desk. "I ask one thing." It was an order.

Edward waited to hear him out.

"Until I receive information from my agent, I want you to remain in the United States. Calamatta is my only sister. Once out of the boundaries of this country, I have little control over her welfare." He fixed Edward with a steady glare.

At first Ward McGannon's acuteness had seemed an impossible obstacle to Edward's ever finding a way to snatch his brother's bride out from under his watchful eye. But against all odds of it happening again as it had in Kentucky, Calamatta's own family had provided him with the means to spirit her away. Overhearing a conversation later that evening between Cala-

matta and her sister-in-law prompted Edward to suggest that he
would like to take her on a short honeymoon. How could her
brother say no to that?

While Edward made his way to the bank, Calamatta sat at
the small painted desk in the hotel suite, tickling her chin with
the feather end of her pen. She had already scribbled off a
short paragraph to Ward telling him of her proxy marriage.
Her missive to a bosom friend was understandably much
longer, and she now concentrated on finishing the letter to
Lucy which she'd started aboard ship. It had been such a rough
crossing that Calamatta had found it difficult to keep a steady
hand to write. She had tried to work on the gloves, but then
she misplaced the scissors and she had no other sharp cutting
tool. Besides, she had lost interest in finishing the gloves after
Edward had told her that he was not her husband.

Oh, she'd been angry and hurt at first, but Edward's eloquent
appraisal of his brother's superior virtues, which continued for
their entire voyage, quite persuaded her in the end that William
was the better choice of husbands.

The disclosure had not truly shocked her, for arranged mar-
riages, it seemed, were quite as common in England as they
were in America. Had not Ward already spoken to Reverend
Dinwiddie on a possible match with his son? And Creed had
certainly not consulted her when he forced her to marry Edward.
No, it seemed that women had little to say in the matter all over
the world. So, considering her alternatives, being married to an
upstanding gentleman like Mr. William Hatcher was a considerable improvement over being shackled to a tadpole like Jeremiah Dinwiddie. Besides, she liked the sound of "Mistress of
Careby Manor."

But no matter how provoked Calamatta had been at first on
hearing Edward's revelation, she could not erase from her memory how handsome he had looked that first night in Richmond.
He'd attired himself in a fine suit of clothes which Creed had

Benjamin pick out for him in Louisville. His hair was washed, and though still long, it was pulled back and secured by a thong in the old fashion. He'd shaved. It was the first time Calamatta had seen Edward's full face, and it had nearly taken her breath away. She could do little else but stare at him throughout the entire meal.

Later when Ward had taken Edward into his study and she and Susanna retired to the sitting room, Calamatta had gazed in puzzlement at her sister-in-law. She'd never seen her brother's wife look so radiant. The petite Queen of Richmond Society, with her tiny slippered feet dangling a full six inches above the floor, was trying desperately not to slip off the horsehair settee where Ward had placed her like one would a china doll.

"Go ahead and say it," Susanna had said, laughing. "I look like Humpty Dumpty on his wall, and like Humpty Dumpty, Ward is afraid I'll break."

With that, Calamatta threw back her head and let out a whoop.

Susanna giggled and patted Calamatta's hand.

How her sister-in-law had changed, thought Calamatta, or had her former assessment of her been wrong? When she saw the way Ward gazed at his plump little wife, she realized how she wished that her husband would look at her like that. Goodness, there was so much she needed to learn about marriage. Calamatta had wanted to ask Susanna about the secret side of the relationship—especially about what happened once the doors closed. Did the kissing part continue? But just then deep masculine voices announced the arrival of the two men.

Susanna only managed an intimate whisper before the men entered. "My dear, we must find you a new wardrobe. That dress really won't do. The color is all wrong and the style is at least two years out of fashion."

Calamatta didn't know why, but Susanna's remark hadn't bothered her as it would have a year ago. But then, things changed quickly and, lo and behold, instead of a simple shopping trip to buy a new wardrobe, Edward had brought her all the way across the ocean to England to meet his brother.

Calamatta picked up her pen and commenced to tell Lucy all about it.

Meanwhile, Edward was exiting the hackney carriage at the corner of Prince's Street and Threadneedle Street in front of the bank. The cold damp wind was so strong that it made it difficult for him to hold onto his hat and the heavy satchel at the same time. It reminded him, too, of the strong gales which had buffeted their ship for the entire journey.

November had been a bitter time to cross the Atlantic, but no other choice had been open to him if he was to steal Calamatta and her dowry away from America before Parnell's man turned up and let the cat out of the bag.

Edward had overheard Susanna's remark in the parlor that night in Richmond concerning Calamatta's depleted wardrobe, and his own had been badly in need of replenishing, also. So his suggestion the next morning at breakfast that he take her for a honeymoon and shopping trip to Williamsburg and towns beyond was all it took to have Susanna persuade Ward to let him whisk Calamatta away. Of course, once Edward was headed for the eastern seaboard, he had kept right on going.

Before they left Richmond, Edward instructed Calamatta to pack items for her amusement to fill any idle hours which they might have at the inns.

Thank goodness she had been so distracted by her eagerness to begin another exciting journey that she had done as he asked without question and packed books and her sewing kit.

Ward had seemed to find the whole conversation about shopping amusing. "If she is anything like my wife, buying new frocks will burn a hole in your pocket. I shall open your account at the bank first thing this morning," he'd said.

Edward had laughed right along with him. But later in the day at the bank in Richmond, he had found himself confronted with a bewildering variety of foreign coins from Dutch rix-dollars to Russian kopecks. He chose what they would allow him of the fifty-thousand in British pounds, then took some American dollars and other foreign currency. Ward was no brain-stick, so Edward stealthily decided not to deplete the savings entirely and left just enough blunt in the account to keep it active.

When they arrived on the coast, Edward had procured rooms in a modest but clean inn. He then sought out a modiste, fresh from France and in need of funds, who for a sizable amount of money was willing to work her girls around the clock to produce in a week's time a few fashionable dresses and a couple of warmer, more practical frocks. He settled Calamatta at the dressmaker's and stole away to the docks.

How Edward had wished at that moment that he had Fitz's services for such skulduggery, but he was comforted to know that the cunning whipjack was back safely in England waiting for him.

Within four days after his withdrawal of funds, Edward had secured passage on a somewhat disreputable cargo vessel which was to set sail within a week's time. It was a British ship owned by a Captain Wetchel, who was quite willing to believe Edward's tale and, for a sound price, take the eloping lovers to jolly old England. For a bit more coin in his palm, the captain was persuaded to bunk in with his first mate and give over his more spacious cabin to the young man and his pretty wife. They were to be the only passengers.

Getting Calamatta on board was easier than Edward had hoped. His suggestion of hopping on a sailing vessel to travel up the James for their return trip to the McGannon's Mockwood Plantation was heartily applauded.

"What a splendid adventure," she had agreed.

Darkness had already cloaked the ship when their numerous trunks and boxes were put aboard, and they set sail sometime around eight bells, midnight. Thank God for her romantic imagination. When her brothers found out he'd kidnapped their sister, Edward knew all hell would break loose.

After Calamatta had gone to bed, Edward spent the remainder of the night on deck wondering what her reaction was going to be when she awakened the next day to find it was not the banks of the James River which greeted her, but a vast sea.

The next morning, Edward had watched with concern as he saw Calamatta's eyes widen when she came out of the cabin and glimpsed the Atlantic Ocean. Explaining as calmly as possible that they were on their way to England, not Mockwood, Edward had watched carefully for signs of panic—or anger. At first, he thought she'd gone berserk, because she broke away from him and ran to the rail just as the ship caught a high wave, rolling dangerously. Edward raced after her. "Look out!" he shouted. To his surprise, Calamatta had whirled and thrown her arms around him.

"Oh, Edward, you are the most surprising of husbands," she'd exclaimed, pulling him toward the bow. "Are we truly going to England?"

Before he could answer, she'd turned to look toward the east. "What a wondrous wedding tour! Kings and queens and grand palaces. I shall see them all!"

He couldn't believe his ears. They'd nearly been cast overboard and the contrary chit wasn't even frightened. Next he'd found it difficult holding onto someone who kept doubling over with fits of laughter. He'd had to fight to merely keep his footing on the heaving deck. Finally he managed somehow to maneuver her to their cabin. Viewing the room for the first time, Edward realized that the captain had vastly exaggerated the size and grandeur of his accommodations. By any means, the cabin was too small to divide as he had planned and there was only one bed. He remembered the sinking feeling in the pit of his stomach.

Then and there, Edward knew that other sleeping arrangements had to be made, but how was he to do it without raising the suspicions of Captain Wetchel? He couldn't play sick forever with Calamatta. No, she would have to back his excuse for wanting another room which would fadge with the Captain. The only solution was to tell Calamatta the truth—at least half the truth. When she learned her marriage to him was a hoax, would she shout an alarm? Accuse him of kidnapping her? There was the danger of the captain's turning on them. If he discovered the fortune Edward had stashed in his trunk, he could very well steal their money and throw them overboard, with no one the wiser.

After the cabin boy brought their evening meal, Edward knew he couldn't delay telling her any longer. She loved stories, so to make it sound as innocent as possible, he had decided to spin a Canterbury Tale.

Calamatta had startled him out of his reverie by commenting, "William will be terribly disappointed you weren't able to find him a wife, Edward."

Without thinking, Edward blurted out, "I did find him a wife."

She had looked up at him in surprise. "Who?"

"You."

Calamatta's eyes reflected her concern. "Poor Edward. You are mixed up. The tumble from your horse in Kentucky must have addled you more than we realized. You and I were married at Dunfree's Corners."

"No," he said, "I had a proxy." Guilt and that new sensation—which he didn't want to explore—made his words sound harsher than he intended. "We just wouldn't suit, you and I. You're married to my brother." He thought he'd be relieved to have the truth out, but the confession made him feel a veritable cad. Rather than face the look of disbelief in her eyes, he'd risen from his seat, and although the ship had begun to pitch and toss like his stomach, he decided he'd rather be on deck. But Calamatta was close behind, holding him around the waist.

"You're my husband, Edward!"

He had felt her grasp tighten.

"I can't be married to William." She nudged him with her forehead. "You must try harder to keep your thoughts focused."

Concentrating with all his might on how to get away from her, he yelled, "I am keeping them focused!"

"No, you're not! I can tell. Your mind is wandering."

Only the creaking of the ship's timbers penetrated the stillness in the room. In his pain, Edward blurted out, "I didn't . . . I couldn't marry you." Silently, he said, *I'm only the second son. I'm of little account.*

Confused, Calamatta stammered, "You said William wanted a beautiful woman—a fine lady—to be mistress of Careby Manor. You said . . ."

Edward held his breath when he felt her nose press into his shoulder blades. No telling what the chit's next words would be.

A whisper no louder than a breeze in the grass asked, "Am I beautiful? Really beautiful?"

The little catch in her voice made his own words stall halfway up his throat. All he managed was a grunt.

"Edward? Answer me."

"Aye," he said. "You are." *And soft and desirable. There are things, too, I want to do to you that a gentleman shouldn't ever think about doing with his brother's bride.* As soon as her arms had slipped from around him, he'd begun to struggle into his sheepskin coat. Hearing the door close, Edward had whirled around and found himself standing alone.

No, he was not alone. Neither was he on a cargo ship. He was in a bank in London, where a short, roly-poly man in black with pinched little cheeks and spectacles on the end of his nose was asking, "May I help you, sir?"

Edward shook his head to clear it of the pictures of the last few weeks at sea. "I beg your pardon," he said. "My thoughts were several miles away, I fear. Can you tell me where I go to open an account?"

Six

Back at Grillon's Hotel, Calamatta raised her pen and listened. Raindrops! How long it had been raining she did not know. There had been a storm that night aboard the ship when Edward had told her that William was her husband. She now wondered how much she should tell Lucy. Should she confess to her how frightened and confused she had been when Edward told her that she was married to his brother, William, and not to him? She did not want Lucy to think ill of Edward. After all, he had been doing what he'd promised to do—find a wife for his brother.

Calamatta clearly recalled how she'd grabbed her woolen cape and rushed from the cabin because she hadn't wanted Edward to see her cry. Never once had she ever seen Ward or Creed or Benjamin cry, and she was a true McGannon.

On deck, darkness and cold had quickly engulfed her and the squalls battered her, but she'd managed to fight her way to the starboard side of the ship, where she grabbed for the rigging to keep from being swept overboard. At first, she'd been certain Edward was funning her, until he'd choked on his words.

"I won't believe you anymore, Edward!" she remembered shouting into the darkness. She felt something had been taken away from her, but she didn't know what. *Married to William? Pshaw! Pretty, hah!* It was getting so she couldn't regard anything that scalawag told her. But what if it were true that she was wed to Edward's handsome brother?

Her imagination had rushed in to lull her with its world of make-believe. "Calamatta Mary McGannon Hatcher, Mistress of Careby Manor," she said aloud. "Like Mr. Darcy's Pemberley in *Pride and Prejudice*." Hadn't Edward described William as forthright and true? Well that would certainly be a rarity among his sex, she'd thought suddenly, giggling. *Quite ridiculous!*

Then the enormity of his confession pressed heavily upon her. Just as she had begun to feel at ease with Edward, this puzzling riddle had presented itself.

Now that Calamatta looked back on it, Edward's behavior had become stranger and stranger ever since his fever. If that were the cause, then she reasoned she could not fault him. But if she were truly married to his brother and he were as perfect as Edward had painted him, would she be found wanting in William's eyes? "Oh, dear," she said. "I must make sure that doesn't happen!"

By the time the wind had made a mockery of her hair and her cloak was wet through, she decided to go back to the cabin. Since it was the sight of his face and the touch of his arms to which she'd become accustomed, Calamatta had decided that Edward would have to be made aware that it was his responsibility to show her what steps she should take next. After all, he'd brought her to the pretty pass she was in and it was up to him to lead her through. There was no one else to advise her on how to be a good wife. Why, she didn't even know how to kiss a man properly!

Having finished his business at the Bank of London, Edward, too, was thinking along much the same lines as he was being pummeled by rain outside on the curb.

When he had clambered topside that stormy night to locate Calamatta, gale force winds had buffeted him. On the opposite side of the ship, he'd spied her facing the water, her cape whipping the air like giant wings, her hair flying in great arcs around her head. He feared she meant to throw herself overboard, but when she turned and fought her way back below deck, he exhaled loudly. What the devil did the chit think she was doing rushing into a storm like that?

He'd known then and there if he were to keep his sanity, he'd have to think of some way to put distance between them for the remainder of the journey.

When Edward thought he'd given her a decent amount of time to regain her composure, he had gone back into the cabin to find Calamatta washing her face in the warm water in the bowl on the brazier. Her back was to him. Her long hair hung down her back past her waist. So engrossed was she in her ablutions that he stood admiring her a full minute before she was aware of him. She'd whirled around so quickly he didn't have time to step away, and Edward found her closeness disturbing. Eyes as dark and round as a doe's looked up at him. He should have been wary of that innocent look.

"I've been thinking about what you said, and I wondered if you'd do something for me."

He felt he owed her something for the shabby way he'd handled things. "Name the boon."

"Let me kiss you."

Guilt again! Edward wished the demon would leave him alone. He turned his cheek.

She laughed, placing her fingers on his lips. "I mean a real kiss."

What was she so jolly about? Edward felt disgruntled. After all, shouldn't she have been more upset to find out that he wasn't her husband? "Cal . . . Mrs. Hatcher. I told you we're not . . ."

He didn't get a chance to finish before she pressed her lips to his. Her touch blazed a path through his entire body. Before she consumed him entirely, he disentangled himself from her grasp, turned, and pressed his forehead against the wall.

He could still hear Calamatta's cry. "I still don't do it right. Do I?"

"M-Mrs. Hatcher," he pleaded into the pungent mahogany

paneling, "you-you seem overly obsessed with kissing." *Hell!*
He was stammering like a schoolboy. "You must understand
you cannot go around kissing men who aren't your husband."

"But what will William think of me if I can't kiss right?"

Brother Will again! Edward had turned to face her. "You
aren't supposed to do it right! That is . . . it is the duty of the
husband to teach his wife such things."

Her eyes widened. "Oh? That isn't what I heard Benjamin
and his chums tell their girlfriends."

"I fear the education you gained from your brothers has mis-
informed you on matters of the heart," Edward said in exasperation.

"But Benjamin is very good at things of the heart," she said
anxiously.

Edward turned his back to her. "I'm sure he is." He was
swimming against the tide and he knew he had to think of something to keep her away from him before he drowned. Another
here-and-therein tale was needed! She had seen his ugly wound.
She'd even remarked about it. So he'd make up a story about
the possibility that he could become a cripple and perhaps bed-
ridden someday. It was all poppycock, of course. The muscle
in his hip was becoming stronger every day, but he hoped the
tale would suffice to get him off the hook.

By then her arms were around his waist. "I will confess
something to you, Edward, if you won't tell."

Edward grunted.

"I have three brothers. I used to sneak up on Ben and his
friends and listen to their conversations," she said, guffawing
in that intimate way of hers. "They'd be skinny-dipping and I'd
peek. You only had one brother and you went to school with
boys and you were in the Navy with men. You never were around
women much. Boys and girls are different."

Beads of sweat broke out on Edward's forehead.

"Now, you can turn around."

Edward didn't change his stance. "Hah!" he snorted.

"You are embarrassed because I told you."

"No, I am not embarrassed," Edward exploded, knowing he must control himself before he turned to face her.

"Yes, you are. I can tell."

"Mrs. Hatcher, don't tell me what I feel or don't feel."

"All right, Edward."

He knew he was being unreasonable. He didn't want her to hate him. "Mrs. Hatcher," he said softly. "I'm—"

"You needn't say more," she said.

Edward decided he'd better leave it at that. But, of course, Calamatta couldn't leave it alone. "I saw your scar," she said.

"Aye. I nearly lost my leg." She'd jumped to some sort of conclusion herself. But was it the right one? "You understand?" He didn't want to make a muddle of this. "I wouldn't be a fit husband for any girl, Callie."

Her voice was all sympathy. "Poor Edward. But I would have taken care of you."

"No, no," he said, making sure his words trailed off with just the right amount of melancholy.

She gave him a hug. "You are very unselfish, Edward."

He wasn't sure that Calamatta was quite understanding what he was trying to convey to her. Perhaps if he limped a bit more, or coughed a few times. No! That wouldn't work. If he did those things, it was likely that she'd insist on seeing him well. Then he'd never be rid of her. "What I'm trying to say is we would not suit, but we can be friends." When she didn't answer, he tried again, "But I shall always be there if you need me."

"Always, Edward? Hope to die?" Calamatta gave him another squeeze.

Edward took a deep breath and turned around. "Hope to die."

"Enough of this talk," she replied. "I can see the subject is very painful to you. Tell me again what this brother of yours is like."

Edward jumped at the chance to shift the attention to William. "Some say that we look like twins."

"But you aren't."

"No. Will is eleven months older."

84 *Paula Tanner Girard*

She looked up at him in surprise. "You mean there isn't one year difference in your ages and he inherits everything?"

"Not everything, but as the first son he would get Careby Manor and all its holdings."

"That's not fair."

Edward laughed. "The ownership of our estate always went to the oldest male. Other members of the family usually are provided for generously. My grandfather likely thought I would keep my commission in the Royal Navy."

"I'll have money of my own someday, Edward, and I'll share with you."

She looked as if that should make him feel better, but it certainly didn't, and his expression evidently showed it.

"Edward," she said, with a generous smile, "if you won't take my money, I'll gladly share my virtue with you."

Edward's heart had nearly leapt out of his chest. He cupped her face in his hands and looked deeply into her eyes. There he saw a question which bothered him.

"Do you mean that, Callie?"

"Oh, yes," she said, searching his face with her eyes as if she were looking for something there. "I think Ward keeps it in the bank with my inheritance, but I'll gladly ask him to send it."

"Oh, God!" He laughed and hugged her to him. He'd forgotten there was still sweet innocence in the world. "You keep it. It's too valuable, but thank you anyway for the offer. It is very generous of you."

Calamatta bit her lip. "There were four of us and my father left me as much, perhaps more in the long run, than my three brothers."

"I know."

She looked surprised. "How did you know that? I never told you."

"Ward must have said something to me about it." Edward decided he'd better change the subject quickly, before he blundered again. The vixen had that effect on him.

He cleared his throat and tried again. "Some say he is handsome."

"Who, Ward?" she asked.

"No, Will."

Her gaze scrutinized his features. "You described him as tall, slender, and very quiet? And you say he looks like you? I don't believe it."

His lips brushed against her hair. "Don't believe what?"

"That he can be handsomer than you."

Edward's heart had pounded against his ribs harder than ever. "They would weep," she continued.

She had him on a seesaw again. "I beg your pardon, ma'am. Who would weep?"

"The angels," she grinned, giving him a punch in the arm. "The angels in heaven would weep if any man were more handsome than you."

He heard the husky guffaw and frowned. Why did her quizzing displease him? Had he painted too glowing a picture of his forthright brother? Will really wasn't all that good-looking. To Edward's way of thinking, Calamatta seemed far too willing to accept a brotherly substitution. Hah! The heart of a woman was indeed a fickle thing.

Calamatta had stepped back and gave him a sisterly smile.

Lord, she was beautiful—and she was married to Will. What had been done had been done. Oh, what a rapscallion he was. But in a day or two, when he delivered his brother's bride with her virtue intact, Edward would have a very well-lined purse. He'd be set for life! What more could a man want?

As he said he would, Edward finished his transactions in Town quickly and before the next dawn broke, a coach and four was in front of the hotel to collect them and their baggage. Bad weather continued to plague them, as it had for most of their voyage across the sea, but Edward urged their driver to proceed at full speed. It was dusk before they turned into a maze of narrow country lanes.

Edward, strangely quiet for most of the trip, now eagerly pointed out the buildings, barely discernible through the rain. "The village of Careby is part of the Hatcher estate," he said. "It covers over fourteen hundred acres."

It was the first time that the timbre of his voice matched the excitement she felt. Calamatta pressed her face against the small window to try to see better, but she could barely make out the shapes of the two-storied stone houses and the old honey-colored church nestled by a small stream. This was to be her home now.

Every day as they had crossed the ocean, she'd heard nothing from Edward's lips except heroic tales of his brother William's wisdom and valor. For a moment, Calamatta turned to gaze at Edward. He was staring out the window on his side of the coach. In a few more minutes, she would meet this gallant husband of hers, this bravest of soldiers, a man who stood above all others—whose face looked so much like the one across from her. Calamatta clasped her hands tightly in her lap to keep them from shaking. Would William like her? Oh, she hoped he would.

The coach proceeded through iron gates which hung open between two tall stone columns. The heavy curtain of rain nearly made it impossible to ascertain the exact appearance of the manor, only that it rose three stories, was covered with thick vines, and was built of the same honey-colored stones as the houses in the village. The house faced grounds which appeared badly neglected, nothing to compare to the impeccable lawns and gardens of her beloved Mockwood.

They had no sooner pulled up before the imposing entrance than the footman, whom Edward had hired in London, was opening the door of the carriage. Before he could assist her, Calamatta jumped out—right into a puddle. The startled servant looked down at his mud-splattered coat.

"Oh, my goodness!" Calamatta cried, trying to shake the water out of her half boots, only to lose her bonnet. While the footman struggled to open a large umbrella to cover her, Calamatta dashed up the steps.

The door opened. From Edward's numerous references to him, she recognized the man standing in front of her immediately. "Mr. Boskins!" she cried, pumping his hand enthusiastically. She thought the smile he gave her would split his craggy face. Behind him stood a plump little pink-cheeked woman who was wiping her hands on her starched white apron, sending a cloud of flour into the air—and with it the aroma of fresh-baked bread.

Edward followed Calamatta as quickly as possible, but not quickly enough to stop her from making such a *faux pas*. Not good *ton* at all. Now she was hugging the housekeeper. William would have a fit.

Quickly handing his wet cloak to the old retainer, Edward helped Calamatta off with hers, only to give the front of his own coat a dusting of flour. *Lord! Now Will will have a double fit.* Edward quickly tried to establish a little decorum. "Mr. and Mrs. Boskins, may I present your new mistress, Mrs. Hatcher."

"My, oh my, oh my! Ain't you the one," the old lady exclaimed, giving Calamatta a hug.

Calamatta hugged back.

Edward wondered why he even tried. No one was heeding proper protocol at all.

"Master Edward," Mrs. Boskins exclaimed, turning her attention to him. "I swear ye grow another inch every time I see ye."

It was all nonsense, of course, because Mrs. Boskins had been telling him the same thing since he was in knee breeches. Oh, who the devil cared! Edward laughed helplessly and accepted her hug.

Boskins was far more circumspect. He bowed elegantly. "The master said to tell you he would be awaiting you in the study off the library, sir."

Edward thanked him and started down the great hall, only to be accompanied by noises that sounded conspicuously like *slosh! slish! slosh!* Calamatta seemed surprised by the noise, too.

Hopping on one foot and then the other, she gave each rain-soaked shoe a hearty shake without shortening her stride. She had thought of removing her soggy boots, but decided she couldn't very well meet her husband for the first time in stocking-inged feet.

Edward took Calamatta's elbow to slow her down and continued into the small room. God help them all.

Seven

Calamatta looked apprehensively across the room at the impressive figure silhouetted in front of the tall window. Even in the dim light, she saw that William did indeed look very much like Edward, but with so much more dash and polish. His side-whiskers were short and his dark brown hair cut in a becoming style. The points of his collar were so highly starched that he could barely move his head, and his neckcloth was tied in such a way as to give him a most aristocratic air. Tan breeches and a well-tailored dark blue coat completed the picture of a perfect gentleman. Immediately, she thought of a passage from *Pride and Prejudice: His friend Mr. Darcy soon drew the attention of the room by his fine, tall person, handsome features, noble mien.*

"Brother, may I present your . . . that is . . . this is Calamatta."

William's brows shot upwards; his eyes grew rounder. Oh, she could see that her husband was impressed with her. He stared at her through a funny little circle of glass he raised to one eye, then stepped forward and bowed stiffly. Not one word had he uttered, and she wondered if Edward had failed to tell her that William was perhaps deaf. To make certain that she did not embarrass him, she shouted, "Edward has told me all about you."

"Madam!" William jumped to attention.

Well, he certainly heard that. Calamatta caught the flash of amusement in Edward's eyes and scowled at him. If he was so embarrassed by his own weaknesses, he should not make light of another's.

In the meantime, William had marched to the wall beside an ornate marble fireplace and pulled a cord.

Almost instantly there was a scratching on the door, and the round little face peered into the room. "Ye rang, Master William?"

"Come in, Mrs. Boskins. Your mistress is fatigued from her long journey and I am sure is ready to be taken to her room to rest until dinner."

Calamatta wasn't the least bit tired. Besides, she wanted to stay and feast her eyes on her handsome husband. "Oh, but I'm not . . ."

One look from William stopped her from saying more. The expression on his face reminded Calamatta of Creed, and for a moment she felt homesick. However, William had already turned to Edward, so with a shrug Calamatta followed the jovial housekeeper from the room and up the stairs. Mrs. Boskin's smile crinkled her eyes, and while she chattered, her hands drew magnificent pictures in the air. They climbed two flights of stairs and traversed a long hallway before coming to a stop.

The room was smaller than her bedroom at Mockwood Plantation, but most pleasant. The bed and the one ceiling-to-floor window were hung with maroon velvet curtains, and the walls were covered with lovely flowered wallpaper. Considering the dull grays and browns Calamatta had seen so far in Careby Manor, it was surprisingly gay.

"The master wanted it done up specially for ye. Of course, Putty suggested a livelier design than Master William chose," Mrs. Boskins said with a wink, "but we managed to put it foremost on the top of the pile when Mr. Peckinworth came to collect his samples. Master William never noticed the difference. Most men don't pay much attention to what's on the walls."

Calamatta's gaze turned to the flames leaping cheerily in the fireplace, warming the room. Nearby sat a pretty escritoire with writing materials laid out, while a dressing-screen cut off one corner of the room. A large wardrobe and a chest of drawers stood along one wall. Nestled between these was a door which Mrs. Boskins promptly opened.

"This be to yer own little sitting room."

"It is lovely, Mrs. Boskins," Calamatta said, wondering who Putty was.

The tall bedroom window had a narrow, cushioned window seat, and since darkness had already fallen and the rain still fell, it was quite impossible for Calamatta to see beyond the driveway. Now her gaze was drawn to the immense arched door opposite the bed. A large key protruded from the lock. Calamatta was about to ask about it when Mr. Boskins and a large, strapping youth began bringing in Calamatta's trunks. Close behind trotted a little maid carrying a tray with a teapot, cups, and a dish of pastries.

"I'll be leaving ye, now, dear," said Mrs. Boskins, heading out into the hallway. "Best I be getting back to the kitchen."

The men quickly placed the trunks in the middle of the room and left.

The girl remained.

"Me name be Putty," she said, making a quick little bob.

Calamatta bobbed back.

A long carrot-colored curl fell out from under Putty's perky mobcap, and as she tried to blow the errant tendril off her forehead, she pursed her lips and punctuated each sentence with a *phewing* sound. The strand of hair always fell right back down, but Putty was persistent, if not successful.

"Mrs. Boskins told me to ask if you have a dress you want freshened up—*phew*—and she says I'm to assist fixing your hair, if you please, and she would have stayed—*phew*—but she has to cook the meal and Mr. Boskins isn't much help in the kitchen and neither is Ficus who is Missus Boskins's nephew—*phew*—and if milady doesn't need me any longer, she'd like me to get back to the kitchen quick as a whistle to stir the soup."

When Putty ran of breath, Calamatta assured her that she

could dress herself. The girl curtsied and said, "Yes, ma'am," and ran out the door.

As soon as the maid was out of sight, curiosity drew Calamatta to the mysterious arched door. She tried to open it. When it wouldn't budge, she gave the key a turn to the right. Nothing happened, so she twisted the key to the left and pulled harder. Still the door remained stubborn. "Fiddlesticks!" She would try later. It was time to dress for dinner.

She decided on the forest-green velvet gown the French modiste had made for her in Virginia. Susanna had said outdoor colors were her best. She did so want to appear at her very best for her first meal with William.

Calamatta's hair, nearly dry from the rain, flowed thick and silky. How she wished her sister-in-law were here to style it. Perhaps she should have asked Putty to help her. Too late for that now. She plaited her hair, entwining a pink ribbon, then twirled the braid into a crown atop her head.

Belowstairs, Edward was having misgivings of his own. When he'd introduced Calamatta to William, he hadn't even had the courage to say the word *wife*. How could he forget the look of adoration she gave Will when she first saw him? Hell! Why should he care if William was going to be saddled with the vixen? Edward watched his brother for some sort of expression. Not a trace of emotion had shown on his damned proud face.

When the door closed behind them, William eagerly turned to Edward. "Did you get the blunt?"

Edward snorted. "What happened to *Welcome home, brother?* And, yes, I have the money. A small amount in Dutch rix-dollars, some Spanish silver, but most of it is in English pounds. I deposited some of it in the Bank of London. Brought five thousand with me. Thought you would want to put some of it in a local bank—Stamford, perhaps? Easier to get to." Edward sank onto the leather sofa. "I also brought your bride. Or didn't you notice?"

"Notice her—a Long Meg like that? Dash it all, how could I not?" William pointed to the puddle of water on the floor by the door. "She dripped all over my carpet."

Edward bristled. "That's not fair. I dripped, too. I want to know what you thought of her."

"You are exasperating, Eddie. How can I think anything of her? Couldn't even see her with strings of hair hanging over her face. If she wasn't yelling, she was staring at me. Isn't dimwitted, is she?" With that he turned to a table, picked up a decanter of brandy, and filled two glasses. "Lord, I hope she isn't a chatterbag."

"Hah!" Edward gave a bark of laughter and drained his glass. He could hardly wait to see his brother's expression when Calamatta really said what was on her mind.

"Does she know about the will?" William asked.

"No. She doesn't even know about the dowry. But it's strange that Parnell's agent didn't get to Ward McGannon by now. Fitz managed to divert the huggermugger to the Carolinas." He looked at William. "By the by, where is the old salt? I expected him to be here."

"How should I know? I took for granted he was with you."

Edward leaped to his feet. "What do you mean? Didn't you get my letter about the proxy marriage?"

"Yes. A young seaman brought it. Their frigate put into port several weeks ago. He said his captain had a letter for me that was given into his keeping at Norfolk in Virginia. He didn't say anything about Fitzgerald."

"My God!" said Edward. "He was shanghaied or he's dead. Those are the only two things that would have kept him from getting on that ship."

"I'm sorry, Edward. Quite liked the old fellow myself."

Edward pounded his fist into the palm of his hand. *What could have happened?* "Parnell's agent got to him. That must be it."

William began to mull the situation over. "After you left for the United States, I found out from Dickering that Grandfather's instructions said no one in America was to know about the provisions of the will until Miss McGannon was notified. The decision of accepting it was to be her own."

Edward ran his fingers through his hair. "Then where is Fitz? I shall return to London tomorrow and start asking questions on the waterfront. Surely there will be someone along the docks who will know something."

William's eyes widened. "And what am I to do with . . . with Miss McGannon?"

"You forget, brother. She is Mrs. William Hatcher now. I wash my hands of her. I've completed my part of this game." Edward walked to the door. "You have nearly all the fifty-thousand-pound dowry. You have your proxy bride, and I assure you she is unsullied."

"Well, I can see why."

Edward nearly yanked the door off its hinges. "If you don't mind, I wish to go to my room and change into dry attire before dinner. First thing in the morning, I'll be gone."

William looked as though he'd been sentenced to prison. "Eddie! You can't leave me alone with her. I don't even know the gel."

"Maybe not, brother, but she thinks she knows you."

Edward was halfway up the stairs when he heard William call out, "I told Mrs. Boskins to serve the evening meal at eight—and, Edward, I want you there when *she* comes down."

An hour later, Calamatta sat at the table with William and Edward. Mrs. Boskins had tried most diligently to offer a pleasant meal. Boskins hovered about, trying to be both butler and footman and keep up with his wife's several removes, while Putty and Ficus ran back and forth, bringing a seemingly endless number of dishes. Ficus was a big, lumbering boy with more muscle than grace who had tried to squeeze into a uniform made for a much slighter man, but he made up in good nature what he lacked in polish.

While Calamatta was thinking it strange that the Hatchers had so few servants, Edward watched Calamatta with no little amount of anxiety, afraid that she would make a *faux pas* in front of his brother. She ate little and kept peeking at William. On the other hand, his brother did everything he could to avoid looking at Calamatta. When he did dart an uneasy glance her way, only to find her gazing at him, he quickly looked away.

However, Edward's concern turned to amazement. She ate daintily. Not once did she pick up the wrong dinnerware. She lowered her eyes like a modest miss and, except for a quick worshipful glance at William now and then, she didn't speak except when spoken to. Edward barely recognized her.

William was as uncommunicative as Calamatta. He would eat a few bites of this or that, dab his mouth with his napkin, take a sip of wine, dab his mouth with his napkin. Oh, Edward could see those two would be having some lively conversations. If he didn't know of his brother's valiant military record, he would say that William was scared to death of his new bride.

Although Edward kept up a steady stream of light banter, his senses were tuned mostly to his brother's wife. Calamatta never looked more beautiful. Only a little over a month ago—or was it a century—at another dinner table a continent away, those brown eyes had dwelt on him in the same way that they now drank in William. He had to admit his brother sat at the head of the table looking every whit like a proper lord of the manor, his dress as impeccable as always, while Edward had had a devil of a time tying his neckcloth without Fitz's assistance. Well, it was of little consequence. If the chit was happy with Will, it only made things that much easier for Edward to return to his former carefree way of life.

When William did speak, it was as if Calamatta were not present. He addressed everything to Edward. "By the by, popped over to Cambridgeshire to a weekend party at Elmsworth a few weeks past."

"And how is Lettyce and her squirrely earl?"

"Don't joke, Edward. Lady Elmsworth is a widow now. Happened last winter. Her husband was ill for some time. The angel nursed him until the end and seldom came out in public, so I didn't know of his illness. The young earl, Frederick, is only four. The household is still in mourning, but Lettyce had a few close neighbors and friends over to meet her elder sister, Miss Patience Rede, who has come to live with her.

With a gleam in his eye, Edward asked. "As pretty as her sibling?"

William snorted. "A bluestocking if there ever was one. Too long in the tooth for you, anyway. Never married. Odd name for her, Patience. Nothing patient about her. She should have been named Miss Propriety."

Silence prevailed for the remainder of the meal until William told Boskins they would have their port in the library. "Must talk to you," he said to Edward. Calamatta began to say something, but William interrupted, "I'm certain you have something to do in your room, Mrs. Hatcher?"

Hardly able to hide his grin, Edward waited for her rebuttal.

"Yes, thank you, Mr. Hatcher. I do have a letter I wish to write."

"I'll be damned," Edward mumbled, under his breath. "Just like that, the underhanded jackanapes is turning her up sweet as honey."

Calamatta halted at the door and asked in her deep, husky voice, a little too loudly, "How do I mail my letter?"

William flinched. "Put it on the table in the entrance hall. Ficus will take it back to the village with him in the morning. Someone will carry it to Stamford to catch the post-chaise."

Edward raised his eyebrows. "On the table? Is the silver salver gone too, Will?"

"That, too," said William, his lips drawn into a thin line. "Can't find much left of true value. Grandfather sold nearly everything."

"I didn't take him seriously," Edward said, "when he told us he'd seen the estate pass out of the hands of our family before, and he'd do anything to see that it didn't happen again."

* * *

Abovestairs, it didn't take long for Calamatta to get ready for bed and seat herself at the dainty desk.

Dearest Lucy,

You will have already received my first letter, which I posted in London, telling you that I was married to Edward's brother William. Do not be alarmed. All is turning out to be a dream to fulfill all my expectations.

William is the most handsome man I have ever seen. I was afraid he would not like me, but the look on his face when he first saw me was one of shock. Do you remember the passage in our Book, where Mr. Darcy tries not to let Elizabeth see how taken he is by her?

"She attracted him more than he liked . . . He wisely resolved to be particularly careful that no sign of admiration should now escape him."

Oh, I could see William was doing everything possible to keep a tight rein on his emotions. Yes, my dearest friend, I do believe my husband is in love with me already.

During dinner, William had much to tell Edward about the local goings-on, and I realized how much they had missed each other.

I tried to remember everything that Susanna taught me about being a lady. Here I must make a confession. I wish I had thanked her for showing me the proper way for a lady to act. In my first letter, I explained to you how surprised I was to find that Susanna is to give birth in December. I am wondering if the blessed event has taken place.

How I wronged her. If I had known how many babies she lost, I would not have been so cruel in my thoughts toward her. She never once let on to me her sorrow. I overheard the doctor telling Ward that he was concerned for her life because she is so tiny. What if she should die,

*Lucy, and I never told her I'm sorry for the terrible things
I said about her?*

*However, I am eagerly looking forward to my life as
the Mistress of Careby Manor—and I know that William
is going to be the most solicitous of husbands.*

Calamatta stopped writing for a moment and stared out into
the night, a faraway look in her eyes.

Eight

No sooner had the two men entered the library than William spoke. "Now that we have the blunt, I plan to see us out of dun territory as quickly as possible."

"Is money all that you think about, brother?" Edward growled. He tried to change the subject by turning to look around the room. The long rows of shelves were still lined with books. "I see that Grandfather's literary collection has not diminished."

The distraction worked as Edward hoped, for his brother loved books above all else. William pulled out a large volume jacketed in deep maroon leather. "You know these are the last things Sir Henry would have let go. I found many of our great-great uncle Thomas's writings here—his treatises and studies of the antiquities. Papers were dated in the middle 1500s. Damned good writing. Went down to Cambridge University Library to see what others I could find."

It nettled Edward more than ever to find that while he was having to endure countless miseries in America, his brother had been fiddling away his time in a library. "Didn't you have more pressing things to do?"

"Like what?" William snapped back. "Didn't dare show my face in London. Hounded at every turn by our creditors." He shook the book under Edward's nose. "A lot of our ancestors were knighted, studied law, or were elected to the House. But thanks to you and your helter-skelter schemes, I wasted a lot of time at school."

Edward wondered how long Will would take him to task on that point. "Well, it's the estate that has to have our attention now," Edward said. "While in America, I saw new methods of farming. There is money to be had if we make the right use of our land. By the by, I brought you a present, brother. The finest American tobacco." Edward pulled out one of Ward's cigars.

William's frown disappeared as he sniffed the exotic leaf. Before lighting it, he poured them both a glass of wine and sat down. A few minutes of silence passed while they savored the fine smoke rising into the air. William filled their glasses again before he spoke.

"The Tredwells of Leicester were at Elmsworth. He is Sir Bartholomew now. Heard that after making a fortune investing in East India Trade, he gifted Prinny with one hundred thousand pounds for his Brighton Palace. Lord Daybrooke and his wife were at the party, too." William concentrated on flicking a cigar ash from his jacket. "Also met the Countess of Mayberry."

Elinor? Edward said to himself. *What was she doing there? God, I hope she didn't tell Will how much she loaned me for my trip to America.*

"Deuced attractive woman," continued William. "Dripping in jewels. She asked when you were expected back. Dashed if I know how word gets around about such things. It did not come from my lips, I assure you. But since she seemed to know, I told her you would be returning within the fortnight. Seemed eager to see you." William raised an eyebrow. "Hope I didn't overstep myself by telling her."

Edward took the drink his brother offered him and smiled to himself. "No, no, not at all, old boy," he replied smugly. "Quite all right, I assure you." With what Calamatta had put him through, the countess was the one bright spot he could look forward to after all those frustrating months.

"Thought as much," said William. "But what an uproar Lady Mayberry caused at dinner when she announced to one and all that the purpose of your undertaking was to acquire a wife for me. Everyone was demanding to meet my American bride. Put me in quite a squeeze, I will have you know."

Edward slapped his forehead with the palm of his hand. That could pose a problem. He'd only told Eli that now that the war with the Colonies was over, he was going to look into possible investments. "You numskull, Will! You told Eli . . . the Countess of Mayberry that I went to the United States to find a bride for you?"

"Oh course, I didn't tell her. I'm not an imbecile," spouted William. "That is . . . I didn't say so directly."

"What does *not directly* mean? How did she find out?"

William started to get up, reconsidered, then sat down again and tugged at his highly starched cravat. "You know that at one time Lettyce . . . that is, the Countess of Elmsworth and I . . . we thought—" He didn't finish.

Edward encircled his glass with his hands and rolled it back and forth. Yes, he knew that Lettyce Rede had been the woman William hoped to marry. However, her father, a baronet, had forced her to accept the hand of a sickly young viscount who soon after became an earl. After that, William joined Edward in pressuring their grandfather, Sir Henry, to permit them to join the fray against Napoleon.

William took another drink and continued, "We were in the conservatory. Thought we were alone. Lady Elmsworth told me that now, with the succession of the earldom secured in their son, as soon as her mourning period is over she will be free to take a husband of her own choosing." He glanced at Edward as if he were to blame for his miserable consequence. "I *had* to tell her about my proxy marriage."

"And the Countess of Mayberry?" asked Edward.

"Was standing behind some gigantic African palms with someone," William said, in exasperation. "Heard her giggling. Couldn't mistake that voice. She kept right on doing whatever she was doing. Had no idea she was paying attention to anything else. Must have heard every word I said."

Edward laughed quietly. That sounded like Elinor. He could never figure out how the woman could make love and at the same time keep up a lively conversation about a totally unrelated subject. "And how is her husband? He had the gout, last I heard."

"According to Lady Mayberry, the earl is a bear to live with, sick or well. Says she left him growling at their estate near Huntingdon and planned to stay in London at their town house to get some Christmas shopping done."

"I go back to my original assessment of you, Will. You are a numskull. That means our venture will be all over London."

"Not necessarily."

"How will it not?" quizzed Edward.

"Tell you what I did. Of course, I mulled it over all sixteen courses, I'll have you know. Spoiled my dinner—didn't enjoy a thing I ate."

"Get to the point, Will."

"Well, cat was out of the bag, so to speak."

Edward shot him an exasperated look. "Will!"

"I tried to think up a good story to tell them."

"And what was that?"

"Told them it was true. Had a proxy bride arriving from the United States." When Edward looked unbelieving, William pulled himself up straight. "Do you think I would tell a fib? Well, must admit I did fabricate a tiddle. Let it be known that letters had been found in our grandfather's papers which revealed a correspondence had taken place with relatives in America." William coughed. "Said our father and a distant cousin had a gentlemen's agreement—promised each other that two of their offspring would marry."

Edward sat forward. Will was revealing a surprising display of hidden talents for prevarication.

William continued. "The gentleman in question had only one daughter. As the eldest and heir to the Hatcher estate, it fell to me to honor the pledge. Since I had to stay in England to settle Grandfather's estate, it was your mission to go to America and

THE RELUCTANT GROOM 103

marry the lady to me by proxy. I thought that was vague enough to cover the situation."

"Ingenious, my boy." Edward relaxed back into his seat. "I should have known that if given enough time to unravel the puzzle, you'd come up with a solution. I'm just surprised you were able to put it together so quickly." He took a puff on his cigar. "Hope the effort didn't exhaust you."

William gave his brother a scathing look. "At least I solved the problem of how to cover up our scheme."

"Now I'm free to go to Town to ferret out what I can about Fitzgerald." Edward winked at William. "And apply myself to other matters."

"Your other matters had better include clearing up our debts with our creditors. I haven't been able to show my face anywhere outside the shire. Hounded by the confounded money-lenders wherever I go."

"That I shall do," said Edward. "The only hitch I can see is the news may have reached Dickering or Parnell already."

Instead of looking worried, William suddenly brightened. "I say, that means I should lose no time getting to Preston North with the proxy papers to have them registered. Yes, I should make a trip to London, too." His countenance looked absolutely cheerful at the thought. "Eddie, I told the Tredwells that you would look them up when you got there. Wouldn't hurt to make a call at Lord Mayberry's town house, either. I'd hate to get in their bad graces. We need their patronage. Good *ton,* you know. The men may get you accepted back into the clubs. At the moment, your reputation still is not unexceptionable even in the Regent's court after your despicable behavior in that Wellington affair in Hyde Park."

Edward laughed. Hells bells! He wasn't worried about his acceptance into Society. Once word of their new fortune reached the gossipmongers, he would be welcomed in every establishment on St. James's Street.

"By the by," William droned on, "I had to let go our former lodgings. You pay off all our debts and have our credit restored.

Now that our pockets are deep again, we can afford something much more top-of-the-trees."

Oh, demme! Why did his brother have to use that expression now? It only brought to mind the picture of a tall hoyden called Tall-as-the-Trees.

William took no note of Edward's silence. "Do believe I heard Lord Daybrooke say that now the war is over, he and his wife plan on touring the Continent next year. Their four-story town house on Wimpole Street will be to let during the Season. Just right for us, don't you think?" He laughed. "I would give anything to see old man Parnell's face when he finds out that we have beat his man to the spoils."

"Your place is here at Careby Manor. I'll take the papers to North."

"No! It's my signature he will need," said William emphatically.

"You can't leave your wife right after she's arrived."

"You stay to show her around, Eddie," William pleaded.

Edward shook his head. "It's time you got acquainted."

William rose from his chair looking like a soldier going into battle.

A sword thrust into Edward's stomach would have been less painful than what he felt at that moment. Grabbing his glass, he tilted back his head and drained it. "Will, about Cal . . . Mrs. Hatcher." He twisted the goblet around in his hands. "She's still an innocent, you know."

William snapped. "That I will find out for myself, won't I?"

"That isn't what I mean, demme it! Go gentle with her. She doesn't know—that is, she thinks—"

"Dash it all, Eddie! I'm not a monster." William wiped his face with his handkerchief and headed for the door.

Edward called out after him. "I'll be leaving for London first thing in the morning."

William stopped, but didn't look back. "Without saying your farewells to . . . to Mrs. Hatcher?"

The last thing Edward wanted to do was to face Calamatta.

"You say them for me. Tell her—well, you'll think of something. You always do."

William's answer sounded somewhere between a squeaky hinge and a growl. After his brother left the room, Edward sat staring into the dying fire.

Upstairs, Calamatta was sealing her letter to Lucy when she heard a light scratching sound. A mouse? She smiled. A big old house such as this must harbor any number of the wee creatures within its walls. A warm feeling embraced her, making her feel she wasn't alone. She looked at the letter. William said to place it on the mirrored stand in the entrance hall. Taking up the candlestick, she opened the door into the dark hallway. Just as she stepped out, she heard the scraping sound again. That was one persistent little mouse.

No sooner had she closed the door behind her than a desperate pounding resounded from the other side of the locked door. "Mrs. Hatcher, I know you are in there. Unlock this door!" Already halfway down the hall, Calamatta mistook the noise for the muffled howling of the night wind.

Less than ten minutes later, she reentered her room, snuffed out the candle, and crawled into bed. She listened. The scratching had stopped. A smile spread across her face. The mouse had gone away.

From where he sat in the library, Edward had thought he heard a whisper of a sound in the entrance hall. He assumed it was Boskins checking to make sure all was secure for the night. Slowly Edward rose and made his way up the stairs. His room was at the far end of the wing. The old section of the house had been closed for years. He paused a moment to stare at Calamatta's chamber door before continuing on to his own apartment.

"My mission is accomplished," he said. "Now I'm ready to

kick over the traces of this uncomfortable affair and get back to a more enjoyable lifestyle in Town, where a man is not thwarted at every turn by a chit's follies." He wasn't sure why the prospect didn't appeal to him by half.

Calamatta was usually an early riser, but this morning, while darkness still held the outdoors captive, she was content to stay under her warm stuffed counterpane. The clatter of hooves and the unbalanced rhythmic timbre of wheels clanking against the stones in the drive in front of the manor house announced the arrival of a large conveyance. Surely visitors would not be arriving at this early hour.

Curiosity pulled her to the window. With her fingers, she rubbed a circle on the damp glass and peered out. Through the swirls of gray mist, she recognized the carriage she and Edward had arrived in from London, and the long-legged, uneven stride of the tall cloaked figure advancing toward it also was familiar. Panic ran through her and she cried out, "Edward!"

As if in answer to her wail, the man looked up toward her window, then turned to enter the carriage.

Oblivious to the chill, she ran into the long dark hallway in her nightshirt and stockinged feet. She picked up her gown and, as if on wings, flew down the two flights of stairs, across the entry hall, and out the open door, which Mr. Boskins was about to close.

The carriage was already careening around the first bend of the drive. She watched it disappear, then appear once more over the rise of a small hill before the early morning fog erased it from her sight.

Wringing her hands, Mrs. Boskins appeared behind Calamatta. "Mrs. Hatcher! Ye'll catch your death. Master Edward be leaving for London."

"He didn't say good-bye!"

"Didn't want to disturb ye and Master William yer first night together." She looked down at Calamatta's stockings sticking out from under her nightgown. "Whatever will yer husband say? Us letting ye freeze on his doorstep and ye not even here twenty-four hours."

Calamatta allowed herself to be led back inside.

"I sent Putty up to start a cozy fire and I'll be bringing some hot chocolate. Now, ye get yerself back up to yer chambers or the master will think we ain't doing our job proper."

Calamatta climbed the stairs much slower than she had descended them and entered her room. Edward was gone. She didn't want to admit the emptiness she felt. After all, she was used to having those she loved leave her.

She picked up her robe from the foot of the bed and wrapped it around her shoulders. Long ago, she had learned to create her own fantasy world. Brick by brick, she'd built a wall around her heart to keep from being hurt. A garden blossomed inside— lovely, warm, safe. Mellow waves of heat from the fireplace pervaded the room. Calamatta walked to the window and pressed her nose against the icy pane, sniffing its fresh-smelling dampness.

She barely remembered her mother. Her death had placed the first brick in Calamatta's garden wall. Only the dim memory of the scent of lilacs and someone rocking and singing lingered with her.

When her mother died, she had Mandy-lu, her wet-nurse, to care for her. But a few years later, Mandy-lu got sick of the fever and died, too. More than she recalled anything of her mother, Calamatta remembered Mandy-lu's broad gentle hands, wide smile, and ample bosom.

After her dear Mandy-lu died, her upbringing was left to the whims of servants and her older brothers. They included her in their hunting and fishing trips, but when it came to business, she and Ben were left at home. Ward's life soon took him to Richmond. When he found a wife, he scarce had time for his little sister. So Calamatta followed Creed and tried to do everything the way he did it, much to Ward's and Susanna's consternation.

Her father had been away on business a lot, but when he came home, she was the first one he kissed. "My little colleen," he'd say, and hoist her high over his head. Then one day he left and never came back. She was told he'd gone to heaven to be with her mother, but when she got older she found he had been killed in a coach accident on his way home from Philadelphia.

Ward was twenty-two and in charge of the family after that, but he was busy finishing college at William and Mary and running the plantation.

Then Ward and Creed had a terrible quarrel and Creed left her. Soon after, Ben, her companion and friend, took a barge down the Ohio River to join Creed in Kentucky. Calamatta's brick wall grew higher, for she decided then that she was not important to anyone—not until Sun Woman and Strong Arm found her in the Cumberland Mountains, half-starved and delirious. The Indians took her in, a stranger, and accepted her as one of their own.

Calamatta thought back to the barn dance and the kiss by a dark haired stranger that had changed her life. Confusing thoughts came tumbling down over her like a soft warm robe and a lightning storm all rolled into one.

Edward had told her, "I came to America to find my brother a wife."

She had evaded the hurt, but now that he'd stolen off without saying good-bye, tears welled in her eyes. Taking a deep breath, she drew the outline of a flower on the glass with her finger. The first crocus of spring could feel no lonelier when it breaks through the freezing snows, ready to bloom but too early for the rest of the silent world to welcome it.

On their way to England, Edward had said, "Wait and see how wonderful my up-to-the-mark brother is. Any woman would be proud to be his wife." He'd boasted that William was a diamond of the first water who had withstood all manner of brutal hardships during the war with France. Shot in the arm, he'd bound it up, and, with no thought for himself, helped carry his wounded men to safety—and never came down with so much as a fever, either. "Much nobler and forthright than I," Edward had said.

Calamatta had to admit Mr. William Hatcher, with his aristocratic demeanor, was a most impressive-looking man. But if the truth be told, it was not likely that William—or anyone, for that matter—could fabricate such outrageous lies as that blackguard Edward had fed her. "I'll always be there if you need me, Mrs. Hatcher." *Hah!*

On the other hand, Edward wasn't very hardy, and if it was the fall from the horse that had made his brain a tad foggy, she should forgive him his lapses. After all, the fault had been partly her own. She thought of how she'd had to hold him in the cabin in Kentucky to keep him warm and the days at the farm when she had spoon-fed him Mama Coleman's gruel. Even on the ship he said he didn't feel well. He must have made a very sickly captain in the Navy. Edward needed someone to take care of him before he really got himself in trouble. She wondered if she should warn William that he shouldn't let his brother go off alone.

Calamatta shook her head and wiped the tears from her eyes. Surely if William was everything Edward claimed him to be, he would take care of them all. Then a frightening picture loomed before her. Would William stay, or would he leave her, too? Well, she'd do her best to make William a good wife, and she would start this very day. The first thing was to get dressed. Then she'd find the kitchen and help Mrs. Boskins make William's breakfast. She'd prove to her husband she was no worthless, slugabed wife.

"Ye'll do no such thing," Mrs. Boskins scolded a few minutes later when she heard Calamatta's intentions. With an apology for their short supply of chocolate, she set a tray with the cup of weak tea down on the bedside table.

" 'Tis yer duty to do naught but look purty as a pitchur for yer husband after the gift ye give him last night."

"Oh, lordy!" Was she supposed to have given her husband a present? Edward didn't say anything to her about that. Goodness knows, she still felt confused about what was expected of her. If she'd insulted William by not giving him a gift, he'd think she possessed no more brains than a cuckoo bird.

She was barely aware of Mrs. Boskins's prattling until the kind woman mentioned that breakfast would be served at ten o'clock. "Master William be coming in promptly from his morning ride when the clock strikes quarter to the hour. Not one minute before, not one minute after. Putty will be bringing up hot water in a few minutes and will help ye dress and fix yer lovely hair."

No sooner was the housekeeper out of the room than an idea leaped into Calamatta's mind. "The gloves. Of course! Where did I put them?" Sewing had been impossible on the ship. She rummaged through one of the smaller trunks. With a triumphant cry, she pulled out the little package and unwrapped the scarf in which she had placed the leatherwork. Holding the soft white skins against her cheek, she said, "Surely these will make a wondrous wedding gift for my husband."

There were three taps on the door, and Putty peeked into the room.

Calamatta, happy now that she had found a solution to her problem, surrendered herself to the maid's ministrations. Soon she was ready to present herself downstairs. Throwing a shawl around her shoulders, she set out to find the breakfast room. That took her several minutes, because no one had thought to inform her where it was located.

William, already changed from his riding attire, was standing inside the doorway with his watch in hand when Calamatta burst into the room. Whipped by the brisk winter weather, his handsome face appeared darker than usual, and his scowl made him look so like Edward, she forgot for a moment that he was not. With a whoop, she threw her arms around his neck to greet him. She realized her mistake too late.

"Mrs. Hatcher! That will never do!"

Nine

As William grasped her by the shoulders and thrust her at arm's length, Calamatta became aware of the strength in his powerful hands. His eyes made a quick study of her, and she felt herself blushing. If Boskins hadn't entered the room at that moment to set a steaming covered basket upon the sideboard, her husband's words—which he'd meant to be helpful instruction, she was sure—would have been more of an endearing nature. Instead, they sounded curt, for, like her brother Creed, he hid his feelings so masterfully.

"This once, Mrs. Hatcher, I shall allow for your tardiness, but," he warned, "I will not abide inappropriate attire at any time."

Confused, Calamatta glanced down at her dress. She had chosen a lovely blue woolen morning dress. The trim was not excessive and the neckline modest. What was wrong with it?

"Unless you are planning on attending a ball, I want your hair covered. You are no longer a green girl, but a married woman."

Her hands flew to her head. "Landsakes!" She'd never given it a thought. "Oh, thank you, William." How dear he was to help her avoid looking foolish in front of the servants. But, goodness, what was she to do? She didn't even own a cap, and she would look silly wearing a bonnet in the house. Until she could see if Putty or Mrs. Boskins could make her some caps, she'd have to make do, she mused, quickly pulling her shawl up over her hair.

"Very well," he said gruffly. "Hope I don't have to speak of it again."

As soon as he'd seen her seated, William brought Calamatta a plate of two plain muffins and one egg, then prepared a similar helping for himself. Mr. Boskins poured her a cup of weak coffee.

Breakfast proceeded much as dinner had the night before. William spoke little, and when he did, it was to give Mr. Boskins a direction.

It was all Calamatta could do to refrain from wriggling in her chair. William must be quite taken with her, she thought, to have the cat get his tongue. For a moment she wished Edward were there to fill the silence with his amusing chatter. She stole a glance at William.

He was staring at her, but instead of looking away, he cleared his throat and spoke, "Mrs. Hatcher, I will see you in the library"—he consulted his watch—"in twenty minutes. My schedule is off with your being here, but it can't be helped." Before she could answer, William quit the room.

Was that all? She stared at her empty plate. Either the British didn't need hearty morning sustenance, or else the household was more in want of funds than she had first suspected.

Questions whirled in her mind. What was the reason William had left so abruptly? Was he still angry that she wore no cap? He had addressed her as Mrs. Hatcher. Was she to call him Mr. Hatcher? Such a contrast to Edward. Why did she keep thinking of that rascal? She shook her head and looked to Mr. Boskins for a clue, but there was no hint in his craggy face of what fate awaited her.

Calamatta pulled her shawl farther over her head and repaired to the library to await her husband. By the time he entered, exactly twenty minutes later, she had walked the perimeter of the large room seven times.

He gestured toward the couch. "Mrs. Hatcher, be seated."

Calamatta eased onto the long sofa and tried not to slip on the cold leather. She noted Mr. Hatcher's gaze darted toward a comfortable wing chair, then back to the sofa. If she had not known of his commanding military history, she would say he was disconcerted. Finally, he seated himself at the far end of the couch.

"Oh, dash it all!" he exploded and, reaching into his pocket, pulled out a long black velvet box, which he held out toward Calamatta.

She had to move closer to him to take it. After running her hand over its rich texture, Calamatta sat transfixed, not quite sure what he expected.

"Well, open it!"

She did. A lovely pearl necklace sat enthroned upon a rose-colored satin cushion.

William's voice jumped a tone. "My mother's," he said, running his finger inside his elegantly tied cravat. "It is yours now."

"Oh, Mr. Darcy . . . Hatcher!" she quickly corrected. He hadn't seemed to notice her slip of the tongue, for the box in her hand claimed his concentration. With the tip of her finger, she dared to touch the beautiful piece of jewelry, then peeked up at him through her lashes. A most persistent urge to kiss him came upon her. Holding the case tightly, she scooted across the space between them with such startling speed that he fell off the sofa.

Surprised, Calamatta looked down at her husband sprawled awkwardly on the floor and wondered if all Hatcher men were prone to accidents. Feeling most sensitive to his plight and not wanting to add to his embarrassment, she decided to act as if nothing unusual had happened. "I have a gift for you, too," she said nonchalantly, "but it isn't finished yet."

Her husband rose and brushed off his coat. "Really, Mrs. Hatcher. No need for such a demonstration. Decorum, you know."

"But I thought—"

"You are now my wife, Mrs. Hatcher. You have no reason to think."

While Calamatta was pondering this puzzling statement, Mr. Hatcher again cleared his throat, "Didn't mean to be so blunt at breakfast, you know. Just that I am not accustomed yet to—" He waved his hands in the air.

She nodded and, wanting to let him know she was sympathetic to his discomfiture, began quoting from her favorite novel, "In spite of the pains you took to disguise yourself, your feelings were always noble and just."

"Oh, I say," he said, a spark of relief in his voice. "You can read?"

She wondered why that should surprise him. "Yes, I read a lot."

"Good! Good!" He stood staring at some spot over her shoulder.

Calamatta nearly crushed the velvet box waiting out the silence.

Then as if he had not paused at all, her husband extended his hand to help her rise. "Thought you might like a go-around of the house."

The remainder of the morning was such a joy for Calamatta that the unpleasant December weather was forgotten. She found that the more her husband became involved in unfolding the history of the family, an astounding change took place. His face became animated and his manner lost much of its stuffiness.

"Though we know our common ancestor, Dr. John Hatcher, came to acquire the estate in the early sixteenth century, the evidence of medieval buildings shows that it was occupied long before that. Later, I will show you St. Stephen's church in the village."

He escorted Calamatta into the great hall.

"Dr. John studied medicine and obtained a law degree from

Gray's Inn, but although he loved Careby, he chose to teach at Cambridge, where he eventually became vice chancellor."

William reached up to touch a faded tasseled cord hanging on the wall. How much, she thought, his movements resembled those of a king in his castle.

"Dr. Hatcher acquired an enormous fortune. A later heir started the reconstruction and built a much larger addition," he said. A sweep of his hand took in the wide staircase which led to the first floor.

She looked up and saw the balustrades along the landings of the upper floors. Anyone standing on the two floors above could gaze down to the ground level. William smiled, and again Calamatta was reminded of Edward.

"It wasn't until many of the family members went to Virginia that the estate fell upon hard times."

His long strides had Calamatta hurrying to keep up with him. She found herself in a large kitchen. Sunless morning light fell like soft cotton gauze from the strange bubbled-glass window panes. Flames whirled about the logs in the great open fireplace which yawned in one wall. A long-haired calico cat, seeking to enjoy the fire's warmth, sat upon the hearth washing her paws. Several doors opened off the room, but Calamatta didn't see another soul. This was too large a house for one elderly couple and two servants to care for.

She was quite aware that Mr. Hatcher was watching her. *My,* she thought, *one minute he seems a monarch, the next a schoolmaster.* Calamatta wasn't certain what sort of reaction he expected her to exhibit, so she pulled her shawl further up over her hair and tried to look as learned as possible.

"This part of the original manor was restored, as nearly as possible, to what it had been." He ran his hand over a granite work surface. "Of course, all later occupants have added their own touches by purchasing the latest of kitchen equipment, but for the most part, it remains a voice of the past."

William continued to tell her the workings and advantages of modern equipment while Calamatta's imagination ran away to pictures of serving wenches carrying trenchers of food to their lord and his guests.

She was shown more ovens of a later vintage built into the brickwork of the chimney, from which Calamatta now sniffed the enticing aroma of baking bread. Beside them stood a kitchen range of more recent design.

As she and Mr. Hatcher walked around the large wooden worktable in the middle of the gray stone floor, Calamatta couldn't help noticing the empty bins and baskets lining the walls. With the exception of some herbs hanging from hooks on the walls and a basket of dried apples, she saw few foodstuffs.

Her husband's scholarly manner contrasted to the ridiculous stories told by Edward of their childhood, but the richness of his vocabulary and the depth of his knowledge made up for his lack of humor. She was well aware that brothers do tend to exaggerate, but there was no way that the little boy in Edward's tales, who got into so much mischief with him when they were young, could have grown into such a serious, fixed-in-his-ways gentleman. She was tempted to reveal some of the tales that Edward had tattled on him, but thought better of it, for if Edward stretched the truth about his brother, could he have fudged about other things?

"Now that the war is over and my brother is home, we have great plans for Careby." After making that statement, William gazed upon Calamatta with as close to a look of benevolence as she'd seen him give her. "And now, my dear, is there anything else that you'd like to know about the house?"

"Why, yes. There is a door in my bedroom that has a key in it, but I cannot seem to open it. I'd like to know what is on the other side."

Her husband's answer was given through clenched teeth. "The door connects our chambers, Mrs. Hatcher. You could not open it because there are locks on both sides." He seemed reluctant to elaborate.

Calamatta thought it wise not to pursue the subject.

* * *

Later, after a light luncheon, Calamatta found herself once more in the library with her husband. The room was lofty and handsome. On passing a window, Calamatta stopped to survey the view. Though the sky was still the color of ice, the fog had taken itself elsewhere, and she noticed a number of people making their way to the house in wagons and on foot, all hunkered over, carrying heavy packs upon their backs. Some held tethers stretched to the point of breaking. At the other ends of them were pigs, sheep, and a cow or two. She pretended to be looking at the books on the shelves, but in truth she was watching William out of the corner of her eye. She waited until he removed a leather-bound volume from a shelf and settled himself in his chair by the fire.

How much like Mr. Darcy he was, she thought. *Steady to his purpose, he scarcely spoke ten words to her through the whole of Saturday, and though they were at one time left by themselves for half-an-hour.* How masterfully he managed to hide his affection for her, because *He adhered most conscientiously to his book and would not even look at her.* How like the handsome lord of the manor in *Pride and Prejudice.* Calamatta watched her husband's book slowly slide down his stomach onto his outstretched legs. His chin dropped to his chest, and a soft snore told her he was asleep. She sighed. She had hoped for an adventurous afternoon.

Trying not to disturb William, Calamatta slipped from the library and, humming a silly little tune, she headed for the kitchen to hunt out Mrs. Boskins. She'd ask the kind lady if she or Putty would sew her some caps to match her day dresses.

In contrast to what the kitchen had been that morning, the room had all the excitement of a country fair, with its hodge-podge of sights, odors, and sounds. Boxes and baskets filled every space on the floor and overflowed the tables. A sack of apples had broken open and its contents, crushed beneath the many feet, filled the air with a ciderlike scent. A panicky chicken ran loose in the pantry, scattering feathers everywhere, while Mrs. Boskins haggled over prices with the merchants and Ficus directed tradesboys to carry crates of produce down into the cellars.

From outside came the squealing and cackling of livestock. There were farmers, butchers, and wine merchants squabbling for attention. While poor bedraggled Putty bustled about trying to follow Mrs. Boskins's orders, Mr. Boskins directed traffic like a general.

Calamatta would have liked to join in the fun, but realizing that the housekeeper was far too busy to be bothered, she stole off to her room for the remainder of the afternoon.

That evening, Calamatta found herself in the library playing a go-as-you-please game of checkers with her husband. She wore one of her prettiest gowns, the color of ripe peaches. It revealed a lot more of her bosom than most of her dresses, but the dressmaker had assured her it was very fashionable. Nonetheless, with the chill that seeped through the drafty old house, she had chosen to cover her shoulders with a warm knitted shawl, the ends of which she tucked into the top of her low neckline. Putty said the vee made a perfect frame to show off the lovely pearls her husband had given her. She was a little disappointed that her husband hadn't noticed them.

At first Mr. Hatcher—for that is how she perceived he wanted to be addressed—said they would play chess. She professed she didn't know how, but she did play checkers. After much searching, he dug up an old set from his nursery days.

Calamatta sat across the small leather-topped game table from her husband, measuring her next play. She found his attention so strangely diverted that she wasn't having much trouble beating him.

She remembered once how Ward had scolded her for bursting into his office to find him doing nothing more than sitting in his chair, staring into space. "Even when they are not speaking, men's minds are occupied with serious matters which a woman cannot understand. And it is a lady's place to cheerfully accommodate these silences," he had said sternly.

Calamatta wiggled restlessly in her chair. She guessed this was one of those times, for Mr. Hatcher had not spoken a word for the last half hour. When he finally did speak, he didn't raise his head, so she thought he was talking to one of his checkers. Not until he spoke her name did she realize he was addressing her.

"If you remember, this morning I told you, Mrs. Hatcher, that the door between our rooms can be locked from both sides."

Calamatta only took her gaze off the checkers for a second, then pushed her king ahead a space. She watched William's hand hover over the board.

"Now that you are my wife"—he flexed his fingers several times—"I want you to understand"—his hand stopped—"Never—"

Contemplating what her next move should be, Calamatta barely listened.

His voice grew louder. "Never lock your door to me!"

"Well, I wasn't the one who locked it," Calamatta said under her breath, wishing he'd get on with his play.

William picked up his checker and was about to slap it down on another square when they were interrupted by a tap on the door.

Boskins entered. " 'Tis getting late, sir. Will you be wanting anything?"

While William was instructing the servant that he would be requiring a bath tonight, Calamatta had time to observe her husband. Edward had alerted her to his brother's habit of puzzling so intensely over a problem that he could concentrate on nothing else. Therefore, she wasn't surprised to hear him repeat, "Never lock your door to me. Is that clear?"

Gleefully, she concluded that her husband was not a very good game player. Calamatta used it to her advantage and smiled agreeably to throw him off track.

Without really looking, William plunked down his king. It was a bad play. "Glad that is understood," he said, running a finger inside his collar.

Calamatta jumped his king and shouted, "I won! I won!" In her exuberance, she nearly upset the table, but caught a checker before it rolled onto the floor and triumphantly held it up. The pearl necklace bounced playfully upon her chest and her shawl slipped off her shoulders. Delighted with her triumph, she pulled the errant wrap back up and, to secure it, stuffed the ends down the front of her dress.

Mr. Hatcher did not laugh. In fact, she began to believe that he was a trifle short on humor. He was staring at the pearls with such astonishment that she wondered if he even knew he'd lost the game.

He pushed himself away from the table. Three quick strides placed him so close behind her she felt his breath warm her neck.

" 'Tis time we retire," he said.

Calamatta glanced at the clock on the mantel and to her amazement saw its hands crept up on midnight. She hoped she hadn't kept him up too late.

"You understand about tonight?"

"Oh, yes, Mr. Hatcher." Calamatta reached out and took his hand. It was hot, and she gave it a squeeze. "Edward said . . ." She stopped when she saw his eyebrows shoot up. Thinking he was embarrassed that Mr. Boskins might still be near enough to hear, she lowered her voice and putting her lips close to his ear whispered, "It is time for us to practice."

Mr. Hatcher's hand closed tightly upon hers. "Practice what?"

Oh dear, Calamatta thought, trying to loosen his grip. *He's worse off than that scalawag brother of his. At least Edward agreed on what had to be done.* She concentrated now on how to enlighten her husband, but before she could think of anything to say, William was leading her up the stairs.

To Calamatta's surprise, as soon as they were in her bedchamber, he dismissed the drowsy Putty, then turned and bolted the hall door. Without looking in her direction, Mr. Hatcher started toward his own chambers. "I shall leave you alone to . . . to prepare, you know."

What a dear husband, she reflected, but what a strange way to tell her to get ready for bed. Before he reached the connecting door, Calamatta ducked under William's arm and turned to face him. She noticed for the first time since she'd met him a lock of his hair was out of place. My goodness, how much it made him look like Edward. For some reason, that thought made her want to touch him. She couldn't tell what sort of problem was bothering Mr. Hatcher, but whatever it was, she sought to soothe him. Reaching up to brush back the errant curl, she said, "Kiss me."

Calamatta kept her eyes open. She wasn't going to make the same mistake she had made with Edward and kiss Mr. Hatcher's nose, but it was he, she was sorry to find, who didn't know what the target was. His lips barely brushed her forehead.

Well, for heaven's sake! Her husband knew less than she did. She saw she was going to have to take matters into her own hands. With that bit of knowledge, confidence surged through her. Boldly she threw her arms around his neck and planted her lips upon his with such force that he fell backwards, cracking his head on one of the heavy wooden bedposts.

William disentangled himself from her grasp and, weaving like a drunken sailor, made his way into his room.

When the door closed behind him, Calamatta was left to ponder the laborious task before her. "Oh, my goodness!" She feared the two Hatcher brothers' education about matrimonial matters had been sadly neglected. Surely all Englishmen were not so uninformed. Now that she knew she wasn't married to Edward, Calamatta was reluctant to think that she had to start all over again instructing Mr. Hatcher.

After she had undressed and washed, she pulled her night-gown over her head and tied the pretty bow at her neck. He couldn't fool her. She'd witnessed her husband's distress when she mentioned practicing. Like Edward, William was too embarrassed to acknowledge that he didn't know how to kiss.

"Mandy-Lu," she said, as if speaking to her old nurse, "you used to tell me not to put off 'til tomorrow what I can do today—or tonight, as it may be." Determined to face this new challenge, Calamatta marched over to the connecting door. Flinging it open, she called out gaily, "Mr. Hatcher, I'm ready. Are you?"

Ten

William stood in a large copper-lined tub with his back to her, his face toward the crackling flames in the fireplace. Boskins had just removed his master's robe to enable him to lower himself into the water. For a moment, Calamatta was certain her heart had turned a cartwheel. Those wide shoulders, the slender hips, looked so much like . . . she shook the memory of Edward from her thoughts. This was her husband.

"Good evening, Mr. Boskins," Calamatta said cheerfully, heading toward them. With their outstretched arms frozen in space, the two men looked like iron hitching posts ready to receive the reins of a horse. She shrugged at their lack of response and proceeded forward. "Mr. Hatcher—" she began, pulling up a footstool, which she placed beside the tub.

Boskins coughed.

"Excuse us, Mr. Boskins. I would have a word with my husband."

William's mouth dropped open, his expression one of disbelief.

While Mr. Boskins's mouth twitched in a strange manner, his shoulders shook uncontrollably. Before William could grab his robe, the elderly man hung it on a hook out of his master's reach and discreetly left the room.

The sound of the door closing brought William back to life. He slipped quickly into his bath, splashing water over the sides of the tub onto the stone hearth. With his eyes squeezed shut and his legs bent, only William's head and knees remained exposed.

Calamatta swung around to confront her husband. "This needs to be said, Mr. Hatcher. Shame on you for working such a faithful servant so hard. In respect for his age, Mr. Boskins should be allowed to retire earlier. He is no longer young, and you are certainly old enough to wash yourself."

Suddenly her tone turned to anguish. "Mr. Hatcher, your face is an alarming red. Aren't you well?" As his shaking body began to make ripples in the water, Calamatta's fears escalated. "Chilblains!" Racing to the side of the tub she placed her fingers on his forehead.

William's eyes popped open and he grabbed her hand. "Madam, I do not have chilblains!"

Calamatta lowered her face to observe his more closely.

William glowered back. "Mrs. Hatcher, will you explain what you are doing in my bedchamber?"

Calamatta shook her head. Men were so embarrassed by a show of concern. Edward had assured her his brother was a hardy soul. So if not fever, it had to be shyness. She saw his gaze fix on her lips. The kiss. Of course, she should have remembered—he didn't know how. "I'm sorry," she said. "I was going to suggest we try the kissing part again, you see." Her answer was stopped short by the strange look he gave her, his expression incredulous. "Now, don't you give it no nevermind," she said, feeling quite worldly. "Edward and I practiced a lot and I'm much better at it now."

William's eyes widened and with a roar he shouted, "Edward?" He grabbed her wrist, and before she knew what happened, she'd lost her balance and upended in the tub. When she lifted her face from the water, she vowed she was nose to nose with the devil himself. "That rascally, yeaforsooth knave!" he bellowed.

Calamatta could see from the glare in his eyes that her husband was determined to have his say, whether it answered her question or not.

"That worsted-stockinged, cuckoldy, good-for-nothing rake-hell!" Trying to rise from the tub, William only managed to pull Calamatta further in on top of him.

"Mr. Hatcher!" she scolded, pushing her hands against his chest. "Your face is blotching. Oh dear, I'm afraid you *are* coming down with a fever."

"Madam! I am not coming down with anything. I am attempting to get up."

"Well, if you cannot do that, then you are weaker than I thought." Calamatta clasped the rim of the tub and hauled herself out.

"Am not! Yes, I am!" he bellowed. "Damn that brother of mine! I'll kill him! Better yet, I'll get my blunt back." Clutching its sides, William raised himself from the tub and grabbed for the towel. "No wonder that bastard ran off to London with the money." He quickly wrapped the towel around himself, then turned to face her. "Did he think I'd not find out his treachery until too late to do anything about it? Hah! Think twice, brother!"

Her mouth agape, Calamatta stood watching him. Mr. Hatcher had seemed such a shy man. Now he was looking at her in the most peculiar way. She could only stare back at him, until he shouted, "You are wet, wife."

"Well, I know that!" snapped Calamatta. She was too put out to hide her annoyance any longer. Did he think her addlepated?

"Go dry yourself, Mrs. Hatcher!"

With her gown sticking to her like a drenched kitten clinging to its mother, she dripped across the floor and into her bedroom. My! What was it about these Hatcher men that caused them to get so riled up?

"I want you dry when you get into bed," he ordered.

If that didn't beat all! Now, after getting her all wet, he started thinking about her health. Calamatta slammed the door and, without thinking, turned the key. Edward may have been right about this marriage business being terribly hard on men, but, by gory, it certainly wasn't a piece of cake for women, either. Mr. Hatcher needed to be taken in hand. She could see that.

The fire had dwindled to no more than a few warm cinders and the air was very cold. Shivering, she stepped out of her wet gown and padded over to the clothespress to find her robe. She took a deep breath to cool her temper. Why was it Mr. Hatcher brought on the same reactions she had to her brother Creed? She would have to be more understanding with him.

Calamatta secured the robe with its sash and found a towel to rub down her hair. At least Edward had cooperated, even though he hadn't seemed to enjoy it. If she didn't know that, regardless of his strong words, her husband cared for her, she'd say that he was vexed. Well, she wasn't exactly overjoyed with his behavior, either. She had tried to act like a lady all day.

After wriggling her feet into her knitted socks, Calamatta crawled into bed and pulled the pillow over her head. Through the thick walls, she could hear male grumblings and lots of banging. She supposed Mr. Hatcher was mad because she'd beaten him at checkers. Finally, all was quiet.

Sleep was about to catch up with Calamatta when she thought she heard a slight scratching from the other side of the room. She smiled. The busy little mouse again. Calamatta pulled the pillow down tighter around her ears and sleep claimed her just before a loud pounding and a blast of muffled growls nearly rattled the door off its hinges.

"Mrs. Hatcher, I'm warning you!"

Calamatta rose before daybreak to accompany her husband on his morning ride. Wouldn't he be surprised? She wondered how many horses they kept in their stables. She'd decided to forgive him for his outburst of last night. Yes, today she would be most agreeable.

Putty had not yet arrived to light the fire, and the chill in her room made her dress hurriedly. A quick peek out the window revealed a light blanket of snow had fallen during the night.

Calamatta ran out of the room and down the corridor. On the ground floor, she ran into Mr. Boskins carrying a leather portmanteau down the hall toward the front door.

"Mrs. Hatcher," he said. "Master William did not expect you to bother yourself to see him off this early."

With those words, they arrived at the library door. Her husband was coming out of the room, fastening the last of his several capes around his broad shoulders. When he saw Calamatta, he frowned.

"Mr. Hatcher!" It was plain enough to Calamatta that he was dressed for a journey and not for an invigorating ride across the fields.

"I'm off to London," he said, snatching his tall beaver off the hall stand.

"Why?"

"Business. Urgent business." As he put on his hat, he avoided looking at her, and, with deliberate steps, continued to march out of the house.

Ficus stood at the foot of the steps holding a black horse. William strapped the portmanteau onto the back of the saddle, placed his boot in the stirrup and, with one graceful movement, mounted.

For a minute Calamatta panicked and ran after him.

He turned to face her. "I have left your schedule and a list of your duties on my desk." He paused. "You did say you knew how to read."

Calamatta was too surprised to answer. She just nodded.

"Good. Do you think you are capable of following simple instructions and preparing the house for the Yuletide festivities?"

Realizing what he said, she smiled with delight. He wasn't angry with her. "Oh, yes, Will . . . Mr. Hatcher. Indeed I am!" With all the excitement of the last few days, she had forgotten Christmas was only a couple of weeks away. "And you'll be here?"

He reined his horse to face the road. "Of course."

"Promise?"

"Be assured, wife, nothing can keep me from returning."

Calamatta clapped her hands. Mr. Hatcher was the first person to leave her who had ever assured her he'd be back.

"What am I to do to the house?"

"Clean it."

She blinked a moment, thinking of the sparsely furnished rooms. "There isn't much in it to clean."

"Move some furniture, if that amuses you. Do whatever a woman does to get ready for Christmas. Add a few sprigs of evergreen. I'm certain it doesn't take too much to prepare for a holiday. Can't remember doing much but eating and playing with my new toys when I was little." He seemed to be picturing that event, but he still didn't smile. "The staff we will need is written on the list. Surely you can interview a few people from the village and hire them."

"But, Mr. Hatcher, what about the money for wages?"

"Boskins has instructions on that matter. You are to report everything you buy or spend to him. He will act as steward while I am gone."

The old man nodded. "I'll see to things, Master William."

Her husband bid for her attention once more. "Open up a few more bedchambers. May bring some chaps back with me from London for a winter hunt." He turned to his elderly servant. "We'll need dogs. How about Darien Munster, Boskins? He raised good hunters."

"Darien be dead nigh onto three years."

"Humph. Well, see what you can find out while I'm in Town." With that, he set his horse into a gallop and was quickly out of sight.

She called out after him, "Will Edward be coming home with you?" He hunched his shoulders, and if he answered her, she didn't hear him. It wasn't until she had seen him out of sight that she realized he hadn't kissed her good-bye. But then, he wasn't very good at that anyway. "Why didn't he take the carriage in this cold weather, Mr. Boskins?"

We'd Like to Invite You to Subscribe to Zebra's Regency Romance Book Club and Give You a Gift of 4 Free Books as Your Introduction! (Worth $19.96!)

If you're a Regency lover, imagine the joy of getting 4 FREE Zebra Regency Romances and then the chance to have the lovely stories delivered to your home each month at the lowest prices available! Well, that's our offer to you and here's how you benefit by becoming a Zebra Home Subscription Service subscriber:

• **4 FREE** Introductory Regency Romances are delivered to your doorste

• 4 BRAND NEW Regencies are then delivered each month (usually before they're available in bookstores)

• Subscribers save almost $4.00 every month

• Home delivery is always **FREE**

• You also receive a **FREE** monthly newsletter, *Zebra/ Pinnacle Roman News* which features author profiles, contests, subscriber benefits, bod previews and more

• No risks or obligations...in other words you can cancel whenever you wish with no questions asked

Join the thousands of readers who enjoy the savings and convenience offered to Regency Romance subscribers. After your initial introductory shipment, you receive 4 brand-new Zebra Regency Romances each month to examine for 10 days. Then, if you decide to keep the books, you'll pay the preferred subscriber's price of just $4.00 per title. That's only $16.00 for all 4 books and there's never an extra charge for shipping and handling.

It's a no-lose proposition, so return the FREE BOOK CERTIFICATE today!

Check out our website at www.kensingtonbooks.com.

Say Yes to 4 Free Books!
Complete and return the order card to receive this $19.96 value, ABSOLUTELY FREE!

(If the certificate is missing below, write to:)
Zebra Home Subscription Service, Inc.,
120 Brighton Road, P.O. Box 5214, Clifton, New Jersey 07015-5214
or call TOLL-FREE 1-888-345-BOOK

FREE BOOK CERTIFICATE

YES! Please rush me 4 Zebra Regency Romances without cost or obligation. I understand that each month thereafter I will be able to preview 4 brand-new Regency Romances FREE for 10 days. Then, if I should decide to keep them, I will pay the money-saving preferred subscriber's price of just $16.00 for all 4...that's a savings of almost $4 off the publisher's price with no additional charge for shipping and handling. I may return any shipment within 10 days and owe nothing, and I may cancel this subscription at any time. My 4 FREE books will be mine to keep in any case.

Name _____

Address _____ Apt. _____

City _____ State _____ Zip _____

Telephone ( ) _____

Signature _____
(If under 18, parent or guardian must sign.)

RG0899

Terms and prices subject to change. Orders subject to acceptance by Zebra Home Subscription Service, Inc.

ZEBRA HOME SUBSCRIPTION SERVICE, INC.

120 BRIGHTON ROAD

P.O. BOX 5214

CLIFTON, NEW JERSEY 07015-5214

AFFIX
STAMP
HERE

"The carriage has a broken wheel, Mrs. Hatcher."

"Then we must get it repaired."

"You just bring the bills to me and I'll mark them in the ledger."

"Let me do that. I'm good at figures," she said helpfully.

"Master William said"—the old man looked embarrassed—"I don't think he meant anything by it, ma'am, but he left strict instructions I be the only one to see to the books. No task for a lady to labor over."

But Calamatta did worry. She'd do what she could to keep the expenses down. She'd show her husband that she could be very frugal. The Indians and the Colemans had taught her that.

Mr. Boskins held the door open and ushered her inside. "The Missus gave Master William a big breakfast this morning. I believe the food might not be hot on the board, but if you wish, the Missus can heat it up."

"Thank you, Mr. Boskins." That sounded good to Calamatta. She felt much relieved, too, because for a minute she had thought Mr. Hatcher was leaving her for good. But he promised he'd be back in two weeks instead.

Calamatta ate a hearty breakfast, but it wasn't much fun sitting all by herself at the table, so she didn't dilly-dally and hurried into the library where she found the papers left for her on the desk. She was glad she'd eaten well, because her husband's ten-page list of things for her to do was going to take all the energy she could muster.

In London, things were not going so well for Edward. He had checked into a room at Fladong's in Oxford Street. Since it was the hotel most frequented by naval men, he felt he might be able to ferret out information there on the whereabouts of Fitzgerald. He would have plenty of time later to rent an apartment in a more desirable area of Town. But all his inquiries during the next couple of days, at the hotel and on the docks, brought no clue to the fate of his faithful servant.

To soothe his flagging spirits, he decided to call on the countess of Mayberry. Elinor was one lady he was certain he could count on to persuade him to forget all the misfortunes that had plagued him of late, but there he had his second letdown. The countess was in residence, it was true, as Edward was informed when he was ushered into the drawing room of her fashionable townhouse on Grosvenor Square, but she wasn't alone. Her venerable husband, the Earl of Mayberry, sat next to her in front of the fireplace. It was a turnabout that Edward had not anticipated. Contrary to his first declaration that nothing would persuade him to leave his residence in Huntingdon, the earl had decided to come to London after all to consult with a physician who had been recommended to him.

"Damned if the man wasn't all that I was told he would be," shouted the slightly deaf gentleman. "Already can walk about a bit," he said, pointing to his bandaged foot with his cane. Ignoring his several servants, he then ordered his wife to bring him another pillow for his back. "Would have liked to have gone to my club, but have this confounded dinner party tonight."

Elinor exchanged glances with Edward from behind her husband's chair. She winked. "Oh, Captain Hatcher," she pleaded most charmingly, "his lordship would beg you to inspect some old manuscripts he is thinking of purchasing for his collection. I told him you are so clever at detecting a fraud." Then, with an aside to Edward, she said, "Takes one to know one, heh?" She tapped her husband's sleeve. "Isn't that right, m'lord?"

The earl grumbled a bit, but agreed, "Right! Right! Need a second opinion." Edward was then invited to come back for the evening. "Dinner—cards. Need an extra man, I'm told. Damned nuisance. Don't know why the ladies can't get their own men— or why it's so disgraceful to have an empty chair at the table."

Elinor looked wickedly smug.

After that silent invitation, Edward couldn't cry off. He turned up at half-past eight, just in time to escort an empty-headed miss in to dinner. He was seated to the right of the countess, who ran her slippered foot up and down his leg throughout the meal, while managing to keep up a never-ending conversation with the gentleman on her left. Elinor amazed him.

It had been a most satisfying meal, after which the men headed toward the earl's den for their port and cigars, while the women repaired to the game room to set up the tables for cards.

The countess waylaid Edward in the hall. "You will excuse us a minute," she called to the others, his lordship wishes Captain Hatcher to look at some old papers." With that, Elinor yanked Edward into the library.

She was in his arms in seconds. Their kiss was a lingering one. Her fingers ran through his hair. "Oh, darling, how I've missed you."

Her slender body had always excited him before. "You're thinner," he said.

Elinor threw back her head and laughed. "You always did know what to say to make a woman feel attractive." She patted his cheek. "Here I was worried that you'd think I had grown into one of those hot-air balloons."

That wasn't what he was thinking. Her dress couldn't soften her lean ribs. Suddenly, Edward fought a terrible inclination to sneeze from her heavy perfume. He had become accustomed to a gentler scent and a more generous body. He drew back.

Elinor placed her hands on either side of his face and thoroughly studied him. Questions appeared in her eyes, but nothing more was said until the voices of the men became louder outside in the hallway.

After a very unladylike expletive, the countess said, "Why couldn't they have stayed away longer?"

When Mayberry entered the library, his wife was picking up a sheet of paper from the table, and Edward was standing innocently on the other side of the room in front of the fireplace. He was seriously examining the watermarks on a manuscript.

"So, Captain," barked the earl. "Think they are genuine?"

* * *

It was after midnight by the time Edward returned to his room at Fladong's. Aside from the tantalizing interlude in the library, it had been a trying evening. The more the earl drank, the more churlish he had become. Edward stayed longer than he normally would, because in the back of his mind William's warning kept nagging him that if Mrs. William Hatcher was going to be accepted by *le beau monde,* Edward dare not do anything outrageous to stir the pot, so he'd been polite and smiled at everyone. *I'm doing this for you. Callie.*

Edward was relieved to get back to the hotel. He shucked his shirt, removed his boots, and was about to take off his trousers when he heard a tap on the door. "Who the hell is knocking at this late hour?" Then, he remembered he'd spread the name of his hotel all over the docks in hopes that someone would bring him a word concerning Fitz. Edward quickly opened the door.

A large, menacing figure with dark devil-take-you eyes glowered back.

Edward gasped, "Will! What in hell brings you to London in the middle of the night?" The haunted look on his brother's face scared him. "Callie! Something has happened to Callie."

A fist crashed into Edward's jaw. He felt as though every bone in his face had been shattered into a million pieces.

"Is this your idea of a joke, brother?" was the first thing Edward asked, after a pitcher of water was emptied over him. His head felt like little gnomes were playing a game of bowls inside his skull. William always did have a deadly left jab. He'd have to remember to be wary of it in the future.

The effort to stifle his brother had taken some of the stuffing out of William, who sat like a lump of soggy mold upon the edge of the bed. As Edward pulled himself up from the floor, he observed, "You look terrible. Now can you tell me what this is all about?"

"I meant to kill you."

"That I gathered," Edward said, shaking his head to clear it. Then, pulling his shirt over his shivering shoulders, he jabbed some fresh coals into the grate. Sparks shot up in protest.

"It's freezing in here," grumbled William.

"Will, get to the point. You didn't come all the way to Town to kill me because my room was cold."

"What went on between you two?"

Several possibilities of what his brother was suggesting ran through Edward's mind. Could William have known that he was at Lord Mayberry's tonight, or that he had been holding his former paramour in his arms only a few hours ago? Deciding to let William clarify himself, Edward glared back wickedly. "Wouldn't you like to know?"

William leaped from the bed and grabbed his surprised brother by the front of his shirt. "You're jeopardizing your part of the fortune."

Lord, he meant Callie. "I am not," spat Edward. "I was to gain you a proxy bride, obtain the dowry, and she was to be delivered to you a virgin." Edward looked his brother in the eye. "She was—wasn't she?"

William's face turned crimson.

"God!" roared Edward. "You haven't bedded her yet. Have you?" Why did he feel miserable and relieved all at the same time?

William relaxed his grip on Edward's collar. "But she said—"

Knowing Callie as he did, reasoned Edward to himself, there was no telling what the chit told his brother. Edward knew that William wouldn't have comprehended a thing she said anyway.

"No matter what you thought, Will, I did not compromise her."

"You kissed her," he accused.

"Yes, I kissed her. Like a sister." That was a lie, but he was relieved to see his brother believed him. "You are the one who is married to her."

William sat down again. "Dash it all, Eddie. I don't feel married. Cannot take a girl to bed without some sort of attachment."

"You cannot, Will? That doesn't sound like you."

"You know what I mean. She's Mrs. William Hatcher, future

mother of my children. Must say I think she was trying hard to suit. Will grant her that. Just don't understand her." He began to loosen the clasp of his cape. "Cannot get used to the gel. Cannot treat her like one of the muslin set, but . . . I mean . . . she's so—" His arms flew out to make a wide circle.

"Voluptuous?" quizzed Edward. For some strange reason he wanted his brother to be miserable. "Long-legged? Earthy?"

"Ring off, Eddie! Don't know why I let you talk me into this harebrained scheme." He finally took off his damp greatcoat and draped it over the back of a chair.

"You know very well why, Will." For the second time that evening, Edward began to undress. "Since you are here, I suggest we both get a good night's sleep and take care of the important business as planned. Did you bring the proxy wedding certificate with you?"

"Yes, in here," he said, patting his pocket.

"Good. North is still staying at the Temple off the Strand. We'll see him first thing in the morning to get the papers signed to make sure you have control of the estate before Dickering or Parnell can muck up our plans." Thinking wistfully of another, more delectable, sleeping partner he could have had, Edward crawled into bed and hoped his brother did not take up too much room. "You can have the damp side of the mattress, brother."

As William pulled his feet up to avoid the soggy spot his rain-soaked coat had made, he asked, "Think the McGannons will make trouble for us from America?"

"They can try, but the law is on our side and we are on British soil. Sleep tight, brother."

William soon succumbed to exhaustion, but Edward lay for some time searching the shadows for answers he knew he would not find outside himself. *What we've done to save our legacy was justified, aye—but was it fair?*

Eleven

Calamatta found the first pages of William's instructions were given over to the daily routine she was expected to follow. *Mrs. Boskins has been given a list of foods you are permitted to eat and what time your two meals are to be served each day,* he wrote. *Discipline is good for the soul.*

"Two meals?" She looked again to make sure she'd read it correctly.

The next pages set forth her duties. Calamatta was to hire a regular household staff, find temporary laborers to help set the manor to rights, have the house cleaned, and prepare extra bed-chambers for guests. *How many?* she thought. He didn't say. *Buy ample foodstuffs for several weeks, and decorate the house for the Yuletide Season.* At the bottom of the page, William noted that he would bring the wines from London.

Among the positions to be filled were four footmen, two footboys to run errands, a man to care for the cattle, and two stableboys to assist him. Calamatta was to acquire a cook and cook's helper, chambermaids, housemaids, laundry and scullery maids. Mrs. Boskins, of course, was to remain the housekeeper in charge of the female help.

Already Calamatta's head was spinning and she was only on page five. She didn't know how she ever was to do all that her husband asked. Oh, why hadn't she paid more attention to Susanna's instructions when her sister-in-law was trying to teach her the intricacies of running the plantation?

William wrote a notation saying he'd apply through a registry office at a later date to acquire a proper personal maid for her. "That's silly," Calamatta said, and was rewarded with a joyous smile when she announced the promotion to Putty. "I have you, and you please me just fine."

Ficus showed her the grounds. Inside the stables, she looked about the big empty room. "But where are the horses?" she asked, watching several doves fly into the rafters, their wings whistling.

"There's only Tulip," the young man said, pointing to a sad-looking donkey.

At one time, the brick walls outside the courtyard must have enclosed good fruit and kitchen gardens. Beyond the bare branches of the fruit trees she saw other outbuildings: a chicken yard, cowhouse, and hogs-court. The newer part of the manor was an imposing three stories high, with its several garrets and tall chimneys protruding like sentinels above it all. She walked around the perimeter of the outer walls and imagined how beautiful it must have been at one time.

When she returned to the house, Calamatta found Mr. Boskins busily opening boxes and laying the contents out on the sideboard in the dining room. "Whatever are you doing?"

The old man pulled out a silver bowl and began to buff it with the sleeve of his coat. "The Missus says we has to count all the dinnerware what's been packed away all these years." He looked at the small array of serving dishes and nodded sadly. "She says there ain't enough chairs in the upper bedchambers, neither." Before Calamatta could respond, Putty came into the room, her arms laden with cloth. Mrs. Boskins was close behind, waving a long shredded piece of fabric.

"The linens," she said. "There ain't a sheet or a curtain in this house that don't need mending. And what are we going to do about uniforms for the footmen, Mrs. Hatcher?"

Calamatta's eyes grew wider. "Uniforms?" she asked blankly.

"Oh, my, yes," Mrs. Boskins chattered. "When Sir Henry was the young master of Careby Manor, the Hatcher footmen were bested by none of the gentry in all of the neighboring shires."

Calamatta tried to remember what the duties were of each of their servants in Virginia. It seemed that everything there was done effortlessly. When her clothes were soiled, they miraculously reappeared in her closet a day later, cleaned, mended and pressed. Savory food appeared on the table through that mysterious butler's pantry. She played at cooking with Abednego, but she never had to clean up after herself.

Now her husband expected her not only to hire a household staff, but to properly attire them as well.

At that moment, Mrs. Boskins marched through the room, waving her torn linen like a flag. "Follow me," she said. "Over the years, I recall old clothes and furniture was stored in the attic. Shall we see what we can discover?"

The three women dug through the cobwebs to turn up a motley collection of old uniforms, colorful costumes, wigs, and bundles of old gowns and shoes. The array of old tables, desks, and chairs perhaps had faults—a missing leg, a chipped corner, a broken back—but with a bit of honest carpentry work and a hard rubbing with beeswax, Calamatta reckoned the pieces could be made serviceable.

Calamatta pulled out a table with one leg missing. "Ficus can haul down the old trunks and Putty can sort out the wearable clothes."

Mrs. Boskins clasped her hands in front of her. "What a splendid idea, my dear. I shall set about cleaning and mending the suits immediately. I can use Ficus to hang the suits on while I see what needs be done."

Putty, who turned out to be capable of sewing a very respectable seam, spent the next few days decorating the coats with ribbons, shiny buttons, gold braid and bright colored sashes. Wigs were brushed and powdered. In the end, the women had six very distinguishable men's uniforms of various sizes hung up to dry in the kitchen.

Calamatta stared at the big farmboy in the green jacket his

aunt was trying on him. "My land, you look so splendid in that coat, Ficus. I shall just have to appoint you one of the footmen."

The boy blushed, and as soon as Mrs. Boskins finished altering the green jacket to fit her stout young nephew, he eagerly paraded proudly into the village in his new uniform to spread the word that they would be hiring up at the manor in the next few days.

Calamatta's greatest desire was to make the house beautiful and merry for her husband when he returned from London with his friends.

Early the next morning, even before the break of dawn, villagers and simple farm folk began to appear from all directions like ants drawn to sugar to apply for work. People with hungry, expectant, eager faces pleaded to be allowed to earn a few pennies to buy food for their families for Christmas. They surged into the large, warm kitchen, and when it could hold no more, they spilled over into the backyard. The weather began to turn nasty, so Mr. Boskins herded the men into the Great Hall and the women into the kitchen.

Mrs. Boskins found many women acceptable for household servants, but no one would come up to the scratch for cook, she said, except her widowed sister, Mrs. Wheeler. Ficus was sent posthaste to nearby Little Bytham to petition his mother to come take charge of the kitchen.

With so many men to chose from, Calamatta decided that she would hire the first three men and two boys who fit the uniforms. In no time at all, she had acquired all the male household staff. True, the tallest of the men, Jeremy, had only one arm, but she could not fault him for that. He said he had lost it fighting on the Continent, and without both limbs, he was afraid he would have a difficult time finding work to support his wife and young son. After hearing his story, Calamatta wiped a tear from her eye. He did look quite splendid in the uniform, even with one sleeve pinned up. She appointed him head footman. That way he could tell others what to do.

For stablemaster, Mr. Boskins hired an old farmer named Fotch and his two redheaded grandsons to help him.

Three dogs turned up at the front door on the second day of hiring. Calamatta answered the knock. The pig-eyed man who brought them stood with hat in hand and pulled at his forelock.

"Hunters? Aye, ma'am," he replied to her question. "Best in the shire, but can't afford to feed 'em." He wiped his eye with the back of his hand "Have to put 'em down if I don't find a buyer." He looked down sadly and shook his head. "Aye, 'tis a pity."

From the moment one of the dogs crawled forward and licked her boot, Calamatta was smitten. The other two, each in various stages of yawning, lay with their floppy-eared heads upon their paws. She patted the drooling hound in front of her and mentioned they all looked a bit sluggish.

"Jest saving their strength for the chase, ma'am."

Realizing now that in the few days remaining before Christmas she would be unable to finish the leather gloves for William, Calamatta grasped upon the inspiration of what a splendid gift the dogs would make for her husband. So, without consulting Mr. Boskins, she signed the bill of sale and told the man to leave the animals in a stall in the stable.

How surprised Mr. Hatcher will be, she thought happily.

When all the permanent positions were filled, Calamatta told the remaining hopefuls that the hiring was over, but for the next week she would have many temporary tasks which would need doing each day. They bobbed to her and she bobbed to them, and before they returned to their homes, she made certain everyone carried a sackful of food. Oblivious to the soggy rain, they felt that truly an angel had come to live amongst them.

Calamatta thought she was alone in the large kitchen when, from out of the shadows, a thin bent woman advanced toward her with a small child in tow. At first, Calamatta was about to tell her she had no more positions to offer when the woman spoke up and assured her she wasn't looking for work.

"Then what can I do for you?"

The woman pulled the shy little creature from behind her. Calamatta couldn't tell at first if it was male or female for the dirty rags it wore.

"I be wonderin'," said the woman, "if'n you could find sumthin' fer this'n to earn his keep? No mum nor dada. He's no kin o' mine. Found him starvin' in a cottage with all his dead kin lyin' around—the good Lord only knows fer how long. I cain't keep 'im. I've a sick husban' what come home from the war without an arm and a leg—dizzy in the head he is, too."

"Aren't there any in the village who can give him a home?"

"Don't know many in the village, m'lady. We be cottagers, and when my man got taken off to war and there wasn't no work on the estate, I could barely keep enough growing to feed m'self. And those I do know ain't much better off'n me. The poorhouse or an orphanage is where they'll put 'im. Fer the likes of him, them as they'll put him in ain't fittin' fer a mangy cur."

Calamatta looked at the dirty, raggedy head. She stooped down to put herself on an even level with the tiny child and felt inside the coarsely woven sleeve for a hand. It was nothing more than bones. Even in the bulky rag garment that hung to the ground, she could tell there wasn't much to the skinny lad.

"My, what a fine-looking young man you are," she said.

Two enormous blue eyes appeared through the mass of matted hair.

"What's your name?"

"J-Jamie."

"A fine proud name you have. How old are you, Jamie?"

Though his head came up a notch, his little body began to shake. Calamatta looked to the woman.

"He may be five or six, m'lady. So puny—cain't tell 'xactly."

Calamatta cradled his little stick of a hand in hers. "What can you do, Jamie?"

His rag-swatched feet shuffled and he looked down at them like he was wondering what they were.

Calamatta waited.

"S-swat flies, ma'am."

Once again, Calamatta's gaze sought the woman's eyes.

"We found him this summer past," she explained. "When my husban' was to havin' fittin' spells—all the time pukin' up all over hisself, and the flies swarming around his face sumthin' fierce—Jamie, he stood with a switch and kept them off'n me mister."

Calamatta's stomach turned over. Taking a deep breath, she rose and reached for the sheet of paper on the table. "Well, let us see what we can find here," she said, seriously perusing the list left to her by William. Her finger ran down the page, then stopped. "Glory be! How did I ever miss it?"

A spark of hope appeared in the pale blue eyes.

"Official flyswatter and spider catcher." She looked over and saw the look of expectation on the thin, pinched face. "Do you think you could catch spiders, too, Jamie?"

The little head nodded up and down with the first enthusiasm she'd seen.

"Well, then! That is taken care of." She took the small hand in hers once again and drew him toward her. "You don't know how grateful I am that you came along, Jamie. My husband's patience would surely have been tried if I'd neglected to fill this important post." She looked up to the woman. "I'll see that he is well taken care of," she whispered.

Tears filled the old woman's eyes. "Oh, thankee, m'lady. Yer a saint for sure."

When Calamatta laughed, Jamie beamed for the first time, and she saw his two front teeth were missing.

Before the woman left, Calamatta filled her apron with food to take back to her cottage.

If at first Calamatta wondered what to do with the little urchin, she needn't have worried. Mrs. Boskins had come into the kitchen and had seen enough. She took charge.

After Calamatta made the introductions the jovial lady said,

"Now, if you have any time from your busy schedule of swatting flies, Master Jamie, you can help Mrs. Wheeler in the kitchen."

Jamie took the plump hand offered him.

Calamatta saw Mrs. Boskins's nose twitch as she admonished, "First, young man, a bath and clean clothes, then a filling meal to start putting some meat on those bones."

Preston North did nothing to hide the fact that he was more than curious to meet William's American bride, and since he was footloose for the holidays, he made certain that before the two brothers left his London law office, he had finagled himself an invitation to the Hatcher family seat for Christmas.

It took only a few comments in the right ears, and like quicksilver the *on dit* spread about Town that the Hatcher brothers' pockets were well-lined, even after having paid off all creditors. Edward soon found himself once more welcome at all the men's clubs, if not by the hostesses of upper society.

He elected to keep his room at Fladong's in case he received any word of Fitz, but William went ahead and made arrangements to rent Lord Daybrooke's town house for the coming Season.

"I came across one of my former staff coming out of the Guard's Club, Captain Farthing," William said. "He said he'd heard of my good fortune in acquiring a well-heeled wife, and I didn't want him spreading the word I married a goose, so what was I to do but invite him for Christmas?" William's scowl dared his brother to comment.

Edward grinned. He'd heard some of the bets on why Will was keeping his new bride hidden away in the country. None of them were complimentary. "So who else did you ask?"

William seemed glad to get on. "Invited Cyril Standish, Viscount Heppelsforde. Found him at Brooke's crying into his cups. He'd just lost a bundle at the gaming tables and lamented he was not up to going home to face his father's wrath or his mother's tears."

For the next several days, William spent a great deal of time shopping. Later, on their way to buy guns in a shop off Piccadilly, William entrenched himself in Hatchard's bookshop until Edward reminded him, "Will, we came to buy guns, not books." While in the bookstore, William had invited another of his acquaintances from Cambridge days, a certain Mr. Sylvester Partridge, to join them on their journey to Careby. Syl confessed to the brothers that his fiancée had just cried off from their engagement, and his broken heart killed any desire in him to attend the holiday routs in Town.

At first, Edward had dreaded the thought of spending Christmas at Careby with just the three of them, but now that he knew there would be others, he was not as reluctant to return. In fact, the anticipation of the looks on their friends' faces when they saw Calamatta was enough to make Edward look forward to the party. Edward watched William pen a letter to Calamatta announcing he and his party would be arriving on Christmas Eve.

"I told her I expect dinner to be ready when we arrive," he said, aloud. Edward shook his head when he saw his brother sign it *Major Hatcher*.

When Edward returned to his hotel in the wee hours of the morning, he found a note from Elinor that had been left for him at the desk before noon, saying that she would be alone all evening and was looking forward to entertaining him. *Entertaining* was underlined. The evening was already spent. Thinking of the opportunity lost, Edward let out a groan and went up to bed.

As soon as he awakened the following afternoon, he purchased an expensive bottle of French perfume for the countess at James Smyth's perfumery and had it sent round to her town house.

It was not until his last day in London, when he was passing a little specialty shop on York Street, that Edward happened to see an item in the window that reminded him of another lady he knew. He entered the store and, after dickering with the proprietor over his unusual selection, made the purchase. He insisted on having it gift wrapped, and, sticking it in his pocket, came out of the store whistling.

Twelve

After Calamatta had selected the household staff, she hired several more laborers for temporary work and organized them into crews to scrub and polish everything in sight.

With a hand as firm as her sister's, Mrs. Wheeler declared, "I be takin' charge of the kitchen now, and I will not have any interferin'."

The women whom Mrs. Boskins found to be skilled with a needle were set to altering uniforms, patching holes in the upholstery of chairs and sofas, and seeing what could be salvaged of the linens and draperies. Much to their dismay, they found most of the latter fell apart to the touch.

On a day the sun decided to shine, Calamatta asked Ficus to hitch up Tulip to the dogcart and go with his mother to the little market town of Stamford. "I have prepared a list of foodstuffs, Christmas ribbons, and bright paper. What you cannot pack into the cart, have delivered."

Within three days after the word got out, Calamatta was delighted to find a string of tradesmen at the door. Fabrics were bought. New cutlery was purchased and the old sharpened. The cellars abounded with barrels of fruits and vegetables. Salted meats hung on hooks from the rafters. Aromas of herbs and spices began to fill the kitchen. When she went outside the house, Calamatta heard the cackling of chickens, the bleating of sheep, the squeals of pigs, and the familiar honking of geese—the sounds and smells of home.

Five more bedrooms on the upper floors were opened and aired, and she asked the servants to carry the carpets into the old section of the house to be beaten before being returned to the scrubbed floors. Mattresses were restuffed and covered with fresh ticking.

To Calamatta's relief, Mr. Boskins took over the training of the footmen and young boys who were to work in the house. He set the stronger men to bringing down the trunks of house-wares and what furniture was salvageable from the attic. An old, one-eyed carpenter was located in the village and set to doing the best he could to mend the broken furniture. If all else failed, a good book or a brick placed under a crooked leg could level a table. Their scratched surfaces were hidden under pretty shawls or tablecloths. Pieces of furniture were moved about to hide cracks in the walls.

Calamatta wrapped a scarf around her head, put on an apron, and worked alongside the servants. By the end of each day, she was so exhausted she couldn't remember if she'd eaten her two meals or not.

Stuffed back in corners of closets, they found crates of china and silver cutlery packed away in old flannel. These were taken out and washed and polished.

When the household cleaning was well under way, Calamatta rounded up the children who came with their parents.

"Go into the forest," she said, "and bring me evergreens, holly and sheaves of pine and fir. I'll show you how to tie bows of red ribbon and string together the evergreens into garlands." An impressive wreath was hung on the tall entrance door. Pine needles and spices were mixed in bowls and then placed round the rooms to chase away the musty odors.

Two days before Christmas, a messenger arrived with a letter for Calamatta. She eagerly pulled off the seal.

Her husband wrote: *My guests and I will arrive on Christmas Eve, and I expect dinner and rooms to be ready for them.*

"Just like a man," she said. "He forgot to tell me how many are coming." Then she noticed his signature. "Oh dear, he wants me to call him *Major* instead of *Mister*. Oh my! I've been addressing him incorrectly." Calamatta began to wonder if she would ever get things right.

The six men set out from London on horseback for the trip to Careby. William had hired a coach with a driver and postboy to carry their luggage and the two valets of Hepplesforde and Sylvester Partridge. Edward rode the horse he had purchased in London. The ever cautious William had announced that they would leave a day early in case they had to stay overnight at one of the posting houses along the way.

"A wise man," he said, "counts on English weather to be capricious."

By the time they had arrived at the first wayside tavern, the sharp pain in Edward's hip forced him to ride inside the carriage. He did not feel it necessary to tell his companions why.

At the end of the first day, the snow was falling so heavily they were forced to stop at an inn for the night. The storm continued next morning. The private parlor the men engaged had a warm fire, and the innkeeper's wife kept them supplied with tasty food and drink. Edward played cards with three of the men and won nearly every hand. Why, he asked himself, did he win all the time now that he didn't need the blunt?

Edward was surprised to hear William ask the innkeeper for checkers. Chess was William's game. Edward watched in amusement as his brother hovered over the checkerboard, unusually intent on winning.

The storm let up. Careby was still a good ride away, but all six men were too top-heavy to care. William's promises to his guests had become so outlandish that as they prepared to leave, Preston North proposed a toast. "To excellent victuals, a well-run house, and your obedient wife to pamper us."

"Hear! Hear!" shouted the viscount.

From his seat inside the carriage, Edward surveyed the barren fields and tried to imagine what he would plant on the Hatcher lands when the growing season began. However, the nearer they came to Careby, the harder he found it to keep his mind on plants and animals. All he could think of was seeing Calamatta again.

Meanwhile, at the manor, the table was set and a large leg of mutton, which Calamatta herself had insisted on spicing, was roasting over the kitchen fire. A punch bowl, filled to the brim, sat proudly upon the sideboard. She knew that William said he would bring the wine, but she wanted to contribute something unique to the Yuletide festivities. Susanna always mixed up a delicious drink and Calamatta tried to think what she put in it.

"Be adventurous," Abednego had always urged her, so she found some bottles in the wine cellar and added a bit of this and a smidgeon of that. The outcome, she felt, was indeed decidedly different to anything she had ever tasted. Almost as good as Miz Abigail's recipe.

Calamatta stood in the formal dining room behind her chair, where she would sit facing her husband at the other end of the long table. Since she was not sure of how many guests to expect, places had been laid for twelve—the number of Wedgewood settings she and Mrs. Boskins discovered packed away in boxes in the attic. There were not many silver items, but they used what there were and devised a scheme to wash the bowls and tureens in between the removes to make it look as if there were more. Her husband would surely think her ingenious. Polished to a fine shine, the silverware looked quite splendid beside each of the blue and white dishes.

She thought the footmen looked elegant in their powdered wigs and brightly colored coats. Though all were different, their uniforms contrasted nicely with the boughs of beribboned pine and fir which had been braided into long ropes and draped from the chandelier to the four corners of the room.

The women had made scented candles which gave off a spicy fragrance even when not lit. Every white napkin beside each plate was rolled and tied with a red ribbon. Sprigs of holly decorated the large stacked centerpiece of fruits and nuts.

Calamatta wore her prettiest green velvet dress. Covering her hair was the lovely cream-colored lace handkerchief which Mrs. Boskins had made for her to match the lace on her sleeves.

"Ye look like a fairy princess, m'lady."

"Thank you kindly, Putty. You look quite pretty yourself."

Giving her freshly starched cap a quick pat, the little maid blushed.

It was to be Calamatta's first Christmas as Mrs. William Hatcher and she wanted it to be a time her husband would never forget. The magical moment was at hand. All was ready.

But no one came.

At Mr. Boskins's bidding, Mrs. Boskins marched into the dining room where their mistress sat chasing a piece of potato around the edges of her soup bowl with her spoon.

"Eat something, child. You haven't had a bite since ye broke fast this morning."

"He isn't coming," said Calamatta.

"Now, whoever said he ain't coming? One thing I know for certain, Master William ain't one to be careless. When he says he'll be somewhere, he'll be there, unless the good Lord has other plans."

Calamatta glanced up quickly with frightened eyes. "He's dead!"

"Now, I dasn't mean that," Mrs. Boskins clucked. "Stop yer fretting and eat some of your soup. It be snowing all day. Dangerous for man or beast. Master William is a cautious man."

Listlessly, Calamatta spooned the broth into her mouth. It was no fun eating alone. She'd found that out after William had left for London. To have someone to talk to, she'd taken to eating her porridge with the kitchen staff each morning.

At first, Mr. Boskins, who ate with the footmen in their own dining room, was quite affronted by the familiarity the lower servants showed their mistress, until Ficus became quite besotted with Clara, one of the new chambermaids, and switched to eating his meals in the kitchen. Then the blue-coated footman named Hubert, a middle-aged former tinker, found out one of the laundry maids was indeed a distant cousin to his mother, and he came along with Ficus.

Before long, it seemed quite reasonable for all, after a hard day's labor, to sit around the long wooden table before the warm kitchen fire to discuss what chores had to be accomplished on the morrow. Calamatta entertained them all with amusing stories about living among the Indians.

Now the big evening they had all worked toward had come—and nearly gone. A few minutes earlier, the big clock in the entry hall had struck the half hour past eleven. The neck of the carved-butter swan had drooped onto the table. The little trees of grapes were turning brown. Calamatta had told Mrs. Wheeler to remove the meat from over the fire two hours earlier when it began to shrivel.

Finally Calamatta picked up her soup bowl and carried it to the kitchen at the back of the house. She looked at the tired, disappointed faces around her. They mirrored her own, she knew. Then she laughed. "Well, if this doesn't beat all! Look at us. Aren't we a sad-looking bunch? And this being the happy eve of the little babe born in a manger."

She sat down at her customary place at the head of the table. "Tomorrow we shall cook another meal twice as grand. Tonight, we shall eat and be merry."

Like magic, activity replaced apathy. Dishes appeared on the table. One of the postboys was sent to the stables to fetch Fotch and his two grandsons. When Ficus returned the large punch bowl to the kitchen, smiles appeared on every face.

"Serve the punch, me lad," Calamatta said, holding out her cup toward the young farmboy. "Carve up the roast, Mr. Boskins." Calamatta raised her drink. "Happy Christmas Eve to all!"

* * *

By the time they arrived at Careby Manor, all the men were cold and hungry. When no one answered William's knock, Edward watched his brother impatiently heave open the heavy entrance door. After they all stomped the slush from their boots, William headed toward the portal at the back of the vast, silent hall. The candles in the large chandelier which hung over the table shed a golden light throughout the spacious dining room. Every place was set with what Edward recognized as having been his grandmother's favorite Wedgewood china. He thought Grandfather had sold it with the other family treasures. The cutlery placed beside each setting reflected the flickering lights as if they were inlaid with tiny jewels. Garlands of evergreens made a canopy overhead. It was a fairyland, but where were the elves?

The chimes in the vestibule clock struck twelve. Had Calamatta given up on their arrival and retired? Edward saw William frown. He didn't seem to be aware of the decorations. Surely his brother hadn't expected Calamatta to wait up.

As if in answer to his unspoken question, William said, "I told her I would return on Christmas Eve."

From what Edward observed, Calamatta had everything shipshape and Bristol fashion, but his brother didn't seem to notice.

"Will, it's midnight," said Edward. "She most likely thought we were delayed. You can see she had everything ready to entertain us."

At that moment they heard loud shouts of merriment erupt from the back of the house. "Well, at least there are servants still up," William said. "I shall tell them to serve my guests while I rouse my lazy wife to wait on us."

Edward shook his head and followed the rest toward the noise.

Calamatta looked up when the door swung open.

All action stopped. Encircling the table, the merrymakers, with their arms raised and mouths open, appeared to Edward to be pantomimists in some medieval silent play. But looking over his brother's shoulder, Edward's gaze was drawn irrefutably to the disheveled, lovely creature at the far end of the table. "The devil take it!" he said, under his breath. "Callie, you are foxed!"

Calamatta narrowed her eyes to focus better on the two blurry faces which came into view. At first they appeared very much alike, except that the one in front was scowling and the one behind had a crooked grin upon his handsome face. She then realized her lacy veil was hanging down over one eye, obscuring her view, but when she tried to push it back up on top of her head, it fell off into a sea of gravy on her plate. Wasn't that amazing, she mused, as she watched the brown liquid ooze slowly through the delicate lace. In fact, it was very funny, she thought, and giggled. She squinted again at the troops now filling the doorway and knew they were trying to confuse her.

"I know who you are," she teased. "Can't fool me. You are Major Hasher." She raised her cup. "Welsum home, hushban!"

Calamatta's mind became befuddled after that. She was not sure how she got into bed or who put her there. She snuggled into her pillow. It must have been Major Hatcher. He had covered her with the soft comforter and gently pressed his lips to hers. It was a much sweeter kiss than his first attempt. She fell asleep happily knowing that her husband had come home to her, just as he promised. It was much later when William's deep scolding voice bore through the thick oaken paneling of the door, "I am disappointed in you, wife." A key rattled in the lock. Then silence.

Down the hall in his room, Edward hit the bedpost with his fist. Why had he kissed her? His anger with his stubborn brother for turning his back on his wife and marching in righteous indignation from the room had caused him to purposely pick up Calamatta and carry her to her chambers. She had felt so good in his arms, as if she belonged there. When they had arrived at the manor, all the men had had to stable their own horses, because the stable hands were in the kitchen, as bosky as their mistress.

Chaos reined belowstairs for quite a while after that. With all those people running about in a dither, Edward realized that no one had been aware that it was he who had taken their mistress from the room. Not even Calamatta. No damage done, thank God, except to himself.

Even though her eyes were closed, Calamatta had smiled when he kissed her. It was when his lips touched hers that he realized he was hopelessly in love with his brother's wife.

What if . . . what if he had done it differently? Married Callie and moved to America? If she'd stayed, she'd have forfeited her right to the inheritance, and Careby would have reverted to William anyway. What price had they paid for their misdirected honor? But it was obvious Calamatta was besotted with his brother, and Edward did not want to see her hurt.

Edward finished undressing and climbed into bed.

"Sleep your sweet dreams, my darling Callie, for if I know my brother, I fear you are in for a royal scold tomorrow."

As soon as he could make it livable, Edward mused, he'd remove himself to the hunting lodge. At least that was his. It would put some distance between them. When all else became unbearable, he would take himself off to London and find his pleasures there.

On Christmas Day, Calamatta awakened to a storybook wonderland. The air was shot through with tiny crystals and the fields and trees were frosted with snow.

She arose and ran to the window, trying her best to recall what took place the night before but, like a sled on an icy slope, her thoughts kept slipping and sliding away. For the life of her, she couldn't remember how many guests her husband had brought home with him—or had he brought anyone? The only picture she could hold in her mind was one of dark twinkling eyes and the whisper of a kiss.

Calamatta quickly washed and dressed herself while, in strong contrast, a tallow-faced Putty dawdled around the fire. The little maid didn't seem at all herself and was taking so long to comb her mistress's hair that finally Calamatta finished pinning it herself and, plopping a lacy cap upon her head, hurried into the hall.

Surely the kitchen would have been bustling since early morning, but the upstairs rooms were quiet. As she ran toward the stairway and started her descent, Calamatta didn't notice the shadow in the alcove at the turn of the corridor where a tall figure stood watching her.

Thirteen

Edward stayed hidden. He'd thought to be up early enough to buffer William's ill temper, but he had underestimated his brother. No sooner had Calamatta entered the hallway than the stiff-necked William was on his way out of his room. He waited for William to reach the stairway, then, keeping well out of sight, Edward followed.

William was standing at the top of the first floor landing when Calamatta's cheerful words spiraled up from below, "Welcome to Careby Manor, sir."

Edward leaned over the banister as far as he could to ascertain which of their guests had risen so early. Below, a white-wigged, blue-jacketed gnome, obviously one of Calamatta's newly acquired staff, was trying to bow and, at the same time, keep his wig from sliding off his head. The knobby man was addressing the tall, black frocked figure in front of him as *m'lord*.

What the devil? thought Edward. The man they were greeting was Vespers, Cyril Standish's valet, and the coat the servant wore was none other than one of Sir Henry's old hunting jackets.

Looking down his lengthy nose, Vespers announced, "I am searching out the kitchen to order a kettle of hot water for Lord Heppelsforde."

Edward had never seen Will move so quickly. He skipped every other step and glared down at the rotund little figure who by now was having to retrieve his traitorous hairpiece from off the stone floor. With a glance that would have heated Windsor

Castle for a year, William ordered his wife to immediately summon the rest of the staff.

God bless her! Calamatta didn't even realize his brother was angry. She shooed the befuddled minion off on the errand, then turned and beamed her husband a welcoming smile.

Keeping himself out of sight, Edward stood on the landing, watching the scene below. Like a mother hen, Calamatta proudly clucked greetings to each of the uniquely-costumed characters as they shuffled into the entrance hall.

Edward tried to guess the positions allotted to the wide-eyed servants. After one look at their stern-faced master, each of them glanced toward Calamatta for reassurance. The most decoratively dressed were surely the footmen. He had never been exposed to such an array of gold and silver ropes, laces and bells, ribbons and emblems, even at the Royal Palace. There were more medals pinned to their chests than he'd seen in the whole war.

Obviously, the men had been chosen to match the color of their uniforms. The tall thin one had a face as red as his coat. "Good lord! He only has one arm." Edward nearly didn't recognize Ficus. The boy's face was as green as his jacket. Even old Boskins, in his familiar grey suit, looked ready to cast up his accounts. Edward stared at the two younger chaps standing alongside the men. If he wasn't mistaken, they were adorned in suits he and Will had outgrown years ago.

Calamatta's eager voice broke the embarrassing silence. She joyfully introduced each of the staff as if they were members of her own family. Only upon William's sharp rebuke of, "Enough, wife!" did she stop.

The maids and kitchen wenches, with their caps askew and flour smudges on their cheeks, hid their hands inside their aprons and looked near to swooning. Edward thought his brother was putting it on a little too thick.

At that moment, an old man rushed in, pulling bits of straw from his sleeves. His white beard, like the last remnants of snow clinging to brown soil, sprouted in patches from his swarthy face. Following closely on his heels were two redheaded fustians, their dark odorous tracks across the flagstone floor making it no secret they had been mucking out the stalls. The shocked look on his brother's face as he looked at the clods upon the floor nearly caused Edward to give his hiding place away.

"These are your new stablemen," Calamatta said, motioning the odorous men to come forward.

When Will covered his nose with his handkerchief, Edward felt it was time to come to Calamatta's rescue. But just then a shorter, fatter replica of Mrs. Boskins came charging into the foyer waving a wooden spoon around in angry circles above her head, demanding to know how she was expected to prepare an entire meal by herself when all her workers were lollygagging about as if they had no other things to do.

Just before colliding with William's rigid figure, Mrs. Wheeler skidded to a stop. She dipped a quick curtsy. "G'day to you, Master William," she shouted in a gravely voice that suggested he was as deaf as the rest of them. "Glad t'see the two of ye home again." She glanced up at Edward on the balcony before he could hide again. "Make sure ye both wash your hands good afore ye sit down at my table. Ye boys always did have dirty hands and ye prob'ly ain't no differ'nt now ye're grow'd." Scooting her minions before her, she disappeared as quickly as she had come.

The hallway was empty except for the three of them.

"Was that Mrs. Wheeler?" asked a mollified William, all the bluster gone from his voice.

"Yes," said Calamatta, her eyes lighting up. "She's come to cook for us.

"Thank God!" Edward said with relief.

Christmas dinner was superb.

When Boskins found out the true number of guests, he removed the extra place settings and the meal began without delay.

Although the servants acted strangely subdued, the meal was served without any great disaster, except when one of the ropes of evergreens fell down upon the table and splashed a bit of gravy on Lord Heppelsford's brocaded waistcoat. But with so many glasses of wine already consumed, they all made light of it.

The fatted goose was succulent, the fish, mutton, and beef equally tender, the vegetables and fruits outstanding. Cakes and pies and custards accompanied the final pudding.

In her enthusiasm, their hostess sparkled like a holiday ornament. It was difficult for Edward to keep from staring at her; more difficult, when he did, to stop himself from showing his desire. So he scowled instead.

All the men, except William, vied to tell Calamatta amusing tales just to hear her husky laughter. Each time she took a deep breath, the men held theirs as all watched the little round pearls dance upon her ample bosom like the tiny beads of perspiration which formed upon their foreheads.

Although her husband sat at the other end of the long table, Calamatta tried to include him in her conversation, and when she spoke all other conversation ceased. The vixen had their guests charmed, and never was Edward so pleasured to see his brother discomfited.

"I planned on making the Christmas pudding myself," she shouted down to him, "but I didn't have the time."

Thank the saints! thought Edward.

Proudly, she told them. "I seasoned the leg of mutton and made the punch last night, too."

Will didn't know how lucky he was that he and his guests were delayed getting home last night. Edward chuckled. That explained the sickly looks on the servants faces and why Ficus kept leaving the dining room abruptly for no apparent reason, only to return a few minutes later looking more ashen than before. The whole kit and boodle were hung over. He wondered why the hoyden never took ill from her own cooking.

"I'm sorry you didn't get here with Major Hatcher in time

to taste it," she said, smiling around at the men. Her gaze came to rest on Will.

I'll be damned, thought Edward with a pang of envy. She only remembers Will arriving last night.

As if she were trying to recall something, Calamatta blinked a couple of times. "Did you taste any of the punch before you carried me to bed last night, Major Hatcher?"

William raised his quizzing glass to look at her and said, emphatically, "No, I did not!" And just as Edward realized his brother was about to deny that act of chivalry, a shout went up.

"Hear! Hear!" cheered the viscount, raising his goblet in the air. "No need for embarrassment, old fellow. I wouldna wasted time on a drink m'self with a pretty wife like yours waiting up for me."

William started to choke on a piece of pie. Edward expected an explosion but, after a quick swallow of wine, it took his steely-nerved brother only a moment of intense concentration before he was able to bring his emotions under control again.

With a wave of his hand, William summoned the one-armed footman behind him to hold his chair. He then rose and advanced toward the other end of the table. "Gentlemen, let us have our port in the library." Leaning over Calamatta's shoulder, William announced magnanimously, "Since it is Christmas, you may join us and we shall exchange gifts."

Calamatta's eyes lit up and, as she turned her head, Edward noted her lips were but an inch from his brother's face. "Oh, Mr.-Major Hatcher, I do have a most splendid surprise for you!"

At that, William actually smiled. "And I for you, my dear."

Edward scowled. Wasn't his brother overdoing it a bit?

Boskins stepped forward and whispered something to William, who turned and looked out the window.

"Right you are, Boskins. The light is fading fast, and since we were not here earlier to do so, we have yet to bring in the yule log." He turned to his companions. "What say I call a couple of the stronger men and we go take care of that task, gentlemen? Then we shall return to the warmth of the hearth."

Before Calamatta could get out of her chair, he added, "My good wife will see that our wine and cigars are ready upon our return."

"Amen to that, old boy," said Partridge.

After paying their respects to their hostess, the men jovially exited the room, leaving Calamatta sitting by herself.

Later in the library, after his guests' comforts were attended to, William dismissed Boskins and the two valets to attend to their own meal and then handed out the gifts which he'd purchased in London for the men. Only after his brother saw that his guests were pleasantly occupied playing a game of whist did Will seat himself beside Calamatta and bring out a rectangular package which he handed to her.

It looked to Edward to be the size of a jewelry box. His heart sank. As the eldest son, Will had the right to do as he wished with the family heirlooms. He glanced at the pearls poised above Calamatta's bosom. He wondered which of their mother's things he was giving her now. Her eyes bright with anticipation, he watched her tear off the wrapper. Inside were two books.

Why hadn't he thought to get her a book? When they were on the ship, Edward had noticed how much she liked to read. He felt the slender package in his pocket.

"You said you liked to read. Hope those aren't too difficult for you," William said, with a hint of doubt in his voice.

Calamatta picked up the first volume and read the title aloud. *"The Ladies Calling, Part One."*

"Though it was written over one hundred years ago," William expostulated, "the bookseller in London assured me that it is still said to be the authority on the nature and duties of women. The first part is about a woman's virtues." He scrutinized Calamatta, as if hoping to find one.

"It looks like a very practical book," she said, halfheartedly. Calamatta then laid it down and eagerly picked up the second volume and read, *The Ladies Calling, Part Two."*

"Oh, good going, brother. You know just how to get right to a woman's heart," Edward said to himself.

Unaware of Edward's scrutiny, William flipped it open. "Have taken the time to glance through them, and"—he pointed to a place on the page—"underlined some very important points on womanly decorum. Ponder them seriously."

When Calamatta started to open her mouth, William raised his hand. "No need to thank me. Felt it my duty as your husband to instruct you." Looking around at the amused expressions on his friends' faces, he cleared his throat and shut the book. "I shall go over the contents with you later."

"I have a gift for you, too, Major Hatcher," Calamatta said. "May I be excused a few moments to go fetch them . . . it?" Her hand flew to her rosy cheeks.

Was she blushing? Before she could rise, Edward walked over to the sofa and handed Calamatta a small package. "First, may I give you my present?" he said. "I fear it, too, is a practical one."

Edward enjoyed seeing his brother's out-of-joint look.

This time she opened the package slowly, as if she were trying to work up an enthusiastic reply beforehand. "Oh, Edward," she exclaimed as a shiny pair of steel scissors fell onto her lap. "Just what I needed." She raised her gaze to meet his.

"Scissors?" quizzed William. "Not a very unique gift, Eddie. Surely there are several pairs around the house already."

Edward watched Calamatta run her finger carefully over the blade. Her look was all he needed. "Not as sharp as these, brother. Not as sharp as these."

With an air of mystery, Calamatta excused herself and left the library. She and the twins each led a hound—or rather pulled it—into the house. Calamatta had wanted the dogs to be a surprise for William, and they were. In less than half an hour, the library was turned into Bedlam. For a moment, she'd worried she couldn't get them onto their feet or move them from the snug straw nests they had scratched out in the stables, but as soon as the beasts felt the warmth seep from the library, they reacted as if they had been hooked up to an electrifying machine.

Calamatta had no more than opened the door a crack than the animals broke their tethers and bounded into the room, leapt upon the men, devoured the biscuits, and knocked over the chessboard. One wag of a tail sent a bottle of wine crashing into the fireplace, causing a lighted hunk of the log to roll onto the threadbare carpet, setting it afire.

Pandemonium ensued while the men put out the fire and cornered the animals—all to no point, because when the ruckus died down, Calamatta found, to her disgrace, she'd been swindled.

"Mongrels!" Major Hatcher declared.

Oh, my, her husband was angry. She helped the twins remove the dogs. Then, squaring her shoulders she marched back into the library ready to take her scold. However, a far different picture awaited her.

William was actually smiling—no, grinning. In fact, all six men seemed to be sharing some secret joke, and for the first time she saw Edward and his brother exchange the mischievous looks of two schoolboys who had just executed a prank.

Calamatta was not one to question her good fortune. Perhaps someday she would ask that rascal Edward for an explanation.

The hounds had no sooner been taken from the room than Boskins and the footmen came in to straighten some of the damage.

While they bustled about, a rippling at one of the heavy draperies at the window drew the attention of the lieutenant, who signaled William with a motion of his head. As Farthing whipped back the velvet drape, William reached in and drew out a small figure. Gripping the child's waistcoat, he raised him up to his own eye level.

"What the deuce? Who is this?"

Edward didn't know the boy, but the black velvet suit looked vaguely familiar. Oh, God! 'Twas one of the pair of suits which had been made for him and William to wear to their parents' funeral.

From the sudden look of pain which he saw pass over his brother's countenance, Edward knew Will recognized it too.

"What is this urchin doing here, and in this—this suit?"

As he stared at the man who held him, the child's look was not one of fear, but of wonder.

To Edward's amazement, it was the usually taciturn Boskins, his face still a strange shade of gray, who stepped forward and dared to speak first.

"That be your flyswatter, Master William."

"My . . . what?"

Now it was Calamatta who stepped up behind the boy and, putting her hands around his slender waist, tried to pry him from her husband's grasp.

"He's your flyswatter."

William didn't relinquish his hold.

Between the two determined people, Edward feared the sprite would be rent in half. All the while, the wide-eyed child was vigorously dabbing at William's shoulders with his shaft of reeds.

Calamatta took a step back and folded her arms across her chest. "The thirteenth item on your list, husband. Flyswatter and spider catcher."

William, trying to avoid having his nose switched off his face, turned and gave her a look that would have assigned her to an asylum.

"Aye! I seen it meself," dared the old servant again. "Mrs. Wheeler, me sister-in-law, says she couldn't get along without Jamie fer all the help he give her in the kitchen."

Calamatta nodded her head.

The mop-headed urchin stopped brushing William's coat and smiled a broad, gap-toothed grin.

Everyone in the room now turned their attention to William. Edward knew his brother was examining every bit of the evidence set before him, but William didn't relax. "We shall see.

We shall see." He then set the child upon the floor as far away from himself as he could.

To Edward's amusement, the tension in the room didn't seem to run over to the small page. From the look of adoration in the boy's eyes, his unwavering allegiance had already been pledged. Instead of leaving the room with the other servants, Jamie determinedly attached himself to his lord and master and followed him everywhere. His little switch flailed the air, daring any sort of pest to come near his liege lord.

William acted as if he didn't notice.

Once more the room fell into a dawdling peace, and Edward, with a wicked gleam in his eye, felt it high time to tip the iceberg again. While the others were occupied elsewhere in the room, he pulled a sprig of mistletoe from his pocket and attached it to the boughs of holly above the entrance to the library. He then settled himself at an advantageous point across the room to watch.

Preston North was the first man to spot the new decoration. With a wink at Edward, he stationed himself near the doorway. Soon after, Calamatta walked that way on the arm of the shy Sylvester Partridge. William followed behind them.

"Oh, I say," said the serious-looking Mr. North, "may I have your attention a moment, Mrs. Hatcher?"

Calamatta stopped and looked directly into the blue eyes of the young lawyer. Not one to hesitate, North pulled her into his arms and kissed her most diligently.

Edward, laughing inwardly, would have been annoyed at his own feelings if he hadn't been so overjoyed at watching the startled look on the face of his unexceptionable brother.

North quickly stepped out of the range of William's fists and with a laugh pointed upwards to the mistletoe. "All's fair at Yuletide, Hatcher."

"Landsakes!" As she too spied the guilty plant above her, Calamatta let out a whoop of laughter and vowed, "I see I shall have to stand here all afternoon to kiss every one of you."

Edward saw William shoot a challenging glance around the room, only to have it greeted by a gleam in every man's eye.

William made to move his wife away, but she sidestepped him with the agility of a practiced pugilist and, pulling his head down to hers, kissed him.

Applause broke out around the room. Even Jamie giggled.

Delighted with the amusing drama, Edward waited for his pattern-saint brother to break the unexpected embrace but, to his annoyance, Will's hands went to his wife's waist and the kiss lasted longer than Edward thought proper. With his one hand still around Calamatta, Will reached up with the other and ripped the mistletoe from its nesting place, then, raising his head, he gave Edward a triumphant wink. Edward's attention was drawn back to Calamatta. With a surprised look upon her face, she drew back and stared at her husband.

Anticipating that his brother would remove the mistletoe, Edward had supplied himself with a pocketful of sprigs, which he schemed to hang in outlandish places throughout the house every time Will tore one down. But damn it! Calamatta seemed to be enjoying the game more than anyone, he decided gloomily.

When he retired to his apartment to dress for supper, Edward pulled the crushed plants from his pocket and, further crumpling them in his fist, threw them into the fire.

Calamatta found herself alone with her husband in the hall-way outside their bedchambers. A perplexing dilemma confronted her, but she decided to meet the problem head on. Placing her hand upon his arm she said, "Major Hatcher, please come into my room. I wish to talk to you. There is something you forgot to do last night."

William avoided looking into her eyes, quickly passed by her bedchamber, opened the door to her sitting room and motioned her inside. He then moved across the room and, after seeing her settled, seated himself stiffly on the opposite end of the dainty settee.

The small sofa dipped dangerously to one side and Calamatta prayed it wouldn't slip off the two bricks she'd used to replace the missing leg.

"Major Hatcher," she began, reaching over to touch his arm, "I don't want you to think I'm not having a very nice time being mistress of Careby Manor, but . . ."

Not a word escaped his lips, but his finger ran around the inside of his neckcloth again.

Trying not to let this habit of his distract her from the thought uppermost in her mind, Calamatta blurted out, "I missed going to church last night and this morning. There was no excuse, husband, it being the birthday of the blessed baby Jesus. Could we go to church, Major Hatcher?"

He let out a sigh. It sounded as though her request had come to him as a relief. Had he thought she wanted something else?

"The little chapel in Careby is sorely in need of repairs," he began. "The roof leaks, and the rector, Mr. Saulthorpe, is ill and in the care of his daughter in Little Bytham. There is no one else to serve the southern part of the parish until he recovers. The villagers may have held their own service last night, but even that aside, our carriage is missing a wheel and we have no cattle to pull it—and a donkey cart is not a proper conveyance for the mistress of Careby Manor."

"I'd like to see it. I don't think God will mind how we go to church."

"But I most certainly do! 'Twould not be the thing! Appearances are very important, wife. Mayhap when the rector returns, we shall see to the repairs of the church. Donate a new organ. Would you like that?"

"Oh, yes! But isn't an organ expensive?"

William's attention suddenly became concentrated on a piece of lint on his knee which he unsuccessfully tried to slap off with the palm of his hand. "Nothing with which you need concern yourself. There's money enough for what's important."

Calamatta reached over and with a flick of her finger sent the piece of lint flying. Giving his leg a little pat, she let her hand come to rest upon his knee. "How generous you are. I feared you were remiss in your commitment to worship. I'm sorry if I misjudged you. Forgive me?"

As if he feared it would burn a hole through his buckskins, he stared at her hand. "I . . . I'll see that a wheelwright is contacted and the carriage repaired, but I fear more than a wheel is needed to return it to its original prime condition. We need cattle, too. Sir Henry was very proud of his horses." Then, as if to make sure it didn't wander elsewhere, he captured her hand with his own. "Would it please you if I promised that as soon as that is all done, I shall take you to church?"

Calamatta nodded vigorously. What a fine man her husband was.

"Well, now that I've put your mind at ease about that"—his voice took a sudden commanding tone—"you will take a rest before supper." He quickly placed her hand back upon her own lap.

My, he sounded like Creed. Do this! Do that!

When she rose, Calamatta watched in amazement as Major Hatcher rushed out the door into the hallway, as if he were deliberately avoiding going through her bedchamber with her. She entered alone. Even though there was a fire burning, the room was dark. Calamatta didn't feel the least in need of a nap, so she lit the bedside lamp and reached for one of the books Major Hatcher had given her. She opened it and sprawled out on the bed to read.

Book Two: *The chief duty of the wife is obedience to her husband.* Humph! "I wonder if Susanna has read this book," she mused. "It's Ward who obeys her, not she him." She flipped the page. *How To Live With A Husband.* That was more like it. But as she tried to concentrate on the book, her thoughts kept wandering back to Major Hatcher's kiss in the library. She had to admit he was improving, but why, she wondered, didn't she get that exciting feeling from him—like fingers tickling up and down her back—the way she did when she kissed Edward?

* * *

In his bedroom next door, his hands clasped behind his back, William stood at the window and stared out over the snow-covered landscape. The moonlight made the battalion of tattered shadows appear to be marching toward the house.

"Dash it all! 'Twon't do!" he said. "Have to admit the gel has a certain attraction, but it isn't what a man should feel for a wife." Certain refinements were definitely needed by his American bride before he could present her in Town, but where was he to find her the training? Calamatta was too old to have a governess.

She was overly loud in her speech and too familiar with the servants. *Good Lord! She curtsies to them.* Then there was the matter of their marriage itself. No matter how legal Preston North declared it to be, a marriage without the proper consent and blessing of a clergyman of the Church of England didn't make it holy in William's mind.

He wanted the next week and a half to run smoothly for his guests. Tomorrow was Boxing Day. He had gifts to distribute to the servants and was prepared to allow a few of them at a time to return to their homes to be with their families. Apart from Mrs. Wheeler, every person his goose-witted wife had hired seemed totally unsuited for his or her station. William had a feeling Mrs. Hatcher would protest if he sent them off, though so far she seemed biddable enough. On the other hand, if he were to let any go, 'twould cause ill will in the parish. He shook his head. Having a wife, it seemed, created more problems than it alleviated. So how was he to go about righting this hobble in an unobtrusive fashion?

William seriously weighed the point. He had planned every day of the holiday to be packed to the hilt with hunts, races, some wagering, cards, perhaps some ice skating if the stream remained frozen. A trip to Peterborough to open another bank account was something to consider. Edward was right. Best not to have their money in one place only.

The six of them could ride over and be back in a day or two. William knew he was trying to find excuses for absenting himself from his wife, for he was beginning to realize that the more time he spent with her, the more pronounced her shortcomings became to him. The difficulty was getting used to the idea of being leg-shackled to a woman he did not know, of being tied down to a nursery full of children. He must delay their union.

'Twas time he faced the fact. Time he took charge of his own household. William hit the palm of his hand with his fist. "Ho! That's it! The solution." He walked across to the door which connected their rooms and raised his hand to tap. "Nonsense! I am her husband. I don't need permission to enter my wife's bedchamber." William unlatched the door and marched toward the bed.

Fourteen

Calamatta looked up when William entered her room.

"Mrs. Hatcher!" he sputtered. "I have made a decision about our future." Discovering his wife sprawled on her stomach, her little bottom sticking up, her stockinged legs revealed to her knees, was so unsettling to William's sense of decorum that he decided to put off the discussion of his program until later.

In the meantime, he found he was unable to turn his gaze away from the provocative sight. He swore under his breath to remember his resolve to postpone any intimacy. Then anger took over—anger at her for causing him to suffer a moment of weakness.

He spun around and hurriedly left the room, calling back, "When the Yuletide festivities are over and my friends have returned to Town, I shall inform you further of my plans."

By the time all the guests had departed Careby two weeks later, Edward was acting like a Far Eastern bey, giving everyone the Turkish treatment. The more he watched Calamatta trying to please Will, and the more his stuffy brother ignored her, the more Edward's disposition soured.

Finally, during dinner one evening, he culminated his foul behavior by declaring, "I'll be moving to the hunting lodge early tomorrow. My belongings are already loaded in the donkey cart in the rear courtyard."

The next morning, the cock had not yet crowed, nor had any

of the servants yawned their way belowstairs for breakfast, when Edward attempted to make his departure through the kitchen. But before he had traversed that cavernous room, an unexpected apparition appeared before him standing over a huge iron cauldron on the hearth, mixing a witch's brew. A roaring fire burned in the huge fireplace, silhouetting the familiar figure.

"Callie! What the deuce are you doing?"

As she swung around to face Edward, the large sheet Calamatta was dousing up and down came with her, as did half the water in the pot. Well, she could see his disposition hadn't improved overnight.

"If you looked closely, you would see I'm soaking a skin."

"Of course," he replied. Nothing she did should surprise him. "Most ordinary thing in the world. I should have known immediately." Mistress of the manor, up before dawn—or was it all night? He recognized the pelt was from the stag they'd shot three days ago. "You're tanning it?"

Calamatta shook her head like he was a little boy not yet out of the nursery. "Indians don't *tan*. They *soften*."

"How?" He couldn't believe he'd asked that, but curiosity edged out his pique, and no matter how hard he fought the urge, he yearned to be near her. How easily and quickly he closed the distance between them.

She twisted and pulled the skin. Then, stretching it over a large log from which the bark had been removed, she knelt, picked up a large knife, and began to scrape, smoothly, rhythmically, like a musician playing a harp.

"After the skin soaks for several days, all the fat and sinew have to come off, then the hair." Softly, she began to hum a tune.

Edward didn't want her to stop, but she did.

"If I don't get it just right, I can make a hole in it. Singing helps me to scrape more smoothly."

Edward pulled up a stool and sat watching her. He wanted to leave. He wanted to stay. He wanted to hear her voice, so he said, "American skins are prized here in England. What makes them so white?"

Calamatta stopped and leaned back. "They are white to start. To get color, I make a bag of the skin and then tie it over a smoke pit. When it becomes just the color I want—yellow, tan, brown—I take it off."

She picked up the fat she'd scraped and tossed it into the fire. Bullets of fat flew in every direction and sizzled when they fell upon hot stones.

Edward shot from his seat.

Calamatta laughed.

"God! Don't you know you can set yourself afire doing that?" He could see she wasn't going to pay any attention to what he said, so he steeled his nerves and settled back down. "That can't be all there is to making the skins feel like velvet."

"It's a secret," she said, deciding to ignore his strange behavior. "Sun Woman and her great-granddaughter knew it, and they taught me."

"You'll tell me, won't you, my brown-haired widgeon?" he teased.

Calamatta studied the problem. "I don't trust you."

One eyebrow shot up. He sat back and crossed his heart.

"Don't you bam me now, Edward. You must admit, you've told me some pretty wild stories. Someday when I can trust you—and not before—then I suppose I'll tell you."

Pots and pans rattled in the back of the kitchen. The servants were up and Edward was reminded of what he had been about.

"I fear that someday will never come," he said, rising.

Calamatta ran to him and threw her arms around his neck, a frightened look in her eyes. "Oh, Edward, must you go? Can't you stay here at the manor house?"

"Nay, widgeon," he said, pulling himself from her embrace. It was one of the hardest things he'd ever had to do. "I cannot stay. I must go. With that," he touched her cheek with his fingers and left her standing on the hearth.

* * *

When William found his rapscallion brother had left, it was with both relief and trepidation that he, too, readied himself to leave for London. Armed with papers drawn up by Preston North and signed by Mrs. Hatcher, William could now claim power of attorney over his wife's substance.

Although he wasn't quite certain she had understood what he was saying, William, with what he felt were quite sensible reasons, had persuaded his wife to agree to his suggestion that, "We postpone our . . . the . . . consummation until after we have had the blessing of the Church."

Seeing her puzzled countenance, William had explained to her, "By spring our rector, Reverend Saulthorpe, should be fully recovered from his indisposition and able to perform a quiet ceremony in the little church of St. Stephen's at Careby. The villagers and tenants feel they have missed out on a celebration; therefore, after the service, if the weather decides to be reasonable, there will be a small reception on the lawn of the Rectory for the cottagers and tenants. Our friends of the neighboring shires and those from London who wish to attend will be offered a more elaborate table and entertainment either in the Great Hall or in the garden of the manor house."

William's ploy didn't come without its bit of remorse, for his actions wounded his masculine pride to let any of his male friends know that he hadn't consummated his marriage. But he felt the delay would give him time to think of how to make his American bride more acceptable to polite society.

William shook his head. There was the rub. If Mrs. Hatcher's performance of the last two weeks was any indication of what he could expect in the future, he had a problem on his hands. For had he not this morning found her sitting cross-legged like an Indian squaw in the ashes on the kitchen hearth, scraping the hide of the stag they had killed in the deer park? It was shocking enough for the servants to observe her thus occupied.

Thank heavens his guests were gone and had not been there to witness the embarrassing sight.

The next day, after her husband left for London, Calamatta tried to figure out what he'd told her. *Consummation?* Major Hatcher said they hadn't had one yet. It sounded much like one of those fancy puddings Abednego learned to make in Paris, but her husband had spoken of it with so much intensity that Calamatta supposed it had to be something a lot more important than dessert.

Could it be anything like a celebration? That was what they did on New Year's and the Fourth of July for Independence Day. Would there be fireworks and music and dancing in the park? She didn't think he meant that, because he said they would have their celebration with the villagers. He spoke as if at the Consummation there would be just the two of them. There was the reception, too. She knew lots about those. Susanna loved them—liked to give them and go to them. William already said they would have the reception on the manor house lawn after the short chapel service. No, this Consummation was something else. She wondered if she had to wear something special.

An hour after her husband's departure, Calamatta sat beside Ficus upon the seat of the dogcart, heading toward the village. When she'd entered the kitchen earlier, she had found Mrs. Wheeler preparing food baskets for her son to deliver to the sick and needy of the parish. Calamatta declared she wanted to go along. All thoughts of Major Hatcher's promise to escort her to St. Stephen's when he returned from London were forgotten.

Their journey took them first to a cottager's run-down hovel, where six people lived in two tiny rooms, poor as Job's turkey from the looks of things, then to the former miller's, a lonely old man who received only a meager pension, and finally to the village of Careby. Ficus said he had several messages to deliver to relatives.

"Then please drop me off at the gate of the churchyard and pick me up when you are finished," she said.

Calamatta didn't know why she disobeyed her husband, but for some reason she wanted to see the church for the first time by herself. Entering the gate, she crossed the hard winter soil, passed the gravestones scattered about the little yard and around to the entrance on the opposite side of the lovely little honey-colored stone church. The splendid door, about ten feet high, had a fine handle ornamented with a pair of lizards. She'd just reached for it when a whinny caused her to turn. Down where the River Glen nestled in the curving arms of its banks, she saw a horse tied to a tree. Was there a worshiper within? In her most practiced Indianlike manner, taking care to make no sound, Tall-as-the-Trees entered the dark church.

To her right, the aisle ran forward to the raised dais. The room was dim, but the light streaming through the stained-glass windows fell upon the figure of a man seated in one of the front pews, hat in hand, head bent. The devout worshiper was evidently so deep in prayer he didn't hear her. Not wanting to disturb his communion with God, Calamatta approached the front of the church as piously as she could. She stood a few feet behind him, not knowing whether to stay or let it be known that he had company.

Then he started to rise, and Calamatta exclaimed, "Edward!"

If God Himself had stood there, Edward would not have been more surprised. Lord! Was he never to be rid of her? And yet, if he was so annoyed at seeing her, why in the reflection of the clerestory windows did she appear to him to shine like a rare beacon on a lonely shore?

Edward didn't know why he had come into the church. Habit, perhaps? For centuries, his ancestors had been baptized, married, and buried at St. Stephen's. It had been a cold ride coming back from Grantham this morning, and he thought to take a respite before riding to the deer park. Never before was he one to turn to the Almighty for direction, but since a vixen named Calamatta Mary McGannon had come into his life, he found himself making a great many supplications in his own behalf. Was he never to have peace? Edward, knowing it was unlike his brother to let his wife out of the house without him, asked, "Where's William?"

"He's gone to London," she said. Then, noticing his grin, she added defensively, "Ficus brought me. We delivered food to the needy, and I thought it a good time to see the church."

"You haven't seen it before?"

"Only a glimpse that first time I rode through the village with you from London."

"Would you like to have me show it to you?"

Calamatta clapped her hands. "Oh, Edward! Yes!"

For the next hour, he showed her the Norman tower, the windows dating back to the 13th century, and the comical carved stone heads on the outer walls. He excited her with tales of ghosts and secret passageways underneath the building. She laughed and cried and eagerly asked for more.

In the chancel was a finely preserved stone figure of a knight in chain mail, a dog at his feet, and a headless lion at his head.

" 'Tis believed to represent a lord of the manor who lived here six hundred years ago," Edward said.

By now Calamatta was floating in her make-believe world, imagining all sorts of romantic goings-on. It was so nice to have someone with whom to share it. For all his deceptions, Edward was truly a good friend.

She clapped her hands and pointed at another memorial in the aisle. "And that?"

Edward enjoyed seeing the rapture on Calamatta's face. "Ah, that!" he said holding his hands over his heart in an exaggerated theatrical pose. They were looking at the figures of an armored knight and his wife, side by side, their hands clasped in prayer, a shield below them. "Those are figures of the 14th century. I don't know their story. Mayhap you can make up a fable about them."

Calamatta was just about to tell him she already had a tale

made up when the tinkling of donkey bells was heard outside. "Ficus is here."

A few minutes later, Edward saw her into the cart. Then, with his joy going with her, he watched the new mistress of Careby Manor ride out the gate and up the hill toward his ancestral home. When the cart reached the top of the rise, she turned and waved.

"Ah, Callie, how did you steal my heart?" he asked.

On his return trip from London, after securing the rental on Lord Daybrooke's town house, the answer to William's dilemma presented itself in the most unexpected way. He stopped at Elmsworth, giving the excuse that he had to take a detour to the university town of Cambridge. The countess was the only true friend of the opposite sex to whom he dared unburden himself. Strange how he could reveal things about himself to Lettyce that he could never tell another human being.

Seated in her parlor, William made the diminutive, dark-haired lady aware of the circumstances which had him hesitating to introduce his wife to the local gentry, let alone the *beau monde* of London. "What can I do to make Mrs. Hatcher acquire a bit of Town bronze?"

Lettyce looked into William's dejected face. She started to place her hand upon his, but propriety made her withdraw it before they touched.

"She is welcome to come here," said the soft-spoken woman. "My seamstress will see that she has the proper wardrobe and I will introduce her to my friends in the neighborhood."

William set off for Lincolnshire carrying a heavy heart for his lost love, but with renewed hope that he could make an acceptable parcel of the vexing woman to whom he found himself bound.

Deep ruts caused by the thawing of the ground made the going slow. It had begun to snow again. The mud hardened. William let Thor, his large black stallion, pick his way among the holes in the road while he reflected on the warmth he'd felt sitting across from the countess of Elmsworth.

A sordid thought plagued him. What would happen should he decide to throw in the sponge? William reasoned that if he and Mrs. Hatcher had not consummated their marriage, 'twas possible that he could get an annulment.

But what if his wife was not a virgin? There was still that niggling thought. If he swore he had not consummated the marriage, there would be those who would like not to believe him and the gossipmongers would leave no stone unturned to put her reputation in question. No, he was not such a bounder. Like so many of his ancestors, William had entertained dreams of someday returning to Cambridge to become a scholar, but now . . . He shuddered to think he would be spending a lifetime breeding sheep and planting grains.

The cold swirled around him, making William hunch farther into his collar. His mind closed in on Edward. There was no answer to it but to continue the path they had chosen. If his brother had shown any inclination toward the girl, any predisposition at all, William would gladly have offered to change places with him. He shook his head. "Impossible!"

Whatever had transpired between the two in America he would never know, but William had noticed how Edward avoided any close proximity to Mrs. Hatcher and took the first excuse to be away from the house. True, he'd presented her with a Yuletide gift—but scissors! Nay, that was not a gift of love. It was plain as a pikestaff that his brother disliked Calamatta.

Too, there was the possibility of some unscrupulous dunderhead setting his sights on the Careby estate and cutting both brothers out by marrying Calamatta just to be able to take over the Hatcher estate. No! If he was to save their inheritance, William could not put off his responsibilities.

On entering the stone village of Stamford on the southern edge of Lincolnshire, William was overtaken by the postrider. He was headed for the George Hotel when the driver recognized him and called out, "The coach ran behind, Major. One of the horses cast a shoe yeste'day. 'Twould save me seven miles if you took your post from me. There be five letters to Careby."

William carried the letters into the hotel with him and placed them upon a table while he ordered a drink. Seating himself before the fire, he pried open the seals of the first two and perused the contents. They were answers to inquiries about sheep stock Edward wanted to buy. William didn't even finish reading them. The third was a bill from the wheelwright for repairs to the old family coach. Absently, he opened the fourth and was halfway down the paper when he frowned. He turned it over to question the name on the other side. It was addressed to *Mrs. William Hatcher, Gent.* The letterhead showed it to be from the office of Obediah Dickering, Solicitor.

William had already perused the page before it dawned on him what he had read. Dickering was informing his wife of Sir Henry's will, making her sole heir to the entire Hatcher estate. The old fox had caught up with them.

He folded the paper and, holding his knife over the candle on the table, reheated the wax and pressed the seal shut. Before opening the fifth missive, he checked the addressee. It was postmarked from the United States. It too was for his wife from her brother Ward. He didn't open it.

William pocketed the letters, swallowed his drink, and pulled on his coat. He could not keep this information from Mrs. Hatcher, but he would delay doing so as long as possible. She really wasn't uncomely, he thought, as he wiped his sweaty hands on the sides of his greatcoat before pulling on his gloves. But he dared not take the chance that his ancestral lands might fall into the hands of others. His duty lay in producing a Hatcher heir. As he mounted his horse, William quickly drew on his recent memory of the demure widow at Elmsworth. Why was it that it was to Lettyce he felt disloyal?

His backbone stiffened, along with his resolve to see first to his wife's social education. He then set the pace of his horse to enable him to arrive back at the manor that evening. No matter what Mrs. Hatcher's reaction to Dickering's news, William had the law of the land giving him control of her monies until she was of age. A lot could be done with seventy thousand pounds. He might even assign her a small allowance to spend as she wished. He'd prove he wasn't as clutch-fisted as his brother claimed him to be.

Within the week, Calamatta and Putty were bundled off to Elmsworth. The carriage had been rebuilt and restored to its original colors. Displayed upon the door was the Hatcher crest: an arm embowed clutching a green olive branch set over a field of azure blue. Four coach horses and two large draft horses had been purchased, but Major Hatcher hadn't yet brought home a mount for her. She questioned him about this.

"You are going away," he stated, "so it is nonsensical to acquire the unnecessary expense of an animal you will not be using."

From her husband's adamant protestation, Calamatta concluded Lettyce didn't have room in her stables for an extra horse. She hoped they wouldn't be putting the lady out to acquire two more souls to feed and bed.

Keeping true to his promise, as they made their way through the village Major Hatcher took Calamatta for a short visit to St. Stephen's church. She soon wished he hadn't. There she was subjected to a quick analysis of every part and particle of the structure which needed repairs. Calamatta tried to change the subject to something more exciting, like knights in shining armor or ghostly visitations. "Can you tell me about the secret passageway?"

William harrumphed. "Don't talk humbug and nonsense about ghosts and mysterious hideaways!"

After that, Calamatta lost interest in all else he had to say and decided, too, that she wouldn't even tell him she'd been there with Edward.

Back in the carriage, he informed her that the countess would see that she was fitted with a fashionable wardrobe and introduced to the gentry of the neighboring estates. "You will attend her most carefully, Mrs. Hatcher."

William refrained from giving Calamatta her letters until they were well on their way to Cambridgeshire. First, he handed her Ward's and prepared himself for a tearful fit of homesickness. When none developed, William dared look her way, only to wince when he observed her bouncing up and down in a most unladylike manner. She waved her brother's letter. "Susanna had twins—a boy and a girl. I'm an aunt!"

She quickly ran down the remainder of the page. So excited was she at the news from Virginia that she paid no nevermind to Ward's scolding her about running away in so unseemly a manner.

William then dared to give her Mr. Dickering's missive.

Her eyes still shining, Calamatta settled back into the comfortable squabs to read it.

William fully expected to receive a sharp wigging over the solicitor's letter. None came, which made William suspicious. He glanced at her out of the corner of his eye. What was the termagant plotting?

Fifteen

The letter from the lawyer named Mr. Dickering was so shot full of legal phrases that it was nigh to impossible for Calamatta to make heads or tails of it. Pleasant thoughts of Susanna's good health and her new nephew and niece overshadowed any significance to the man's announcement that she had inherited Careby Manor. A surprise, yes, but, fiddlesticks, she knew little about running a farm, only that it was a great deal of work, and she was glad she had signed over that responsibility to her husband. There were some compensations for being born female after all, she decided. With that thought, she turned and gave her surprised husband a broad smile.

When they arrived at Elmsworth, William handed Calamatta down from the carriage into Lettyce's care with a decided look of relief on his face. Even with Lettyce's supplications and Calamatta's urging to stay over, he was quick to make his escape back to Careby the next day.

In the ensuing weeks, the two women took a profound delight in one another's friendship, and Calamatta took an instant liking to the little Earl of Elmsworth as well, and he to her. But Lettyce's sister, Miss Patience Rede, was a puzzle—a tall, silent creature who stayed much to herself and didn't seem to care to enter into light conversations in the parlor with the ladies who came to call.

"You know, dear," Lettyce confided to her sister when they found themselves alone, "I can find little to fault in Calamatta.

I cannot think what William sees in her to cause his disapproval. Perhaps with her quick laughter and honest spirit, she is just the sort of wife William needs to joggle him from being such a pattern-saint."

In the meantime, Calamatta made a commitment not to make a fool of herself and to try diligently to remember everything that Susanna had taught her. More and more, she found herself grateful for her sister-in-law's training. In fact, Lettyce reminded her a great deal of Susanna. True, one was dark haired and the other light, but they both were petite and shared a sunny disposition.

For the first time, Calamatta found someone with whom she could share the secret gift she was finishing for her husband, and Lettyce, truly fascinated, didn't object to her working on the leather gloves. "Why, they are quite lovely, my dear. You can work on those while I do my stitchery."

Occasionally when the winter clouds decided to withhold their rain, the ladies of the surrounding area made quick use of the pleasant weather to go visiting. Lettyce's large mansion was filled with friends and neighbors, and, more often than not, by overnight guests.

Elinor, Countess of Mayberry, a girlhood friend of Lady Elmsworth, was one of the important personages to frequent the gatherings. Both women, it was said, had made excellent matches. It was soon evident to Calamatta that Elinor knew the Hatcher brothers quite well, for the countess made pointed inquiries of their whereabouts, especially as to Edward.

Having to answer innumerable questions about her husband was becoming quite wearisome to Calamatta, for in truth Major Hatcher did not generate much to talk about. In contrast, she admitted that she had worried ever since Edward told her that he had an *affliction*. Elinor seemed genuinely concerned for his welfare, too. And so it was when several ladies and their young daughters were gathered in one of the large sitting rooms for afternoon tea, Calamatta decided to confide in the lovely Lady Mayberry.

"We all know he was wounded in the war, my dear," Elinor said. "For a while we didn't know if Captain Hatcher would ever walk again."

"Oh, I know about that," Calamatta said in hushed tones which carried in the still air the way the memorable Mrs. Siddon's voice soared through a crowded theater at Covent Garden. "Down here." Pointing toward her skirt where it covered the most intimate section of her body, she drew, in dramatic exaggeration, an imaginary line up and around her hip. Not one word, not one gesture was lost upon the gaggle of ladies who sat about the parlor trying to appear innocent of eavesdropping. "But that is not all that bothers me. There are other things."

If the sudden quiet in the room was noticed by Calamatta, the Countess of Mayberry saw no indication of it. Elinor's own wide-eyed silence seemed only to encourage her to continue. "He fell off his horse in Kentucky and whacked his head—well, actually, I nearly shot him—that is, my gun did. He has a scar on his forehead," she said pointing to her own. "Then he was in bed with a burning fever for over two weeks. And, oh, I nearly forgot. He became quite weak on our trip across the ocean." Calamatta shook her head sorrowfully. "Poor Edward. He told me that his affliction may get worse and he would not make a proper husband."

Elinor's whirling thoughts returned to the night she had flown into his arms in the library. Calamatta's innocent remarks explained Edward's strange reaction—or lack of it. That was why he had turned down her invitation for a late-night tryst and left Town with no more than the delivery of a bottle of her favorite perfume to mark his departure.

Rusticating in the country had never been his habit before, and Elinor, remembering their many adventures together, experienced a deep sense of loss and regret. Up until his departure for America, Edward's wound had posed no problem to their lovemaking, but if he'd suffered a fever and was relapsing . . . well, damages of that nature were known to trigger strange behavior in some men. *Poor Edward* was a mild way of putting it.

Such an essential, virile spirit to be lost among the sheep and grain.

Elinor glanced about her. She hoped that Calamatta's testimonial had not been overheard, but the angelic expressions displayed by the pidgeon-faced women in the room told her otherwise. To spread such a humiliating tale was not Elinor's habit, but she knew others gathered in the salon were not as scrupulous. What a rattle! As soon as this latest *on dit* got back to London, many a scheming mama who looked forward to a nursery full of grandchildren would be steering their daughters clear of Captain Edward Hatcher. Well, Elinor had to look out for her own pleasures, and her mind wandered off to other possible liaisons. She only half listened to the chatter of the delightful girl beside her.

For several weeks, Edward worked long and hard, submerging himself in his long-range plans for Careby. While it rained, he busied himself with renovating the inside of the large hunting lodge. It was well-built and sturdy, with enough bedrooms on the first floor to handle a hunting party of twelve or more. The ground floor was given over to a great hall for dining and entertaining and a connecting room large enough for library or office. Living quarters for a year-round caretaker and his family were off the kitchen, and there were rooms under the eaves for additional help.

On dry days, he rode the boundaries of the property, reacquainted himself with the tenants who still remained, found men to begin replacing the broken hedge posts around the deer park, and saw to the mending of the stone fences and hedgerows which separated the pastures from the crop fields.

Not certain what William's plans were for Jeremy, whom Calamatta had hired as a footman, Edward asked his brother to allow the one-armed man and his wife to move to the lodge to attend to his household needs. With their son, a willing lad of ten years, they were adequate help, but Edward missed Fitz and

wondered how he had come to his end. In the evenings, he
pored over the books on farming he'd borrowed from the Peterborough library, but even that paled after a time.

Then a letter arrived for Edward. It read:

> *Your part in the capturing of Napoleon's spies at the
> end of the war has been made public by the War Office
> and I am pleased to say that you have been exonerated
> from any accusations of wrongdoing against Wellington.
> I expect you will be welcomed back by all the patronesses
> of the* ton, *as well as our friends on St. James's Street.*
>
> *With the excitement building for the royal wedding of
> Princess Charlotte in May, all of London is gearing up for
> an early season. Sir Bartholomew and his wife are already
> preparing their lavish residence for what is anticipated to
> be one of the outstanding winter routs of the year.*
>
> *Say you will come.*
>
> *Preston North*

Now that his pockets were well lined, it would not do for the
debonaire Captain Edward Hatcher to lose his well-earned reputation and be branded a hermit. He would join North in Town.
The popular young barrister was on every hostess's invitation
list and would make a devilish companion for the disgraceful
larks they would enjoy sharing.

With the Countess of Mayberry's husband once more at his
country estate, Edward decided he'd look up Elinor as soon as
he was settled. She was always one of the first to arrive in
London at the beginning of the Season to order her new gowns.
Edward had no doubts that a few honeyed words of apology
for his inattention over the last months would send her sailing
back into his arms in no time at all.

A few days later, Edward headed for London. On his way
through Stamford, he decided to stop at the magnificent Eliza-

bethan mansion Burghley House and pay his respects to the Cecil family, long-time friends of the Hatchers. Escorted into the dining room, he found himself being greeted by the present owner's son and several local friends, who had been enjoying a light repast. Now full of more than enough victuals and warm wine, several of the men were standing before a set of portraits upon a wall, making ribald remarks to one another as they scrutinized the names on each.

"I say, Hatcher," chortled George Palmer, a rotund, jolly-faced individual, "we was just admiring our ancestors' pictures. All members of the old club *The Honorable Order of Little Bedlam.*"

"I was led to believe it all started with John Earle of Exeter in 1684," broke in Bradford Nevil, coming up to peer at the portrait labeled *Fox.*

"All of them took on a name of beast or bird," added Peter Robbinson, squinting at the painting in front of him through his quizzing glass. "Glad that my great-great uncle was a buck and not an elephant like your predecessor, Palmer."

"Well, Hatcher's great-uncle Thomas was a bear," that gentleman said, trying to divert the attention from his own girth.

Edward glanced over the wall. For a moment, the bear was replaced by Will's stubborn face. "I think our uncle passed similar traits down to a certain member of our family."

"Captain," said Palmer, "now that you and your brother are amongst us, might it not be a splendid notion to get the club activated again? Heh?"

"And if we should," expostulated Lord Lexington, looking at Edward, "no doubt your irascible brother will lay claim to your uncle's name, the bear. So what animal would you choose to be, my boy?"

Edward didn't have time to answer before Palmer, his custard pudding chins bouncing about inside his highly starched collar, choked out, "By Jove! What else would the captain be but a stallion?"

Myth or not, the statement renewed Edward's vigor. Why was

he pining over something that could never be when he could have London's most desirable women at his feet?

Two days later, Edward rode into London. After that jovial afternoon with genial friends, the gloom that had gripped him at Careby was dissipating as quickly as the fog over the city. Maneuvering his horse through the congested traffic, he grinned. His notoriety as a nonpareil had not been won easily, but it was well established. Now that his loyalty to his country was proven, he determined to put his recent disappointment behind him.

Yet, to his dismay, although anticipation accompanied him all the way to St. James's Street, nothing but confusion greeted him. At the Guard's Club, as well as the Whiggish White's, his former acquaintances acted damned strange. North was especially solicitous and said no more than, "Sorry, ol' boy."

Edward found himself avoided at dances by the married flirts, and the mamas of the single ladies pulled their tender young charges away from him. Nonetheless, he decided to attend the rout at the Bartholomews' stately mansion. Perhaps there he could uncover why his proudly upheld reputation was in a shambles. He wasn't about to ask anyone, especially Preston, who alternately shook his head and smiled too brightly.

On the night of the ball, Edward accompanied North in his hired carriage, hoping that after a couple of hours of doing the pretty they'd extend their evening to other centers of entertainment. He was ready. He had to get Callie out of his system.

His and North's relationship seemed back to normal until they were approaching the Bartholmew residence. As they alighted from the coach, the barrister leaned toward Edward and said in a confidential tone, "There's a soiree tonight at the Cherry sisters' after the theater closes."

Such promise of a diverting evening had Edward's full attention.

Then North's voice assumed that odd confidential timbre Edward could not quite decode. "But if you prefer, we'll hit only the gambling hells later. Want you to know it's all one and the same to me, old fellow."

Too late, North was halfway up the steps of the mansion before Edward could react. North was not one to turn down a hard-to-come-by invitation to the house of the most notorious sisters in London. Still, trying to unravel his friend's meaning as they approached their hosts, Edward received another setback when he was given a solicitous pat on the shoulder from Sir Bartholomew and, at the same time, saw a tear in the eye of his wife.

Things began to look up when Edward spotted Elinor. Perchance this intolerable melodrama would be cleared up, but the countess only squeezed his hand and, with a sad shake of her head, walked away on the arm of the high-heeled Lord Penwhittie.

The sympathetic glances he received during the next half hour added to his confusion. He had expected a far different reception back into Society. In desperation to remove himself from the maddening crowd, Edward escaped outside onto a balcony to blow a cloud. The cold air made his breath crystalize into more vapor than smoke from his cigar. To warm himself, he walked back and forth the length of the porch, coming to rest beside the long casement windows leading into the game room. It wasn't until his hand was on the handle, ready to make another go at it, when he overheard the by-talk of four card players seated inside. The leading article under discussion was poor Captain Hatcher's Condition.

Edward stepped forward and listened. He was treated to four different tales of the possible causes. The macabre variations consisted of everything.

"I hear it was a tropical fever the poor man picked up in the jungles of America."

"Oh, no, my dear! He nearly lost a leg to those heathenish pirates off Jamaica."

"You're right. I hear he has this long scar"—there was a feminine twitter—"don't ask me where now."

God's blood! Nearly swallowing his cigar, Edward muttered, "Calamatta!" Only she could have been the source of his humiliating downfall, for only she had the personal knowledge that could have brought his reputation to such a low level. Was she still so angry with him as to wreak such revenge?

With his eyes blazing a challenge for anyone to stop him, Edward barged into the room. He bumped into a table, sent cards into the air and the ladies into fits of the vapors. Like a dark storm, with nary a word to anyone, he came a hairbreadth from colliding with several players, which only added to the *on dit* that if the captain's virility wasn't in question, his sanity might well be. No wonder North asked if he wanted to bypass the Cyprians' ball.

Too furious to bid his hosts farewell or enlighten his friend of his departure, Edward ordered his cloak and hat from a startled servant. With his fists clenched murderously, he set out to walk the considerable distance to his lodgings, ignoring the steady rain that had begun to fall. Edward was determined to get to the bottom of this fiasco. If anyone would tell him the honest truth, it was Elinor.

The next afternoon, Edward presented himself at the Mayberry mansion on Grosvenor Square.

Finch, the butler, opened the door. "Captain Hatcher. Good to see you, sir." After the warm greeting, he was ushered into the green salon.

Shortly thereafter, one of the maids appeared and said, "Her ladyship is preparing to go out for the afternoon, but if you will follow me, she will receive you in her parlor."

Edward had no sooner entered the room than Elinor appeared, a smile lighting her face at the sight of him.

"What the hell is going on? Why am I suddenly such a pariah that no one will associate with me?"

Elinor took him gently by the arms. "Sit down, dear, and let me tell you what has the gossipmongers all a-twitter."

Edward seated himself on the corner of her purple velvet lounge. His deep frown spoke louder than words that she had better not make a long tarradiddle of it.

Elinor looked at the angry man and decided she'd better explain as far as she could without involving a certain young woman for whom she'd developed a deep affection. "Yes, there have been some wild rumors flying about, but don't try to fault anyone but yourself, Edward."

Edward glowered threateningly.

He didn't frighten her one bit. "After all, 'twas your absenting yourself from all your acquaintances and social activities that gave rise to the stories."

"And you believed them?" he said.

She leaned over and kissed the fading scar on his forehead. "You must admit, my dear, that you have been limping more than ever since you returned to England. And that was less than a passionate embrace you gave me the night of our dinner party."

The touch of Elinor's seductive lips was a balm to Edward's ego. He decided she looked particularly lovely this afternoon. Taking her into his arms, he kissed her deeply. When he released her, he chuckled and asked, "Have I lost my touch, Countess?"

Elinor sighed. "Not at all, my gallant knave. Not at all." She smoothed out her gown. "But now, though I am reluctant to leave you, I must get to Lady Hampston's. Do you wish for me to spread the word about town that Captain Edward Hatcher is as much a man as he ever was?"

"You were never one to spread gossip, Elinor, and I know that there is no use for me to ask who did start such a tale."

She only smiled. "You will stay in Town, won't you?"

Edward placed a kiss on Elinor's cheek. "Didn't you know? I have become a farmer."

Before the crack of dawn the next morning, Edward made ready to leave London for Careby, swearing to strangle a certain mischief-maker if she dared to cross his path again. He had not been fooled for a minute as to where the rumor had started about his disabilities.

Sixteen

It promised to be an early spring. The hills were turning green, and out of the warm earth, yellow and purple blossoms were pushing up their colorful faces. Calamatta had been at Elmsworth for two months when Major Hatcher finally came to call.

The moment she caught sight of him from a second-story window, it was all she could do to keep from rushing down into his arms. *Get your wits together,* she told herself, *or you'll spoil everything Lettyce has taught you.* She squeezed her eyes shut for a second, took a deep breath, and, with as much dignity as her racing heart could muster, descended the stairs.

She waited for a sign showing how impressed William was with her modish clothes and fashionable hairstyle, but after he'd looked her over, the cool kiss he placed upon her lips was less than she had hoped for. He'd certainly lost ground since Christmas. Calamatta kissed him again, but received as much assistance as she would from a wooden Indian.

As he held her away from him, she couldn't help but compare her reaction to a kiss she'd received a long time ago at a barn dance from another dark-haired man who looked very much like him. She blushed. *Shame on you,* she chided herself, *for thinking of that rascal Edward when your handsome husband stands before you.*

Lettyce also witnessed the greeting, but only saw the strong arms of the man she loved embracing the statuesque, brown-haired beauty. The blush which rose in Calamatta's cheeks did not escape her observation, either.

Major Hatcher spoke impassively. "If you will excuse me, Mrs. Hatcher, I wish to go to my chambers to change from my traveling clothes." He'd only gone up two steps before he stopped and descended to where Calamatta stood watching. After shuffling about in his pocket, he produced a small box and handed it to her. "Wear it so you and others don't forget you are my wife," he said before continuing on his way.

Calamatta opened the box and gasped. Inside on a blue satin cushion sat a gold ring set with a circle of tiny diamonds. She slipped the ring on the third finger of her left hand and held it out to gaze at it. Landsakes! Who would have thought Major Hatcher so extravagant? How he must love her to spend so much of his money on a ring.

Later in the parlor, the two women settled back into their chairs. Lettyce ordered tea, then glanced over at her protégée. Calamatta looked lovely, but she sat nervously twisting the ring on her finger. Lettyce waited for an explanation. She knew it was sure to come, for as quickly as they formed, the young American's thoughts usually popped out of her mouth.

Calamatta asked, "What does it mean when you kiss a man and your knees go all weak and you're sure your brains have turned to custard?"

Lettyce gazed at the ring. "It means you're in love," she said with a tightening in her throat.

"Oh," was all the response she received.

Her husband stayed a week. No matter how hard she tried, Calamatta thought herself a regular skitterbrain. Under Major Hatcher's critical gaze, she did everything wrong, and he was quick to point out every *faux paus*.

He explained that since he was taking several trunks of their clothes with him to London, he had come in the family carriage. He had brought his favorite riding horse, Thor, and asked permission to stable it at Elmsworth when he continued to Town with the coach.

Calamatta's gift for Major Hatcher, the white leather gloves, were finished. To her delight, Lettyce had declared them quite dashing. Calamatta rolled the gloves carefully in her hands and waited at the stables for him to return from his morning ride. Gaining her husband's favor was uppermost in Calamatta's mind, so she wanted him to have them before he left for London. She watched him hand over the reins to the stableboy and smiled widely in anticipation of Major Hatcher's delight, but before she could make known her intentions, his stern face turned to her.

"While I am gone, I shall expect you to behave."

Something snapped in Calamatta. "I always try to behave like a lady, *Mister* Hatcher." She wouldn't even give him the honor of his rank.

She saw him blink, but it didn't shorten his retort.

"No, you do not! You speak up when you should be silent and you are disrespectful of your husband. But what can be expected of someone with a name like McGannon?" There, it was said.

Calamatta's eyes narrowed. No one, *no one,* made fun of a McGannon. She might carry the name of Hatcher now, but through and through, her Gaelic blood was that of a fighting McGannon. As the gloves burned in her hands, her fingers closed around them and, with a look of defiance, she stuffed them into the front of her dress. Oh, how she wanted to fling a tirade of lusty words at that man, but he had already turned and was marching, ramrod stiff, across the lawn to the house.

He flung one last sally over his shoulder. "You could use some lessons in restraint, madam!"

If that didn't beat all! Calamatta turned and stomped toward the stables, but not before she shot back a volley of her own. "Well, when it comes to kissing, Mister Hatcher, I'll have you know that you could use some pointers on that yourself." As she continued to watch her husband storm toward the house and his waiting carriage, she mumbled to herself, "If you must know, your little brother, Edward, kisses a lot better than you." She knew he couldn't hear, but it made her feel better to say it.

William saw only the countess of Elmsworth, who stood awaiting him in the drive. Although he felt certain she had not heard his words with his wife, Lettyce had witnessed the confrontation. From the moment he saw her sorrowful look, William's gaze softened. He took one of her hands in his.

"If I could, my lady, I would ask for a divorce. But for reasons I cannot tell you, my honor would not permit it," said William.

"I would not ask it of you. She is in love with you."

"Mrs. Hatcher told you that?"

"Not in so many words. More in her innocent questions." Lettyce paused. "She is very young, William. We have become good friends and I have her confidence. I'd not betray that. I was much of the same vent at that age." She looked up pensively into the intense eyes of the tall man in front of her. "Was it that long ago when we asked the same questions of each other?"

William began to pull her toward him, but Lettyce tried to withdraw her hands. A rumble of thunder interrupted. With a worried look upon his face, William glanced up at the threatening clouds forming overhead, turned, and hurriedly entered the carriage.

Calamatta watched her husband take leave of Lettyce. The distance was not great enough to hide her husband's address to the small lady in black. Calamatta gladly would have slammed a fist into his aristocratic nose, but for lack of that target she looked about her and her eyes fell upon the great black beast, Thor, being led to the stables.

Giving the stableboy no time to protest, Calamatta yanked the reins from his hands and led the horse to the mounting block. There she pulled her skirts up between her legs and tucked the hem into her sash. Then, leaping into the saddle, she turned the surprised stallion away from the stables and headed across the lawn. Her feet fell short of the stirrups, but, undaunted, she hugged her knees to the leather and did not consider that the flapping metal acted like sharp spurs against the flanks of the animal.

Waving his arms wildly, the stableboy was soon left far behind.

Escape! Calamatta gave Thor his head, not caring in which direction the stallion took her. Rain began to fall, but the raindrops did less to blind her than the tears welling in her eyes. She was married to an exasperating man who was always ordering her about and telling her how clumsy and provincial she was. She didn't understand. The harder she tried to please, the more of a trial she became.

An opening into the thick wood appeared and she turned Thor toward it. The lane proved to be no more than a footpath winding its way through thick underbrush. Low-hanging branches from the ancient trees grabbed at her hair, tore her clothing, and whipped her horse into a frenzy. A thick cloud of mist enclosed them before the terrified horse burst from the forest through a break in the hedgerow and onto a rain-soaked road, nearly colliding with a mud-splattered carriage. The six frothing horses which pulled it veered into the ditch, where the carriage, careening precariously upon two wheels, came to an abrupt halt. The coachmen tried to calm the frantic horses to keep them from overturning the vehicle completely.

Mounted soldiers preceding and following the coach shouted all sorts of blasphemies, some never before heard by Calamatta, and a deep commanding voice cried out, "An attack! Ho! Watch on the left of the wood!"

When confronted with the oncoming cavalry, Thor whinnied, reared up, and pitched Calamatta unceremoniously into a puddle in the middle of the road. As she watched helplessly, the frightened horse galloped off. From her embarrassing position, Calamatta saw a great retinue of scarlet-coated soldiers advance toward her, brandishing all sorts of ugly weapons. It was too much. The tears began to flow, and there was nothing Calamatta could do to stop them. William's cowardly beast had deserted her, leaving her to fend off these brigands by herself. Her eyes closed to shut out the sight of them.

Calamatta wanted to go home, but where was home? Mockwood Plantation belonged to Ward and heaven knew he most certainly wouldn't want her back. Creed slept wherever his head came to rest, and Edward had deserted her to live in the deer park all by himself. Major Hatcher said he had the right to send her away from Careby Manor because of the papers she'd signed. It seemed nobody wanted her, and she didn't know why.

The clammy moisture of the ground began to seep up through her skirt and so increased Calamatta's misery that she only became aware of the portly gentleman, huffing and puffing beside her, when he patted her arm. She squinted up at him, curiosity overcoming any fear. He was definitely no knight in shining armour. In fact, the poor man was quite disheveled himself.

Instantly, she felt sorry for him. His neckscarf was askew and a button on his fine coat hung by a thread. Bravely, he was trying to swat away the weapons pointed at her and, at the same time, attempting to wipe some of the filth from her clothes, smearing his gloves with mud for all his trouble. She struggled to keep her emotions in check, but when Calamatta looked up into his kind eyes, she lost the fight and tears started all over again.

With concern in his voice, he said, " 'Pon my soul, if this ain't a fine how-de-do! What have we here?" Settling his heels firmly into the ground, he offered her his hand to help her rise. "M'dear child, are you hurt?"

"I don't think so," she sniffed, twisting around to look at her soaking backside. She couldn't miss the smile which flitted across his face.

He abruptly waved away the remaining soldiers. She tried to tell him she was sorry, but the words blubbered out and sounded like nonsense. She could only point in the direction of the disappearing horse. Oh, Major Hatcher would kill her if anything untoward happened to that cowardly beast!

The kind gentleman gave sharp orders to one of the men, who turned his horse and took off after the fickle Thor.

"There, there!" said the courtly gentleman. "Our man will retrieve your mount before he goes too far." He led her to the side of the road where two footmen had placed one of the large chests which had been thrown from the top of the carriage. It was quickly covered with a thick fur robe and, with a creak and a groan, the large man settled his ponderous body upon it. He looked down at both sides of the trunk and seemed rather surprised to find he had taken up the entire surface of the makeshift seat. Snapping his fingers at one of his servants, he whispered something in his ear. A carriage rug was spread across his lap and, with a twinkle in his eye, the man took Calamatta's hand and patted his knee. She sat. Immediately, another minion popped open the largest bumbershoot she had ever seen and held it over them.

"Now," he said, handing her a lacy handkerchief he pulled from his sleeve, "tell us what a beautiful young gel is doing riding all by herself?"

Calamatta didn't trust her voice, so she shook her head. While raising the handkerchief to her nose for a hearty blow, she exposed her ring.

"Let me guess," he said, taking her hand and scrutinizing the massive gem in her ring. "A quarrel . . ."

Calamatta let out a wail.

"With your husband?"

Calamatta cried louder.

"Ah," he patted her hand. "Husbands are such beasts at times. I know."

Her gaze fell upon his muddy gloves. "They're ruined," she said.

He dismissed the problem as inconsequential by dropping them to the ground just as their tête-à-tête was interrupted by the return of Thor.

"Zounds! What a magnificent animal," he exclaimed, boosting Calamatta from his lap. Two liveried attendants helped him up, and while he was still admiring the stallion, a coachman approached and spoke. Her new friend ordered one of the officers to assist Calamatta into the saddle, and as she threw her leg up and over Thor's wide back, the officer didn't attempt to hide his frown of disapproval. In contrast to the soldier's dour looks, her flying skirts brought an appreciative grin to the face of her rescuer.

"We see that our carriage has been uprighted and seems none the worse for the little upset. Now, we suggest you hold your head high and return to that husband of yours and make up." He gave her a wink. "No problem should be so great that such a lovely young lass cannot persuade a man to see her way of thinking."

Now, why couldn't some other men of her acquaintance be as charming? she thought. When Calamatta raised her hand to pull her jacket close about her, she felt the bulge in the front of her dress. The gloves! She had forgotten them. "Wait!" she called, her voice made low from her crying.

The man turned back.

On impulse, she reached down inside her bodice.

Eyebrows shot upward on the expressive face in front of her.

Calamatta pulled out the small roll of leather and thrust it into his hand. "Would you take these to replace the gloves you ruined on my account?" As she paused, a pleasant blush bloomed in her cheek. "I made them—" She caught her breath, for she had nearly said, *for my husband.*

He took the little packet and, with a wide sweep of his arms, made a leg. "M'lady. May we assure you, it is you who should be thanked. What started as a tedious journey has turned into a most tantalizing misadventure."

Calamatta burst into a husky laugh.

Bowing again as chivalrously as he was able with his great bulk, he winked at her and whispered, "Whatever 'tis you gift us with, we shall treasure it all the more because you made it."

Calamatta gathered the reins and turned Thor back toward the wooded path. The rain had stopped. Patches of blue checkered the cloudy sky. Now that William had left, the day looked as if it would be most pleasant.

So wrapped up was she in her own problems that Calamatta didn't think until later she'd forgotten to ask the kind gentleman his name.

Four days later, Major Hatcher returned to Elmsworth and announced, "The Prince Regent has just come back to London, and we have received an invitation to a reception to be held in one week's time at Carlton House, the royal residence. If you are to have a proper gown made in time for you to be presented, you must make haste to get ready to leave."

By his high-stickler countenance, she couldn't tell precisely if Major Hatcher was irritated or enthusiastic about getting back to London.

"This is your opportunity to make your husband proud," Lettyce whispered to her. "You are just as grand a lady as any of his friends."

Later that day, Calamatta settled herself in the coach beside Putty. Her husband sat across from them, staring out the window. In an unguarded moment as he watched Lettyce walk back to the house, she saw his pain.

There followed several days of exhausting fittings to have her court costume ready. How was she to ever get such an enormous hooped skirt to fit through the door of the coach, she thought?

To avoid having to wear the ridiculous buckled shoes and the knee pants required of the men for court appearances, Major Hatcher dressed out in his most colorful uniform for, Calamatta had been told, the Prince Regent loved lavish dress of any sort.

The night of the party, Calamatta stood before her husband with great trepidation. Major Hatcher raised his quizzing glass to look at her. The hall clock was drowned out by the beating of her heart, and she feared for the first time in her life that she would swoon. Finally, when she thought her lungs would burst, he said, "You look *en grande toilette*. Quite up to fashion, wife."

There was no endearing smile, yet as he placed her cape around her shoulders, he extended his arm in a most chivalrous manner to escort her. It was the first time her husband had given her a compliment.

The crush of carriages continued along Regent Street toward the royal mansion. After what seemed an endless number of twists and turns, their coachman finally maneuvered into a spot where a flock of society's most privileged plumed and bejeweled peacocks was being disgorged into a magnificent garden. Like a gaggle of noisy geese, they flowed down the path toward a tall arched doorway.

They were well back in the crowd, but Major Hatcher's broad shoulders broke a path for them. Handel's music, resounding from somewhere above, added to the cacophony. In his zealous pursuit to teach her the correct court etiquette, her husband had omitted any reference to the magnificence of the Royal Palace. "We are on the ground floor," he whispered. "The Prince entertained two thousand guests here in 1811 in celebration of his Regency."

Calamatta was without words. It seemed Major Hatcher was more in awe of the numbers than of the genius which inspired this beauty. Above the heads of the crowd, she could see the ornate columns and the hanging lanterns bordering the endless corridor. As she clung to her husband's coattails in fear of their being separated, she stared up in wonder at the high, fan-vaulted ceiling made of cast iron and glass. Only when the anthem started did the assembly hush.

"The Prince is coming!" someone whispered.

A real prince! Calamatta stood on tiptoe and hopped from one foot to the other, trying to get a better view. It was hopeless. The deeper hum of men's voices and the high twitterings of the women's told Calamatta the royal entourage approached from the eastern end of the long hallway. Here and there, the party seemed to halt for the Prince to greet a guest. The murmuring stopped near them and a vaguely familiar voice called out, "Ah, Major Hatcher! Haven't seen you 'round London for some time."

A narrow path opened for her husband, and as he stepped forward to greet the Prince Regent, his body blocked Calamatta's view. She took advantage of the shield afforded by Major Hatcher, closed her eyes, and practiced her curtsy over and over in her mind.

"May we extend our condolences to you upon the death of your grandfather, Sir Henry," the voice droned on. "Such a dear friend to our father and mother. We are sure the Queen will miss his friendship more than most, for they have been near neighbors in Scotland these last eight years."

Then the Prince peered around William's commanding form and teased, "But let us not dwell upon unhappinesses. Understand congratulations are in order. Surely you are not going to keep your bride hidden from us."

Calamatta stared at her husband's back, not quite catching the words spoken. Then Major Hatcher stepped aside and, taking hold of her arm, pulled her forward. A long pause followed. When she looked up, her brain had gone to mush. She stared at the Prince. He stared back. *Lord-a-mercy! The pudgy man from the ditched carriage!* She'd blubbered all over the next king of England and offered him a pair of homemade gloves to replace . . . to replace . . . surely a more expensive pair which she, with her carelessness, had caused him to ruin. How he must have laughed when he unrolled her gift.

"Curtsy!" William's desperate whisper penetrated her foggy brain, for all the good it did. She had no more knees than a rock in the road. Little hazy speckles danced before her eyes. She vaguely saw a retainer hurriedly approach the Prince and in little staccato notes say something in his ear. The Regent, his gaze still directed toward Calamatta, looked aghast, frowned, whirled, and left her standing there exposed to all.

Seventeen

The muttering commenced as a low rumble, and then the room became a raucus mocking monster. Calamatta's feet refused to obey her, but somehow Major Hatcher managed to get them through the throng. He called for their carriage. While she pondered what possible excuse she could give for her unaccountable behavior, a suffocating fog of silence engulfed them on their journey back to Daybrooke Hall. There, William quickly deposited her in her bedchamber. The door closed resolutely behind him, and Calamatta knew she would always remember those three words he cast at her.

"You are hopeless!"

For once, Calamatta agreed with him. How could she have been such a bumblehead? Lettyce had had so much confidence in her, and she'd forgotten everything that Susanna had taught her, too. She'd let everybody down. She wished Edward were here to tell her what to do.

A wide-eyed and for once speechless Putty undressed her mistress and prepared her for bed. Calamatta knew she'd insulted the Prince Regent and humiliated her husband, and after everything that Major Hatcher said he'd done for her. Oh, what a mess she'd caused! He would never forgive her. Calamatta blinked several times, but managed to keep a placid countenance until Putty left the room. Then she crawled into bed. As if to shut out sniggering innuendoes, she pressed her hands to her ears. The tears finally came. She pulled the pillow over her head and cried herself to sleep.

The next morning, Calamatta was awakened from a deep sleep by a frantic tapping on her bedroom door. Before she could arise, Putty burst into the room. "Oh, miss, there's a fancy-dressed man in the entry hall with a message he insists he is to deliver to Mrs. William Hatcher and no one else."

"Goodness! What now, Putty?" With shaky hands, Calamatta quickly donned a morning frock and, securing her hair back with a ribbon, hurried to the foyer. Major Hatcher was already out of his bedroom door, dogging her steps and demanding to know what the disturbance was.

The liveried messenger recited his message. Mrs. William Hatcher was to appear alone at Carlton House at three o'clock that afternoon for an audience with the Prince Regent. A carriage would be sent for her.

Her husband, looking like a firecracker trying not to explode, listened and, as soon as the royal servant exited, turned on her. "See what shame you have brought down upon our heads by insulting His Royal Highness! He may have overlooked your provincial manners when you didn't curtsy, but to insult him in front of a roomful of notable guests without so much as a word of greeting or apology? That was more than outside of enough!"

Oh, lordy! Major Hatcher didn't know the half of it! And in his agitated state of mind, Calamatta certainly wasn't going to tell him the all. The Prince probably thought her to be a wanton woman when he'd met her on the road. Now she had turned up in his court to publicly insult him. She thought of that murderous look in his eyes at the reception before he had turned and strode off. In days long past, those who angered their sovereigns used to have their heads chopped off at the Tower of London. Calamatta wasn't sure of the punishment now, but wondered if she should pack a bag and be ready for a long stay in prison.

That afternoon, a beautiful carriage with the royal crest emblazoned upon its doors and pulled by four fine horses, drew up at the Daybrooke town house. With unsteady hands, Calamatta was readjusting her bonnet for the fifth time in the foyer mirror when she was startled to see her husband's reflection behind her, his expression unreadable. Was this to be the last time she ever set eyes upon his handsome face? At that moment, she was tempted to tell him of her havey-cavey encounter with the Prince, but that would mean also confessing to taking Thor, and she knew he would never ever forgive her indiscretion of riding his horse after he had strictly forbidden it.

Just as she thought she'd have to walk to the coach alone, Major Hatcher was there beside her, taking her arm and handing her up. For a moment before closing the door, he took her hand in his. Was she mistaken that he gave it a little squeeze?

Calamatta glanced back through the window and waved to him. He stood at attention and didn't return her farewell, but she saw his sorrowful gaze follow the carriage until it rounded the corner. As she settled back into the luxurious squabs, she vowed she would do anything to return a smile to his woebegone face. "Come to think of it, he seldom smiles about anything," she mumbled. She clasped her hands in her lap to try to keep them from trembling. Yes, she promised herself, she would do anything if she could see the same adoration which she had seen on his face when he had looked at . . . when he had looked at Lettyce.

After the royal coach disappeared around the corner, William walked slowly back into the house and retreated to the library. A fire had been lit, but its warmth did little for his consternation. How could one provincial chit make such a turmoil of his life? She had to be doing it on purpose! But she had looked so forlorn, so distressed, that for a moment he was almost moved to take pity on her. A fit of conscience niggled at William—a very unsettling feeling for him. He rose and began to pace the floor. If he knew the *ton,* the bets were already being placed in the books at Watier's on what would be her punishment. What a *faux pas!* If Mrs. Hatcher received no more than a setdown from the Prince, William vowed he would have her removed to the country immediately, before she could cause any more damage.

He would take care of his business in Town, then return home to Careby and have their marriage vows repeated in the chapel. The only woman he could ask to stand up with his wife, the only woman William knew pure enough of heart to overlook their humiliation, was Lettyce. As soon as he had the blessing of the church, he would quickly make Mrs. Hatcher his true wife and, as he was an honorable man, keep her protected in their country home away from the vicious tongues of the gossipmongers. When the future Hatcher heir was established in the nursery, he would go his separate way, spend more time at his beloved Cambridge.

William sank into the wing chair before the fireplace. Grandfather had sorely misunderstood him. Eddie was the cutup. Before this whole sorry flimflam began, William had fully intended to do as Sir Henry had wished—restore the ancient family seat at Careby, and then settle there to find pleasure in his books as a country gentleman. He had even contemplated not marrying if it meant he could not have his true love, Lettyce. Then Eddie came up with his poppycockish, farcical scheme. *Marry the American heiress and our problems will be over.* Well, their problems had just begun.

Upon her arrival at Carlton House, Calamatta dared to peek out of the coach windows and realized they had gone around the edifice. They weren't coming in the same way they had the night before, but were approaching the magnificent Corinthian columns of a portico.

After the royal carriage drew to a stop, Calamatta found herself escorted up the steps between two resplendently uniformed, dour-faced guards. Wordlessly, they passed on into a Great Hall surrounded on all sides by open screens of Ionic columns. Light fell from the coffered top-lit ceiling upon a thin figure standing in the center of the tiled floor, a crotchety-faced man dressed in a costume Calamatta thought more appropriate to a scarecrow staked out in the middle of a cornfield. Fear of her impending confrontation with the crown prince was all that kept her from being amused.

The scarecrow bowed.

Calamatta quickly curtsied. From the man's stiff response, she wondered if she'd done it wrong.

With no more than a twitch of his head to indicate she was to follow him, he about-faced and led her into an octangular, two-storied vestibule.

She hurried to comply. Without a pause, he continued straight ahead, giving her only a moment to register the decorative, wrought-iron balustrade encircling the second-floor balcony above. Through the red draperies pulled back from an archway, she caught a glimpse of a spectacular oval staircase leading to who knew where. She wondered if such a magnificent place had a dungeon in its cellar.

They didn't stop there, either, but entered into a much less spectacular room, painted bright blue. Accusing eyes gazed down at her from the portraits of plain-looking young ladies and proud men which lined the walls. This proved to be an anteroom, the end of the long procession of rooms, for Calamatta saw the tops of trees through the two floor-to-ceiling windows.

With a punctilious peek at the watch in his hand, her escort scratched on one of the ornately paneled double doors, then opened them.

A bodaciously mustachioed gentleman, whose walrus head, hunched into his padded shoulders, and scowl bode no good from within, stomped out.

Like a reed blowing in the wind, the scarecrow turned and motioned Calamatta into the room, closing the doors behind her.

Her first impression was that everything in the room glowed.

Dark blue velvet panels set in peach-colored borders with gilded frames created a perfect backdrop for the large masterpieces which covered the walls.

Calamatta blinked. In spite of the gold and glitter, all was overwhelmed by the personage standing beside the ornately carved desk, but one look into the Prince's intelligent, twinkling eyes told her she had nothing to fear.

His deep laugh broke the silence, and he stepped forward to raise her gloved fingers to his lips. If they lingered a little longer than necessary, Calamatta wasn't one to question.

"M'dear Mrs. Hatcher," he said, splaying his right hand over his heart.

Calamatta would have sworn he had tears in his eyes.

"We wish to apologize and apologize we will. Our manners were abominable, most abominable, last evening. 'Tis not often we are given such a significant gift as you gave us, and we did not mention it."

With his plump fingers encircled with several jeweled rings, he made a grand sweep of the room. "Oh, we get gold vases from India, silks and porcelains from China." He gestured to where a pair of Chinese vases sat poised daintily on green marble and gilt-bronzed pedestals. "Brocades from Turkey, gold chains from Spain, and beautiful statues from Italy and Greece, but no one takes the time to make us something so personal. Do you know what it did to our heart when we unrolled your gloves?" He drew a handkerchief from his sleeve and wiped his eyes.

"Then to have you stand before us last night and receive not one word of our appreciation." He held up his hand to silence her. "No, 'twas inexcusable! But you will surely excuse us when we tell you we were called away by an urgent plea for help. Our chef was threatening to quit in the middle of the preparations for our banquet. We personally had to go to the kitchen to soothe his rumpled feelings."

He took her hand and patted it. "Please say we are forgiven."

Calamatta nodded happily. "My husband thought—"

"Ah, yes! Major Hatcher," interrupted the Prince. "Fine man! Fine family! Sir Henry would be extremely proud of his grandson were he to know that he was to be knighted. Oh, dear!" He stopped when he saw Calamatta's eyes widen. "Didn't mean to let the cat out of the bag."

"Major Hatcher?" Calamatta cried. "My husband is to be knighted?"

"Shh!" The Prince pressed his index finger to his lips. "Shall be our little secret. Heh? Promise us you won't breathe a word of what we've said here today. All sorts of reports and inquiries about his intercepting secret communiques from old Boney during the war, you know. So complicated, but *they* insist. Much easier when someone gives us a few hundred thousand pounds sterling and we can reward him with a title or a little property."

She was going to ask him if she could tell her husband about some of their visit, just leave out the knight part, when he interjected, "Now, let us hear about you. First, your name. M'friends at Watier's seemed most interested in speculating on what it was."

"Calamatta," she answered. "And what is yours? Surely your parents didn't name you *Prince*."

He held his belly and laughed. "George . . . George Augustus Frederick."

"Why, that's a splendid name," she said. She placed the tip of her finger on her chin. "But rather long. I think I shall call you just plain George."

There was a tap on the door and the retainer entered and announced, "Your Majesty, the carriage has arrived for your afternoon ride."

" 'Pon my soul! Where's the time gone?" He turned to Calamatta in apology. "Always ride at four o'clock, y'know."

The formidable scarecrow didn't even give Calamatta a chance to say good-bye before he hurried her out.

"Wait! Wait!" called the Prince. "Be most honored to deliver you to your door, m'lady."

A few minutes later, Calamatta passed the brilliantly dressed palace guards on the arm of the Prince Regent. "D'you like their uniforms? Designed 'em m'self."

"You didn't! Oh, they are most splendid."

"Thought so, too. We adore red. Fastest scarlet dye comes from your part of America. Did you know that?"

She nodded. "Dye-flower. Dye-flower and laurel leaves make a bright orange-red." Lucy had told her that.

" 'Course, there's a little scaly insect in Mexico—only the female, of course," he said, giving her arm a little pinch. "Makes a magnificent red, too." His laughter shook his entire body; then, like a child who's had his candy taken away, he stopped and stuck out his lower lip. "Blockades of your ships during the war made it very difficult to get any decent dyes. Wars cause so many inconveniences."

"I didn't start the war," said Calamatta, apologetically.

" 'Course you didn't, child. Neither did we. We abhor fighting."

They approached the *vis-à-vis*, a small unpretentious carriage, and, with the assistance of two retainers, they were settled in.

And so it was, sitting face to face and knee to knee, Calamatta rode through the streets of London with the Prince Regent. With the blinds sheltering them from the outside world, the future king of England proved to be a rapt audience. He listened attentively, only breaking in now and then while Calamatta entertained him with her tales of running away, living with the Indians, and how she learned to soften deerskins fine as silk.

"Knew it! Knew the gloves were from the white-tailed deer," he expostulated, slapping his knee. "Continue, m'dear. What's the Indians' secret? We confided in you; surely you can confide in us."

Calamatta leaned forward and whispered, "It takes brains. When all else is done, a batter of deer brains is rubbed into the skins."

"By Jove! Takes brains, eh? Must remember that. *Au fait!* Clever, those Indians." They laughed together.

Calamatta told him she liked to read, and when she said the book which kept her company on her long trek across the wilderness was *Pride and Prejudice* by an unknown author, the Prince roared. "Her name's Jane Austen, m'dear. We have every one of her books. She dedicated her latest, *Emma,* to us. If we'd known, would have shown it to you," he said proudly.

My! Calamatta was finding it as easy to talk to George as to Lucy. Edward was right. She was finding a lot of friends in England.

When she told him she'd been married by proxy, he admitted that he, too, was the victim of a proxy marriage. He patted her hand and said, "But you, m'dear, have been lucky. Some are not so fortunate." She wondered why he looked so sad, but instead of pressing him further, she decided to speak of only happy things. She regaled him with tales of her adventures with her brothers on the James River in Virginia; watched him wipe a tear from his eye as she recited Benjamin's poetry extolling a land full of mountains and streams and never-ending forests; then had him slapping his knee again with a few rather spicy ditties she didn't quite understand but which she'd overheard Creed tell some of his cronies. And since they sent the Regent into spasms of laughter, she thought her time well spent.

In no time at all, the carriage came to a halt. The Prince peeked from behind the curtains and said, "Well, here we are at Daybrooke Hall, m'dear."

Major Hatcher awaited her in the library. Thinking happily of the secret she shared with the Prince, Calamatta entered. For all the movement he made or the emotion he showed, the rigid man could have been a permanent fixture, along with the andirons standing before the fireplace. With his right arm resting on the mantelpiece, he remained where he stood, only his dark eyes showing any movement. His caustic voice caught her unawares.

"Well, Mrs. Hatcher, since you have returned with your head

still attached to your neck, do I surmise that His Majesty was in one of his benevolent moods and saw fit to excuse your provincial behavior?"

Lord-a-mercy! Now that he mentioned it, she realized she had forgotten to curtsy again. Well, she wouldn't mention that omission to her husband. "Yes, Major Hatcher, he did." She thought she noticed a slight relaxing of his jaw muscles, but Calamatta felt it wisest to be as formal as he, play her cards close to her chest, and let him make the next move. That was, if he ever planned to detach himself from the mantelpiece.

"The Regent is an overgenerous man. What penance did he ask?"

"I can't tell you."

"If your comedown was so bad you cannot repeat it, the disgrace you have brought upon the Hatcher name is not to be rectified." Her husband's arm dropped to his side. "While you were gone, I told your abigail to pack your belongings. Tomorrow I'm sending you back to Lincolnshire."

"But you don't understand."

"No! It is you, wife, who don't understand. You have appreciated nothing I've done to make you acceptable."

Calamatta looked at him askance.

As he advanced, his voice grew louder. "You are to remain at Careby until I have finished my business here in Town."

"But—"

"Do not interrupt your husband, wife. Have you learned nothing from the books I bought you?"

"Persnickety, ickety," muttered Calamatta under her breath.

"Be prepared on my return to Careby to have our marriage vows blessed by the church. That will make me feel that something holy has come about from this here-and-thereian alliance."

Calamatta saw there was no talking sense to him. The man was almost as ornery as Creed.

Major Hatcher continued, "There still may be those near neighbors in the country who will not have heard of the scandal or those who will prove to be true friends and still wish to attend. The small reception will take place afterward as planned. Then I shall do my duty and make you Mrs. William Hatcher in more than name only." He turned to yank the cord to summon a servant, not even trying to hide his display of indignant humor at that horrendous thought.

Well, if that didn't beat all! Calamatta's mouth dropped open, and by the time she'd formed her lips into words which could be repeated, Major Hatcher had marched out the door. She shouted after him, "I'll have you know, George told me—"

From the hallway, she heard a howl. "George? Oh, God! Tell me you did not call the Prince Regent *George!*"

"That's his name, Major Hatcher!" Calamatta yelled back. She heard his footsteps clumping all the way to the second floor.

Eighteen

Once again, Calamatta found herself back at Careby, surrounded by those she called friends. As quickly as it took Mrs. Wheeler to toss bread crumbs out the door to the chickens, the little misunderstanding in Town was thrown from Calamatta's mind. She'd tried her best to tell Major Hatcher his concerns for her consequence were poppycock, for she was of too little import to be fodder for long to the tittle-tattlers of London. Glory be, but she wished she could have told him of the good tidings her new friend George had shared with her. *Knighthood! Imagine that!*

The Prince had told her, "You will be a Lady."

She laughed to think of it. Wouldn't that news just make her husband pop right out of his skin?

Now, the entire estate was all abuzz about the goings-on that she and Major Hatcher would be having at St. Stephen's church. The main street of Careby was whisked clean in anticipation of the quality folk who would be attending. Each colorful garden was lovingly tended and the soft honey-colored stones of the cottages scrubbed.

The grounds of Careby Manor had undergone an astounding transformation, too. When Calamatta left for Elmsworth, the country scene had been covered with gray slush. The new caretaker, a bent old man called Badger, showed Calamatta the freshly tamed greenery, the flowers popping up in their rightful places on the terraces and the carefully edged, pebbled paths.

While he ran his fingers through his stubbly gray beard, his eyes sparkling, he outlined his plans to restore the grounds to their former splendor.

The manor house was wearing a new face, too. The great brass doorknocker at the entrance was polished to a high shine, and all the broken panes had been replaced and the windows cleaned.

Mr. Boskins pointed out the new slates on the steeply hipped roof. "Master William had 'em brought in from Colleyweston, near Stamford. They been quarrying slate there for over two thousand years. Cut the stone into large blocks, they do, and water it down all winter. The frost splits them natur'ly into slates. Burghley House be roofed with them, too."

She could tell it was a very important bit of information to the old servant, and smiled to show him she thought it most interesting.

Though the older section of the house remained little changed, Mrs. Boskins, her arms moving as animatedly as her mouth, showed Calamatta around inside the manor house—all freshly painted, waxed, and scrubbed. New furniture had replaced the few rickety pieces they had pulled from the attic at Christmas. Richly patterned woven rugs covered sections of the floors and a large silver salver now sat proudly upon the receiving table in the foyer.

"It all be Master William's doin's. Ain't it fine?" stated Mrs. Boskins proudly.

Calamatta had to agree her husband's selections were unquestionably top drawer. My! While she'd been away, Major Hatcher had been busy. She decided she'd forgive him for not telling her all that he'd done.

Large paintings hung on the walls circling up beside the stairs. They were of handsome, proud men: one on horseback, three separate paintings of different noble-looking gentlemen standing before the same library fireplace in the background, the fourth of a man walking in the forest surrounded by his hunting dogs.

"Master William tracked down those old family portraits like a regular detective and bought them back," Mr. Boskins informed her.

Upon her arrival, Calamatta had been met by the entire well-dressed staff lined up in the entry hall to welcome her. She greeted each of her old friends with a hug and gave a hearty handshake when introduced to those who were hired after she'd left for Elmsworth. The women bobbed and curtsied and the men bowed and tugged at their forelocks, so Calamatta bobbed and curtsied in turn. She wasn't going to make the same fool mistake again that she'd made with the Prince Regent.

At the end of the line stood Jamie, proudly showing off two new front teeth and a fine blue velvet coat with matching pants. William had not sent him to the foundling home after all, as she had feared. Surely the lad had grown three inches since she last saw him, and Mrs. Wheeler's food had put several pounds on his skinny bones. When Calamatta reached to embrace him, he blushed and held her off with a long, magnificently carved pole, twice as tall as himself, which was topped with long red and green feathers.

"It be me flyswatter!" he said proudly.

"Well, I swan!" Calamatta said with great admiration. "Wherever did you find the likes of that?"

"The Master hisself give it t'me."

"Major Hatcher?" asked Calamatta, not hiding her astonishment.

Jamie bobbed his head up and down. "Brought it all t'way from Lund'n Town, he did."

It was a surprise to her that for all of Major Hatcher's saber-rattling, not one member of the staff she'd hired had been sent away. True, many of them had new assignments, but she realized they had been given tasks much better suited to their talents. She understood why her husband had made a good officer. Maybe he didn't love her, but somewhere behind his severe countenance, she decided, there was an honorable man.

Excitement over the preparations for the coming social event ran throughout the estate, and with such exuberant activity all about her, Calamatta could not be expected to remain with a case of the sullens for long.

"The villagers be looking forward to the family tradition of a medieval wedding," Mrs. Boskins informed Calamatta. "The bride always rides to the church on the back of a white horse. 'Course, they all knows ye no longer be a bride, but they're jest as happy to go along with the fairy tale as long as the Master wishes it," she cooed. "There weren't no white stallion, but Mr. Fotch found a docile old dappled draft horse on a farm near Bourne that'd do jest fine."

Major Hatcher and fairy tales. Now there was an odd combination if ever there was one, but Calamatta could see that there'd be no shaking Mrs. Boskins's fanciful illusions about her employer.

Calamatta soon discovered there was much to do—the fitting of her old-fashioned attire, the planning of the feasts and entertainments. In the two weeks she'd been home, Calamatta's only disappointment was that Edward hadn't come to see her. When she asked after him, Boskins told her, "No steward was hired. Master Edward hisself manages the estate from the lodge in the deer park. He seldom comes to the manor house."

Later Calamatta climbed upon the donkey, Tulip, and set out to search for Edward, but no matter where she rode, across the fields or along the roads, it seemed she had just missed him.

In the village, all the cottages had new roofs, the churchyard was weeded, and wild roses cascaded over the fence and around the solemn grave stones. Farm workers were in the fields, craftsmen were setting up shops, and new families now occupied the formerly deserted houses. Freshly sown fields sprouted their new grains like fuzz on a baby's scalp. Stone fences were repaired and birds carried twigs in their beaks to build nests in the neatly clipped hedgerows. She laughed when she saw the newborn lambs bouncing about on their little stilt legs, butting their heads together, while the open faces of daffodils announced to the world that spring had come. But, though she watched for Edward, she still didn't catch so much as a glimpse of him.

Edward was purposely keeping away from Calamatta. He knew she had to be behind the puzzling behavior of the *ton* toward him in London. How long had it taken her to plot her diabolical scheme to embarrass him?

That morning during his inspection of the south fields, he'd seen her plodding along the hedgerows on the little donkey. To avoid a confrontation, for he was sure his first inclination would be to commit mayhem, he decided to stay at the deer park after lunch to repair a strap on his saddle. The fact that he had hired a young man for that sort of work conveniently escaped his reasoning.

"The woman is dangerous," Edward spouted. Aside from his short reunion with Elinor, he'd remained a bloody monk for months because of her. Three months of traipsing all over that godforsaken wilderness called Kentucky looking for his brother's intended, being poisoned by her, having to contend with being beaten up by her barbarian brother Creed, and then suffering all sort of indignities at the hands of two women while he recovered from influenza. He should have made William go after Calamatta. Now, because of her, Edward's well-earned reputation lay in ashes at his feet.

Completing the leather repairs, Edward began vigorously currying one of the horses, but no matter how hard he combed, Edward's thoughts kept coming back to Calamatta. He was trying to puzzle out why she'd been sent home.

His brother had no patience. He'd even told him so the last he'd seen him off to Elmsworth. *Be a little more understanding, Will.* Hell! He himself couldn't understand her, either.

"Lord!" Edward grumbled, kicking the dirty straw about the stall. "After what you did to me, you little hoyden, I can't believe I asked my brother to be more sympathetic."

He'd heard some mention of Carlton House, but since he

seldom went to Careby Manor, much of the gossip flowing throughout the great halls didn't reach the hunting lodge. At twilight, he preferred to settle in with his ledgers and the three worthless hounds he'd inherited, Wynken, Blynken, and Nod. Whatever possessed him to give them names like that? The thought of Callie bringing in those fool dogs at Christmas, completely destroying the tranquillity of their afternoon, made him throw back his head and laugh.

Just from the look they had given each other, Edward knew Will, too, had been reliving the memory of a day long before that, when two small boys had trundled a basketful of eleven puppies into that same room and excitedly dumped them at the feet of their parents' guests. But now, Will had changed. No sooner had these worthless vagabonds refused to stay in their new kennels and were discovered to be sneaking into the house to sleep beside the library fireplace than the stickler had said they had to go.

"Don't want fleas and dog hair about," he'd said.

Except to journey to the neighboring villages to hire more workers and order supplies, Edward hadn't been off the estate since he'd returned from London. Who would have thought the flamboyant, debonair captain, the dashing courtier, would come to this? He glanced down at his bedraggled attire and attempted to slap some of the orange-gray dust off his trousers. A farmer, a jack-of-all-trades, rusticating in the country. The irony of it!

He picked up a pitchfork which was leaning against the wall. Consternation hit him when he saw what he was doing. No gentleman mucked out stables. With a snort of disgust, he stomped through the foul-smelling straw and exited the stall. The witch had him thoroughly disoriented. Her harebrained ways made a man forget his station. But what was his station? He didn't seem to fit in anywhere anymore.

How long had it taken him to build up the daredevil image he'd enjoyed after all the battles, the challenges, the horrors, the glory? One saber wound put an end to that part of his career. Then he'd healed enough to be cleared for a year of undercover work. Five turbulent years had honed his tastes for a much faster way of life than that afforded a country gentleman.

As the eldest son, it was Will's responsibility to find a wife and start his nursery. But at that time, they both thought the entail on the Careby estate to be intact.

Playing the Corinthian had aided his undercover work. Side-stepping jealous husbands and frequenting the more unsavory dens along the waterfront brought excitement to the game. Espionage had proved to be a more dangerous career than his naval one. He'd been warned. *If you ever fall under suspicion by our enemies, the Department won't recognize you.*

Finally it did happen in the Wellington affair in Hyde Park, when he was accused of threatening Castlereagh in a drunken rage. Of course, the incident had been planned to fool their enemies into thinking that Captain Edward Hatcher was no longer a friend of England.

Little did anyone know, not even her husband, of the Countess of Mayberry's help in this. Edward was fortunate to have been assigned such a willing partner, in more ways than one. Elinor—undoubtedly out for the excitement, for she surely didn't need the blunt—had proved to be a very talented and amusing spy. Their liaison had lasted long after their government assignment was completed, but now he knew that was over.

It did not matter that Preston North had written that his heroics in capturing enemy spies had been publicly recognized by the War Office, nor that he was no longer *persona non grata* at his clubs. Somehow he found the game of little interest anymore.

"Grandfather, you soft-hearted old bellyacher, if you'd just lived a few months longer, none of this unbelievable tale would have happened. You should have known Will and I would have come home."

The war had stolen their salad days. Granted, even Sir Henry's attempts to bring a hornet's nest down around their ears hadn't brought them to bay, but it had taken only a few dissembling words out of the mouth of an angelic-looking she-devil named Calamatta to bring the beasts to heel.

"Well, I hope your revenge is sweet, Mrs. Calamatta Mary McGannon Hatcher. You've got yourself a husband of good family and a beautiful old mansion to run. If I hadn't taken you out of Kentucky, what would you have? A freckled-faced, overgrown fustian named Sauly chasing you."

In the library at Careby Manor, Calamatta wriggled into one of the oversized leather chairs in front of the fireplace to contemplate her problem. The church ceremony would be tomorrow, and she still didn't know how to kiss correctly. Major Hatcher was to arrive this very evening. He was everything she'd pictured her ideal man to be—handsome and reticent, intelligent and commanding like Jane Austen's Mr. Darcy. But he wasn't Mr. Darcy. Had she been wrong trying to fit herself and Major Hatcher into make-believe characters?

She placed her chin in her hands and stared at the dancing flames.

Exactly when had she figured out that Major Hatcher loved Lettyce and not her? Oh, Calamatta thought he might care a smidgeon for her, but not the way he adored the little Countess of Elmsworth.

Calamatta held out her left hand and looked at the sparkling gem on her finger. Was it on the stairs at Elmsworth when she knew? When he'd given her the ring and then looked solemnly past her to where Lettyce was standing? Oh, he didn't think she saw, but she did. Or was it before he entered the carriage to go to London, when he tried to kiss Lettyce's hand? Calamatta paused a moment. Perhaps the pained expression on Major Hatcher's face was because he didn't know how to kiss. At first that thought gave Calamatta heart, but she soon dismissed it as daydreaming. She did remember, though, that all had not been bad between them.

When they first met at Careby, Major Hatcher seemed more

than pleased to show her about the manor house. In fact, she recalled, he smiled once on the tour.

Calamatta had thought when they went to London things were beginning to change between them. Major Hatcher had given her his first compliment. It wasn't what she had dreamed of, but she knew he had looked at her a tad differently. Then, of course, there was that little misunderstanding at Carlton House which put a strain between them again.

Reaching out, Calamatta grabbed the poker and began to jab at the logs in the fireplace. Her fault was in playing make-believe and letting her temper run away with her tongue. Well, she would correct those two flaws. She wouldn't pretend any longer, and she'd be more amiable to her husband.

Now that she had admitted her own faults, Calamatta was certain that when she pointed out Major Hatcher's shortcomings to him, he'd realize the error of his ways.

But, oh, dear! There was so little time left! Well, Calamatta wasn't going into marriage so deficient. She wanted to be kissed, and one of them had better know how. So if Major Hatcher wasn't going to assume that responsibility, she would.

That made her think of Edward, and she once more compared his kisses to those of Major Hatcher's. She and Edward were just about to get it right when all that nonsense came up about it not being proper for him to kiss her, she being married to his brother and all. She'd like to explain to him that it would not be a sin for him to give her more instruction. After all, being married hadn't stopped her brothers, Creed or Ward, from telling her what to do. Landsakes! Why should it be any different with Edward? He was her brother-in-law.

That problem straightened out in her mind to her satisfaction, Calamatta set off on foot in the direction of the hunting lodge. That it was a good three miles from the Manor didn't deter her from her purpose.

Just as the deer park came into view, another thought occurred to Calamatta. She still hadn't had her Consummation.

She must remember to ask Edward if he would help her pick out the proper attire for it.

Edward was leaving the stables when he saw Calamatta making her way through the forest. What was her game now? She'd already wreaked her revenge on him, yet the determined set of Calamatta's countenance piqued both his interest and his suspicions, and he decided to hear her out.

He invited her into the lodge and asked her to be seated on the comfortable leather sofa before the fireplace. The three large hounds sprawled before the hearth raised their heads, grinned, then dropped back to their initial languid state. Edward had to step over Wynken's inert body to find himself a spot on the sofa.

"I know you've never been married, Edward," Calamatta said, scooting in his direction, "but I want to ask you a question." She took his silence for encouragement to go on. "About my wedding night—"

What had William done? Had he hurt her? Edward spoke uneasily. "It isn't my place to discuss that night with you."

Calamatta reached over and placed the tip of a finger on his sleeve and began drawing little circles.

He winced. A red-hot poker would have done less damage. Where had she learned that trick? Not from Lettyce. Elinor? Decidedly not! That lady was more direct. Calamatta's hesitation should have warned him.

"Do you know what to do?" she asked.

Edward stared at her until the significance of what she was implying began to dawn on him. "You mean you haven't . . . he hasn't . . ."

"Oh, Edward!" she said, her hand clasping his sleeve, "You mean you don't know, either?"

Edward pulled away to a safer distance from her and crossed his arms. "Aye, I believe I do."

She looked relieved to hear him tell her that. "Can I confess something to you?" She bit her lip. "I don't. Oh, I know, more or less, what they do, but I really don't know how to go about it."

A flush crept over Calamatta's face. A twinge of remorse put the blame for this ruse squarely in Edward's lap, making him uncomfortable, but he waited to hear what she had to say.

"I don't suppose—no!" She shook her head as if she were answering her own question.

For God's sake, he wished she'd get on with it!

"I was going to ask you, could you—would you show me what to do?"

Nineteen

Edward started out of his seat. "No!" he exploded. Good Lord! His suspicions were true. Will hadn't consummated the marriage. Edward never would have thought—no, he couldn't believe it of his brother. Will was no wooden spoon when it came to women. He could turn any lady up sweet when he put his mind to it. True, he was a stickler for the proprieties in his address to the fairer sex, but God's blood! This was his wife!

"I can't." He sat back down and tried to control his voice.

"Can't you give me just a little hint?"

"No!" The vixen had him shouting again.

"Why?" she shouted back.

"Can't be done. It isn't proper."

"Why is it proper for you to know when you're not married, and it's not proper for me to know and I am married?"

"It's different for men. A woman has to think of the consequences. A man does not."

Calamatta mulled that over. "That doesn't make sense to me, Edward."

Edward watched the quixotic emotions play across her face. Then her expression brightened and she whispered, "Is it a secret?"

Suddenly, Edward had one of his lightning inspirations. Why hadn't he thought of it before?

"Aye! It's a secret."

"Oh, I knew it! Like a surprise birthday party," she cried,

clasping her hands. "My *Consummation* party. Then I suppose I'll have to wait, won't I?"

He didn't believe what he was hearing, but as Edward let out his breath he nodded his agreement. She was so adorable he wanted to kiss her right then and there.

"You won't tell Major Hatcher I asked, will you? I wouldn't want to spoil the surprise for him."

Major Hatcher? Edward's eyebrows shot up once more. She still didn't call her husband William. This realization made his mind fly somewhere up in the rafters, but he managed to raise his right hand and vow, solemnly, "You can trust me."

"Oh, you're such a good friend, Edward. I thought my husband was angry with me, and you've helped me see it was only his way of getting me away from the city without letting on that he was preparing a party for me."

That Edward had been made privy to the knowledge his brother had yet to bed Calamatta was more than enough. He didn't know whether to laugh, cry, or shout to the winds.

Her hand on his arm began to shake and Edward covered it with his own to give her assurance.

Crazy thoughts sailed through his brain. He could so easily comply to this green girl's wishes—or was she as innocent as she sounded? Whichever way, a scandal would complete Calamatta's ruination, but why should he care? She would belong to him. He would take her away to the Continent or Jamaica. North America was out of the question—her brothers would kill him if he stepped foot on those shores again. Given time, he was sure he could make her love him.

But could he compromise Calamatta? Make William cry off? No! Edward knew that for everything else he was, he could never again cause her hurt nor make a cuckold of his brother. But some way or other, her mind had to be put at ease.

"No one has told you, Cal . . . Mrs. Hatcher?"

She shook her head.

Of course! The reason was clear to Edward. Calamatta feared the bedding. Most girls did. Calamatta's mother died when she was an infant. There were no aunts or older sisters to instruct her. She was around servants and brothers all her growing up years, who definitely gave her a very unladylike slant to the man-woman relationship. When she had been forced to marry so quickly, her women friends in Kentucky and her sister-in-law most likely concluded she had already consummated her marriage.

"You're the only close friend I can ask, Edward."

"What about Lettyce?"

"She isn't here. Besides, Lettyce is in love with Major Hatcher."

Edward's head jerked up.

"Oh, she doesn't know I know," she continued, "but I think I understand what being in love is now. I'd catch her gazing at him." And, Calamatta thought, *I saw by the look in his eyes that he returned her affection with his whole heart.* "So you see, I couldn't ask Lettyce. It would have hurt her too much—my being married to him and all."

Edward began to stroke his jaw. How much did Calamatta know of Will's *tendre* for the Countess of Elmsworth? Surely she didn't know how long he had loved Lettyce—had loved her since they were children.

Calamatta tugged at Edward's sleeve to regain his attention. "You're the only one I can ask. You said I always was to count on you to be there for me." She moved closer. "If you tell me the truth, Edward, I'll tell you the Indians' secret of making soft leather." It wouldn't hurt, she thought, to throw in a little incentive.

As she placed her other hand on his, he felt it tremble. The self-sufficient, self-confident girl he thought she was was not there. How blind he'd been! Edward realized it was a wall, a facade, she had built around herself. Now it was crumbling before his eyes, and he couldn't do anything to help her rebuild it without tearing down his own defenses.

Her forehead furrowed. "Edward? You are my friend, aren't you?"

Why was she doing this to him? No, what had he done to himself? He had fallen in love with her, and for him there could be no other.

His head began to spin. Edward bounded from his seat, clasped his hands behind his back and began to pace around the room.

Calamatta leaped up and followed him.

He was too wrapped in his own thoughts to notice. If he cuckolded his brother, he thought, he might be doing him a favor. That would leave Will free to marry Lettyce and the blame would fall upon Edward's shoulders—but what would that do to this innocent who persisted in asking him such damnable personal questions?

But Edward was sure that Calamatta loved Will. Perhaps, Edward thought, he could woo her and turn her to his favor. Hadn't Calamatta felt a tenderness for him when she thought she was married to him in Kentucky? No, it was too late. The religious ceremony was to take place on the morrow. Once she'd seen Will, there had been no one else as perfect in her eyes.

Edward had been certain that once Will got her to London, away from the smothering attentions of Mrs. Boskins, away from Elmsworth and Lettyce and all those that knew him when he was still in skirts, he'd quit being so stiff-rumped. Obviously, Edward had been mistaken. How could any man resist her? Calamatta was the most desirable girl he'd ever met. She had wit, she was kindhearted, she had gumption. And her lips were the most damnably kissable lips he'd ever encountered.

He stopped in his tracks, did an about-face, circled around Calamatta without really seeing her, and commenced to pace in the opposite direction.

Calamatta nearly bumped into him.

Will was a pattern-saint, but this sudden insistence on the blessings of the church was beyond Edward's ken. Will had never been that religious. Their vows would be repeated tomorrow. In fact, the service would probably be four times longer than the one in front of the fidgety preacher Isaiah Butters. The feast was prepared and the villagers had been looking forward to this day ever since William had announced his plans. Guests were coming. Not many, but their closest friends. Some, like Preston North and Hepplesforde, were most likely traveling on the post road and were already halfway here from London. Will had sent word he would be in late today with the carriage, bringing Lettyce and her sister, Miss Patience Rede. Edward felt he'd done his part to restore their lands. Why was this problem being dumped in his lap?

Calamatta, exasperated with his snorting and tramping about to nowhere in particular, balled up her fist and thumped him on the back.

Edward whirled about, only to find himself nose to nose with Calamatta.

"You're not being helpful, Edward. Why can't you show me?"

A man could only take so much. Show her? Yes, he'd show this beautiful minx why she tread on dangerous ground. Edward gripped Calamatta's shoulders and yanked her toward him. With a half-cocked grin, he leaned down and with brash force kissed her.

He hoped he had not been too ruthless, only severe. Slowly, seductively, his left hand rose to cradle the back of her head. But Edward felt no resistance from her. Damn! The chit was supposed to resist, be shocked. Edward took a handful of hair and eased Calamatta's head back until he looked into her eyes. She was lovely. His voice lowered. "That's why, Callie! That's why!"

He felt her tremble.

Now he knew she was bewildered, but he hoped he hadn't scared her too badly. Edward shuddered to think what all those men she had kissed before could have done to her. That disturbing picture in his mind compelled him to give her a reassuring hug before he held her out and away from him.

Her eyes closed and a soft pink glow tinged her neck upwards until her face glowed. That was more the thing.

Recalling his purpose, he gave her a none-too-gentle shake. "Have you learned your lesson now?"

Calamatta opened her eyes so quickly, Edward found himself staring into two brown mirrors, amazed to see they reflected his own desire. Quickly, he lowered his gaze, only to be mesmerized by her lips. They were spreading into a smile more devilish than his could ever be. It was enough to put a ship on her beams-end.

"Let me see if I have the right of it," she said.

It had been an old path Edward thought he'd traveled many times. He often told himself he knew every nuance of a woman's mind and body. He'd studied enough of them, but this sly creature was pulling the same old Indian trick she'd tried on him in the mountains of Kentucky. Well, he'd show her she couldn't get him going in circles this time. So sure of what he thought Calamatta's intent to be, Edward had not counted on his own beliefs being blown asunder.

Blast if she didn't begin mimicking every one of his less-than-gentlemanly actions. She moved toward him. The confusing girl wasn't playing the game according to Hoyle. Her hands traced on his body the same path his had traveled on hers. He was defeated. As her hands slipped down his chest and around to his back, he kissed her again and again. How had this hoyden in an angel's disguise stolen his heart so completely? As he pulled his lips from hers, he buried his face in her hair, for he couldn't bring himself to look into her eyes again. It would be the undoing of them both.

"Am I getting it right now, Edward?"

He didn't—he couldn't—answer. Edward played a game that he'd taught himself when he was very young. He had even carried the practice over into his adulthood and used it during the war. When faced with an encounter which he knew was inevitable, whether it was to take a setdown from his grandfather, admit an offense to the headmaster, or face an attacking enemy ship, he would count. On the count of three, he had to go forward to conquer or to take his punishment. The practice was so ingrained into his consciousness that it was an automatic response. Edward took a deep breath and started, "One . . . two . . ."

He didn't release her for quite a spell, and when he did, he could barely hear her words. "Are you counting, Edward?"

Edward scowled at her, but continued. When he reached three, he set Calamatta away. "There," he said, too quickly. So much for his attempt at *savoir-faire.* He turned his back to her and, trying to cover the quaver in his voice with a gruff tone, he rasped, "How do you feel now? Hope I've taught you something."

Sorely shaken, he strode swiftly out the door, leaving Calamatta standing alone before the fireplace.

Calamatta grabbed the back of a chair to steady herself and watched him go. He'd smelled of wood smoke and leather, and his chest was hard against hers. *Lord-a-mercy! All of him is tough as whitleather.* Excitement pulsed through her. Also guilt. Had she hugged him too hard? Edward's health was never very hearty and yet, as poorly as he was himself, his parting thoughts had been of her.

"How do you feel?" he'd asked. All she could think of was tongue-tied and cross-eyed, because the rapid shower of changes that had happened in her body defied description. One minute, she'd felt like a fine-tuned string on a fiddle, the next like flowing honey. Then, the twain became inseparable. Two conflicting sensations, all at the same time. Calamatta wanted to sing and she wanted to cry. Instead she wrung her hands until her knuckles ached. What was wrong with her?

"Hope I've taught you something," Edward had said.

What had he taught her? He had taught her that she did not love Major Hatcher. She loved—Calamatta clapped her hand over her mouth. She loved Edward! That was what Lettyce had tried to tell her when Calamatta asked what it meant to kiss a man and have your knees go weak. The little countess had responded, "It means you're in love."

What a muddle she'd made of it. She ran out the door after Edward. He'd tried to be her friend, and now she had hurt his feelings and frightened him away. When she caught up to him, she would make amends.

Calamatta found Edward in one of the stalls, vigorously rubbing down his horse again. "Edward?"

He didn't turn her way. "Go away, Mrs. Hatcher." He knew she had come up behind him, for although she hadn't touched him, he felt her breath warming the back of his shirt. He ached to turn and take her in his arms.

"Will you walk down the aisle with me tomorrow? None of my brothers are here, and you're still my best friend."

"I can't, Mrs. Hatcher, I promised to stand up with my brother."

Calamatta wanted to say, *I love you, Edward.* She wanted to tell him to hold her forever. Instead she said, "Then I think I'll ask Mr. Boskins. He's my next best man friend."

Edward noticed she didn't mention Will. "I'm sure Boskins would be most honored." When he heard the crunching of the straw on the floor, he knew she was moving away from him.

"I must be getting back to the house," she said, a little breathlessly. "Major Hatcher will be arriving this evening with our guests. Will you be there for dinner?"

"I think not . . . not until church tomorrow." Edward waited. When he knew she was out of the stables, he turned and watched her walk with that long, flowing stride he had come to admire— and love.

She didn't look back.

He'd taken her money, but he knew he could never take her virtue or her pride. He'd sign over to her what blunt he still had left in the bank. At least he could do that. His cheeseparing brother would probably be too pinchpenny to give her money for her own use. Aside from the clothes he'd bought, the only other funds Edward used had gone into the estate, and that was hers already. Hers and Will's.

Once again, Will had won. No matter how Edward tried to flimflam his brother, Will always seemed to get the whip hand.

After the ceremony, he would leave. And go where? Jamaica? Canada? India? Somehow, he'd start over.

For several minutes after Calamatta was lost to his sight among the shadows of the forest, Edward stood transfixed, seeing only the ghost of Tall-as-the-Trees. "I love you, Callie," he called softly.

Twenty

Late that afternoon, two carriages carrying Lettyce, the countess of Elmsworth, her sister Patience, and their personal servants, drove up to the manor house. Looking for all the world like the lord of the manor, Major Hatcher followed closely behind on his great black horse, Thor.

The atmosphere in the village and the manor rang with excitement, but it wasn't heard by the principals in this drama. Although Calamatta was genuinely pleased to see her closest woman friend in England, and the sweet Lettyce was nothing but kind and solicitous, as they clung to each other, an air of melancholy embraced the two women.

Major Hatcher, with his usual efficiency, checked the arrangements. "Boskins, is the house ready for our guests?"

"Everything you ordered, Master William. Found a good horse fer the mistress, too."

William nodded. "I trusted you and Mrs. Boskins would see to it." He found Mrs. Wheeler in the kitchen up to her elbows in flour.

"Now don't ye be worryin' yerself about a thing," she said jovially. "All's ready for both the reception at the Rectory as well as Careby Manor."

"Well and good. After a light supper, I will request that everyone retire early, so that we will be ready for the ceremony at St. Stephen's tomorrow." William looked for a moment as though he was tempted to stick his finger into the confection bowl. Then he straightened his back and walked stiffly from the room.

The following morning, as the wedding procession neared the village, the sun greeted rich and poor alike.

"Glory be!" exclaimed Calamatta. "Is all of England coming to my wedding?"

"Indeed, it looks that way," agreed Lettyce, from where she sat on a small roan mare next to Calamatta.

As was the custom, the ceremony was to be performed in the morning, so that the afternoon and evening could be given over to merriment. William and Edward had gone early to confer with the rector, Reverend Saulthorpe.

Calamatta sat atop a sturdy old dappled gray—not quite white, but the nearest Mr. Boskins could come to it. A caparison of rich blue, like that in the Hatcher coat-of-arms and beautifully embroidered along the border with the family crest, covered the horse.

Calamatta wore a filmy cream-colored gown, embroidered with seed pearls and trimmed with lace and pink velvet ribbons. A crown of wild roses held the long veil, which not only covered her face but flowed behind her and over the rear of the horse, nearly touching the ground.

Wondering what made her companion wriggle, the countess asked, "Are you all right?"

Calamatta nodded to set her friend's mind at ease. If she only knew the truth of the matter, thought Calamatta.

"No, wife, you will not ride astride like a man," her husband had commanded that morning.

She remembered her promise to herself to try to be more thoughtful and conceded to his wishes, but she had stubbornly refused to use a sidesaddle and insisted on riding bareback. Therefore she was finding it difficult, even on the broad, hairy-heeled draft horse, to balance herself with one leg bent in front of her. *If you had to ride in so ungainly a manner, Major*

Hatcher, she said to herself, *you'd realize how uncomfortable it is. God will surely reward me for being so obliging.*

Lettyce rode in the conventional manner, but nonetheless in keeping with the medieval theme. Her mourning period was over and her costume, a deep maroon gown, set off her dark beauty. On her head she wore a cone-shaped henin decorated with embroidery and gemstones, swathed in a fine gauze which hung down like a waterfall from the single point.

Each of the women's horses was led by one of stableman Fotch's twin grandsons, dressed as squires. Two mounted footmen, brilliantly arrayed in the armoured suits of medieval knights, accompanied the women. All the horses were blanketed, plumed, and belled, as was befitting the occasion.

Looking over the countryside from the rise on which their party rested, Calamatta surveyed the vast panorama of gentle hills dotted with thatch-roofed stone cottages, high hedgerows, country lanes, and the meandering River Glen. As far as she could see, there were many people afoot, families in donkey carts, men on horseback, and carriages of every description, from barouches to fine gilded coaches, all converging upon the tiny village. The newly leafed trees didn't hide the fact that the small churchyard was already nearly full.

Mr. Boskins had left the manor house a little earlier with Jamie, who, dressed resplendently in the costume of a medieval page, was to strew rose petals in the aisle ahead of the bride. No one had been able to persuade the reluctant boy to relinquish his cherished flyswatter long enough to perform this task until Major Hatcher, in his most militant voice, commanded him to do so. He laid down further orders that Jamie was to resume his responsibilities as household flyswatter and spider snatcher at the reception. Only then did the boy stand at attention and, without so much as a twitch, give up his long pole.

The celestial sounds of organ music reached them long before their party entered the village. From the heavenly sound of it, Calamatta knew it was a new organ which played.

"Major Hatcher told me that he would buy a new organ," she told Lettyce. "He promised."

"He is an honorable man, Calamatta," the small lady said quietly.

The notes of the composition blended in so harmoniously with the sweet tuning of the bells and joyous trilling of the songbirds that Calamatta couldn't distinguish which came from nature and which from man. She glanced over at the unreadable expression on her companion's face. Ordinarily, the fairy-tale pageantry would have set Calamatta's spirits soaring, but even so, as compelling as the hymn sounded, her heart was heavy. This ceremony was to seal forever her fate with a man she didn't love and she now knew didn't love her.

At that moment, a breeze sprang up like a saucy nymph to tease her veil. For a moment Calamatta's delight in her struggle to keep the fine cloth from taking wing and flying away gave her respite from her lonely thoughts and brought the first laughter to her lips.

As if the sound was his signal, her young groom began once again to lead her horse down the path. The spectacle before her of the crush of carriages trying to squeeze through the narrow gateway and into the already crowded church yard was so startling that Calamatta gave but a passing glance to two riders sitting their horses on an opposite hill. One was a huge man, his scowling face covered with a red briarpatch beard. He wore a stained suit of buckskins and clenched a cigar stub in his teeth, while the other man was darker-haired, younger, more fashionably dressed, but nonetheless as weary looking and in need of a shave as his companion.

The procession made its way along the village street lined with a cheering throng of country folk. When they arrived, dear Mr. Boskins was waiting to escort Calamatta and Lettyce into the church. The doors closed behind them, shutting out many locals who were trying to get a peek inside.

The little chapel was crammed with members of the Quality who not only filled up the pews, but jostled each other along the walls, trying to find a place to stand. Calamatta and Boskins stopped at the head of the aisle. The organist played louder, and Jamie, his eyes bright as pebbles in a stream, stood at the ready, clutching his basket of flower petals.

The morning sun played musical colors through the three stained-glass panels above the altar. Calamatta fixed her sights on the front of the church, where, under the high vaulted arch, Edward stood like a dark statue at the bottom of the three steps leading up to the dais. Although both men, who looked so much alike, were silhouetted against the early light streaming in through the windows, she knew which was he.

Lettyce started down the aisle, urging the shy Jamie in front of her. Calamatta, on the arm of Boskins, followed, and as her eyes became more accustomed to the interior of the church, she could see Edward's solemn eyes drawing her to him like a magnet. But a few minutes later, it was Major Hatcher who moved to her side and turned to face Reverend Saulthorpe.

The rector shook his head and frowned as he gazed down upon the four miserable-looking young people. He'd known the Hatcher brothers since they were infants. Though the man of God told Master William that he was glad they had chosen to have the marriage sanctioned by the church, they already were considered by law to be man and wife.

"Heavens above," he said in an aside to the church warden, "this is supposed to be a happy occasion! I do believe the congregation is in a more festive mood than the principals involved. If this is to be only a token pledge of their love, I have grave doubts about the union itself."

The young matron's veil didn't hide her tears. She kept looking not at her husband, but at his groomsman, Master Edward, who looked at some mysterious spot on the altar cloth. The groom, Master William, kept his eyes turned toward the bridesmaid, the countess of Elmsworth, and her pitiful gaze did not leave his sad face.

The rector cleared his throat and began the ceremonies. He smiled at the two young people, but when he received only wooden reactions from both, he raised his eyes to the ceiling. Then, with a shrug, he began again, but the sound of his voice was drowned out by an uproar outside the church.

The door crashed open. Another scuffle ensued at the entryway, which evidently resulted in a few sore skulls and some wounded pride. All in the congregation turned to view the back of the holy edifice, only to find themselves staring down the barrel of a rifle.

The rector saw the deadly weapon pointed at him. "Dear Lord," he said, "for whatever has been my indiscretion, I pray that my end will be swift and painless."

From the rear of the church came a roar so loud it drowned out the organ music. "Hold everything!"

The barrel seemed to be advancing down the aisle by itself until it acquired a body with a thatch of red hair.

Handkerchiefs were raised to the noses of those seated near the intruder.

"Creed!" Calamatta cried. "You've come to see my ceremony!"

"Ain't going to be no ceremony! There's going to be a murder!"

By now, Creed, followed closely by Benjamin, who carried a pistol, had traversed the length of the aisle, climbed the three steps and elbowed his way between the couple to confront the rector. With his cigar still sticking from the corner of his mouth, rifle in hand, and a pistol in his belt, he growled, "They ain't married!"

Ignoring his sister, the big American turned to confront his adversary. He looked from Edward to William. His mouth dropped open. The cigar butt fell to the floor.

"Gawd a'mighty! There's two of you!" He squinted his eyes. "Which one of you heathen Tories is Edward Hatcher?"

Edward didn't think it a propitious time to instruct this barbarian that the Hatcher family had always been more Whig than Tory.

Creed didn't wait for an answer to his question, but came

down with his rifle butt on the one nearest him, which was Edward, but who, being familiar with the redhead's fiery temper, had ducked. Propelled by his tremendous strength, Creed dropped the shotgun and flew over the low balustrade.

However, Edward, readying himself for another assault by Creed, failed to anticipate the action of the milder-looking Benjamin and found himself leveled by a well-placed facer.

William, trying to make some sense of this outrageous attack, stepped forward, "How dare you—"

Before he could finish his diatribe, a fist smashed into his face.

"Ben!" shouted Calamatta. "That's my husband!"

While William was picking himself up from the floor, Creed was attempting to climb back over the railing, but Edward was ready. Just before Edward struck him full in the nose, Creed flung at her, "Ain't your husband! They's a bunch of low-life thieves!"

William had recovered enough to stand up when Benjamin catapulted himself over his brother's back and rammed William in the chest. Their bodies locked and rolled across the pulpit, toppling the startled rector.

Calamatta, seeing Lettyce was about to swoon, threw her arms around the smaller woman and did all she could to shield her from being knocked over by the flying fists.

Benjamin's foot caught in the train of Calamatta's dress, ripping it. Reverend Saulthorpe, having righted himself, pulled the two ladies into the safety of his sanctuary.

There the rector asked for a quick explanation of the catastrophe erupting at that very minute in the outer room. When he found neither lady was harmed and in no wise could shed any light on the fiasco, he bid them stay where they were and bravely charged out to put some order into God's holy church.

In the meantime, the battle had accelerated.

Reverend Saulthorpe picked up the two pistols and shotgun, which had dropped to the floor. "Father, forgive me," he intoned, "but drastic measures are needed."

He then placed one pistol and the shotgun upon the altar and, pointing the remaining gun at the ceiling, closed his eyes and fired. The ricocheting bullet and the ensuing silence gave the good man a space of time in which to order the four culprits into his sanctuary to sort out this debacle.

Like schoolboys caught in the act of mischief, they responded to the voice of authority and marched forth. The rector, following closely, closed the door behind them, the pistol still in his hand.

"Sit!"

Since the women occupied the only two chairs in the small room, the men were obliged to settle on the floor with their backs to the walls. Benjamin sat down one side, William and Edward on the other. Each pair of brothers glowered at the opposing set.

Creed spread his legs wide, thrust his thick neck forward and growled, "I'll stand."

"Creed!" shouted his sister, rising from her seat, "where is your respect? You're in the presence of a man of God!"

"Indeed you are, sir," scolded the rector.

Creed eyed the pistol, sat down, and fell silent.

No sound was heard in all of St. Stephen's.

In the sanctuary, Calamatta and Lettyce were advised to say nothing while the good rector listened to the charges and confessions of each man.

Creed glared at the Hatcher men, then turned to Reverend Saulthorpe. "Old Mr. Butters weren't no preacher, only the houseman for the parish house."

"This makes no sense at all," the rector mumbled to himself, but wisely nodded and waited.

Creed pointed a finger at Edward. "He kidnapped my sister and stole her fortune."

All four men began to shout, but when accusations and denials became too heated and threatened the peace, Reverend Saulthorpe waved the pistol. "Amazing how one little piece of metal demands such obedience," he mused. Then, facing William and Edward, he continued, "These are grave charges. And although her brothers have every right to demand satisfaction, I believe it is up to Miss McGannon to determine what penalties will be forthcoming."

The four men were led out and told to seat themselves in the front pew on either side of Mr. and Mrs. Boskins. The rector signaled to the church warden to keep an eye on them, then stepped back into his sanctuary.

Half an hour later, the two young ladies and Reverend Saulthorpe, holding a gun in one hand and papers in the other, emerged from the inner room.

"Gentlemen," he said. "I have here documents relating to the recompense asked by Miss McGannon. She is willing to drop all charges against Captain and Major Hatcher—"

Edward and William sat up. Creed scowled and half rose from his seat, while Benjamin looked worried and pulled his brother back down.

"—if they will just sign these papers without reading them." The rector watched as uneasiness etched the Hatcher brothers' faces. "The redress is not monetary, I assure you."

At that, William's countenance brightened and he quickly nodded his assent.

Edward was more skeptical. Men were willing to chop each other's heads off and be done with it. But women? They relished the idea of punishing a sinner over and over again—the length of his natural lifetime, if necessary—just to enjoy hearing him confess the error of his ways.

One glance at his brother's relieved expression, though, and Edward, too, gave his nod of agreement. Then he dared to glance at Calamatta. If she thought to frighten him, she was mistaken. What her intent was, he couldn't fathom. The challenge in her eyes made him feel uneasy, but if she thought he'd play the coward, she was mistaken.

Maintaining a look of complacency, the Hatcher men rose and wrote their names on the documents. Creed grinned. Benjamin winked at Calamatta. All four looked quite pleased—until they heard the verdict.

Before Edward and William were aware of what was happening, both were addressed by the rector. "Gentlemen, you have just signed your marriage agreements. As the only church official in a large isolated part of the parish, I am an appointed representative of the archbishop, and therefore I have the authority to write special licenses."

A few minutes later, Reverend Saulthorpe stood conducting a double wedding ceremony. He smiled down upon the congregation, as though there was nothing unusual in the switch of partners. Although she had to hold her torn train over her arm, Miss Calamatta Mary McGannon looked lovely. As she gazed adoringly into the eyes of her intended, she appeared quite calm, giving no outward sign that there was anything unusual in her groom's purple eye, which was already beginning to swell to alarming proportions.

Master Edward may have looked a little odd with the right sleeve of his coat dangling from his shoulder—and if, when he kissed his bride, he held her a little longer than was necessary, and if the rector had to clear his throat three times to get him to take his lips from hers, well, what could one expect when the man had been living in the wilds of a savage country for a good part of a year?

Then, with a lusty laugh, he picked up his bride and strode from the church. There were a few raised eyebrows. Overall, the women sighed and the men punched each other in the ribs. But one lady was heard to whisper, "I dare say, I am persuaded that Captain Hatcher is as much a man as he ever was."

Reverend Saulthorpe rushed outside in time to see Master Edward bypass the carriage gaily decorated with ribbons and bells, and, instead, settle his wife upon her large horse. Then, leaping up behind her, he galloped straightaway over a hill, leaving the villagers all agog.

The guests poured out behind the rector into the churchyard, where they awaited Major Hatcher and his wife, whose manners were far more British, and who therefore could be counted upon to do what was expected.

Later, back at the manor house, they feasted and danced all afternoon and into the late evening. Full of good wine and an abundant repast, no one seemed to give a tiddle that the young American, who was the true mistress of Careby Manor, and her husband never reappeared.

Many of *le beau monde* set off on the mark for London without staying the night.

"I suspect," the rector said to his warden, "that the most urgent thought on our distinguished guests' minds is that those quickest to return to Town will be the first to be credited with the *on dit* of the reluctant groom."

Epilogue

Careby Manor
June, 1816

My Dearest Lucy,
I am married! Truly married! To Edward, not to Major Hatcher. Lettyce agreed to take him, but that is another story. Foolish me! It was Edward I loved all along.
The ceremony was just beginning in St. Stephen's Church in Careby when Creed and Benjamin arrived to tell me I was not Major Hatcher's wife. What an uproar Creed must have caused in Kentucky when he found out my marriage in Dunfree's Corners was not legal. Poor Mr. Butters was only the preacher's houseman and had been too frightened to say so. Edward explained to me that since Major Hatcher and I had not had our Consummation party yet, no harm was done.
After the rector said we were married, and our husbands had kissed us, Edward whispered in my ear, "Enough of that!" He picked me up and put me on a magnificent white horse and carried me off to the hunting lodge. It was like a fairy tale. No! Now I know real life is much more exciting than make-believe.
When we got to the lodge, we practiced some more. Edward had been so anxious to get on with our lessons we did not stay at the manor house for the reception and

consummation parties. I am certain Major Hatcher was just as happy to have Lettyce at his instead of me, because he has always loved her. This is her second one, so it would not be as much of a surprise to her. The fact that Lettyce has had a little more experience might be better in the long run because, as I mentioned to her, Major Hatcher needs a great deal of instruction in that direction. She seemed a little embarrassed, but she kissed me and said she would have patience with him. I told her she would need it.

I know that a person should not applaud her own accomplishments, but Edward did say I was such a fast top that in no time at all we were beginning lesson number two. It's fun, Lucy! Now I can see why married people keep it such a mystery. If the secret got out and about, all the young people would be doing it in no time.

Imagine how surprised Edward was to find he did not have an affliction after all. He had no one to tell him, you see. When I said I was sorry that he had worried all that time, he got to laughing and kissed me and whispered, "Love conquers all." Was not that a lovely thing to say? Especially after the trick I pulled on him to get him to marry me.

When I told Edward that I really enjoyed learning what followed and hoped we could do it often, he said he truly had a good time, too, and assured me it would be all right to do it as often as we pleased. I never knew Edward was such an earnest student.

How relieved we were to find out Mr. Fitzgerald was in Kentucky married to Miss Abigail. Creed told us they have established a successful inn on the Ohio River where the main calling card is the black-cherry cider made from Miss Abigail's secret recipe.

For all their fighting, Major Hatcher and Benjamin have become fast friends. Benjamin wants to attend Cambridge and Major Hatcher said he would sponsor him with a recommendation to King's College, where he and Edward attended. A lord of the manor at Careby who was one of our ancestors, Dr. John Hatcher, was a professor and then vice chancellor of the university in 1579, so Edward said Ben need not worry about connections.

Now that Creed and Edward are not bashing each other's faces in, Creed is going to stay on a while to see if he can make some trade agreements for Kentucky products. Edward and Major Hatcher told him they would introduce him to some very influential men, and Edward said he may buy some ships to take advantage of the increased trade. Creed insists American-made ships are faster.

Oh, Lucy, I must tell you—I met a real prince! His name is George—only they call him the Prince Regent, and sometimes, Your Royal Highness. He is really a very nice person, not at all puffed up with his own consequence, as some say. He was busy planning for the May wedding of his daughter, Charlotte, but he still took the time to send me a copy of Emma *by Jane Austen, who, he told me, had written our favorite book,* Pride and Prejudice. *Inside the cover he wrote, "To my mudsprite, Calamatta," and he signed it, "Your friend, Plain George."*

Major Hatcher was knighted for the heroic service he performed in the war against Napoleon. Now I shall have to remember to call him Sir William. Since I did not marry him, I will not get to be a Lady. I am only Mrs. Edward Hatcher, but that is all right with me.

Edward and I moved into the manor house and Sir William went to live with Lettyce at Elmsworth. He is quite happy, because he will be nearer Cambridge University and can study and write all he wants.

Our little orphan boy, Jamie, the flyswatter and spider catcher, has gone with him. Indeed, the child was so in the dismals at the thought of being separated from his master that Sir William made the boy his official page. It was only make-believe, but just before they left Careby,

Sir William and Lettyce held a ceremony to make the appointment official. Although Jamie looked quite resplendent in his new uniform and was advised of his new duties, no amount of persuasion could make him give up the flyswatter his master had given him, so when the child insisted on kneeling before him to make his pledge, Sir William renamed it Jamie's lance and used it to tap his shoulder.

Did you know? Careby is all mine! Edward said he was ashamed of himself for playing such a dastardly flim-flam on me to get it back. I told him he should be, but since I pulled a few shenanigans myself to get him to sign a marriage agreement, I supposed we should cry even.

I have it in writing that he is to give me some say-so over how my money is spent until I have control of it when I am twenty-one, and for as long as we both shall live he is to be a dutiful husband and never leave me, unless he assures me that he will come back. He said he suspected there had to be some trickery when I didn't say obey before Reverend Saulthorpe pronounced us man and wife. I whispered to Edward he didn't have to say it, either— except he has to obey the part about always coming home to me. That is in the document he signed.

Edward has been gone over two weeks with Creed to London, but I expect him back any day now. He promised.

The best part I have saved until the very last. My congratulations to you! You cannot imagine my delight to hear that soon after I left for England, you and Zachariah McGannon were married. All along, I thought you had set your heart on Benjamin. I should have known something was afoot when my McGannon cousins were so often at your house.

Give my tenderest regards to Mama and Papa Coleman.

Your devoted friend,

Calamatta was about to sign her name when a scratching was heard on the door which connected her bedchamber with her husband's. No longer believing it to be a mouse, she looked up, but before she could call out, the door opened and Edward stood in the portal. He was back! His damp hair showed he had just bathed. A splendid embroidered satin robe covered most of his body, but the bare feet sticking out below told her he wore nothing underneath.

Sporting the humblest of countenances, Edward attempted a sweeping bow, but managed only to show more of his calf. Calamatta tried not to laugh.

"Captain Hatcher reporting for duty," came a deep voice from somewhere under the dark mop of hair. Still bowing, he raised his face and glanced at the paper on her desk. "Unless, of course, m'lady is too busy for more lessons."

"Oh, Edward!" Calamatta pushed Lucy's letter aside and jumped up so quickly her chair went tumbling. She flew across the room and into his arms with such abandon that before he could regain his balance they were catapulted back against his bed.

"You've come home! Just like you promised."

Edward knew that never again would he have to crook his finger at Calamatta. He let her push him down into the thick feather mattress and, as he sank into it, he pulled her up to lie on top of him.

Calamatta gave him a quick kiss. "Are you always going to be such a dutiful husband, Edward?"

His arms encircled her and hugged her closer. Then, tenderly his hands cupped her face, and while he took in her sweet scent, her softness, her dearness, his eyes feasted on her.

"Aye, my love! Always!"

AUTHOR'S NOTE

Although the love story of Calamatta and Edward is fiction, the Hatcher family was a very distinguished one in England and early Colonial America. Their old manor house with its beautiful gardens and the small honey-colored stone church of St. Stephen's still remain on the former lands of the Hatcher family in Careby, Lincolnshire, England. The Hatchers were wealthy landowners, the landed gentry of their times, their estate extending over fourteen hundred acres. The author has taken romantic liberties to take the house back to Norman times. The men were educated at Eton, Cambridge, Oxford, and Gray's Inn in London. Possibly a younger son, the American William Hatcher came to Virginia before 1636 as an adventurer. He became a wealthy planter, ship owner, and was elected four times to the House of Burgesses from Henrico. This William Hatcher was an ancestor of the author.

The McGannons came from Ireland in the 1700s, moving from Culpepper County, Virginia, to Kentucky after the Revolutionary War. In 1818, in the state of Kentucky, U.S.A., Lucy Coleman McGannon and her husband, Zachariah, great-great-great grandparents of the author, recorded in their family Bible the birth of a daughter. They named her Calamatta.

I'd love to hear from readers and know how you liked Calamatta and Edward's story. My E-mail address is: PaulaJTG@AOL.com. Or write to me at P.O. Box 941982, Maitland, FL 32794-1982.

BOOK YOUR PLACE ON OUR WEBSITE AND MAKE THE READING CONNECTION!

We've created a customized website just for our very special readers, where you can get the inside scoop on everything that's going on with Zebra, Pinnacle and Kensington books.

When you come online, you'll have the exciting opportunity to:

- View covers of upcoming books
- Read sample chapters
- Learn about our future publishing schedule (listed by publication month *and author*)
- Find out when your favorite authors will be visiting a city near you
- Search for and order backlist books from our online catalog
- Check out author bios and background information
- Send e-mail to your favorite authors
- Meet the Kensington staff online
- Join us in weekly chats with authors, readers and other guests
- Get writing guidelines
- AND MUCH MORE!

Visit our website at
http://www.zebrabooks.com

More Zebra Regency Romances

Put a Little Romance in Your Life With
Fern Michaels

Put a Little Romance in Your Life With
Janelle Taylor